THE GLADD...

"This is one sassy and smart series with a colorful gang of senior sleuths." —*Mystery Scene*

"Beyond the skillful blend of Yiddish humor, affectionate characters and serious undercurrents…picks up speed and flavor with some **twists worthy of Agatha Christie's archetypal dame detective, Miss Marple.**" —*Publishers Weekly*

"What gives the book its warmth is the way Lakin has turned this group of friends into a family who are there not only for the fun and laughter but also for the heartbreak and tears." —*Romantic Times*

"Yo... love
this ...s.
This ...ystery...

"An... v-
able ...g
plot ...
Retire... ne
with...

"Ri... ...
The... ife
amo... es
very...

"This is a **funny, warm, absolutely delightful** tale...a must read." —*Mysterious Women*

"An unforgettable romp...Lakin's characters are zany, her writing is **witty and crisp,** and anyone who's ever visited one can attest that her peek at life in a Jewish Florida retirement center is portrayed both accurately and tastefully." —*Cleveland Jewish News*

"**Wonderful dialogue and a touch of romance** enlivens this delightful breeze of a tale." —*Kaw Valley Senior Monthly*

"**Sassy, funny and smart**...Lakin sprinkles humor on every page, but never loses respect for her characters." —*New Hampshire Senior Beacon*

"**It is a tribute to Lakin's talent that she is able to mingle comedy and murder successfully.**" —*Dade County Jewish Journal*

"If getting old is this much fun, maybe I won't mind! **Miss Marple, move over.**...Rita Lakin's witty romp through a Florida retirement community is just the thing for what ails you!" —PARNELL HALL, author of the Puzzle Lady mysteries

"So who knew a retirement community could be so dangerous—and so much fun....Lakin handles her characters with **dignity, compassion, and love,** while allowing them the full extent of their eccentric personalities." —VICKI LANE, author of *Old Wounds*

"A truly original voice. **Great fun from start to finish.** Plan to stay up late." —SHELDON SIEGEL, *New York Times* bestselling author of *The Confession*

Fate took RITA LAKIN from New York to Los Angeles, where she was seduced by palm trees and movie studios. Over the next twenty years she wrote for television and had every possible job, from freelance writer to story editor to staff writer and, finally, producer. She worked on shows such as *Dr. Kildare, Peyton Place, The Mod Squad,* and *Dynasty,* and created her own shows, including *The Rookies, Flamingo Road,* and *Nightingales.* Rita has won Writers Guild of America awards, the Mystery Writers of America's Edgar Allan Poe Award, and the coveted Avery Hopwood Award from the University of Michigan. She lives in Marin County, California, where she is currently at work on her next mystery starring the indomitable Gladdy Gold.

www.ritalakin.com

ALSO BY RITA LAKIN

Getting Old Is Murder

Getting Old Is the Best Revenge

Getting Old Is Criminal

Getting Old Is To Die For

Getting Old Is a Disaster

Getting Old
Is Très
Dangereux

A MYSTERY

Rita Lakin

A DELL BOOK

NEW YORK

A Dell Mass Market Original

Copyright © 2010 by Rita Lakin

Published in the United States by Dell,
an imprint of The Random House Publishing Group,
a division of Random House, Inc., New York.

DELL is a registered trademark of Random House, Inc.,
and the colophon is a trademark of Random House, Inc.

ISBN 978-0-440-24542-1

Cover design: Marietta Anastassatos
Cover illustration: Hiro Kimura

Printed in the United States of America

www.bantamdell.com

2 4 6 8 9 7 5 3 1

Getting Old
Is Très Dangereux

ON MARRIAGE:

Marriage is not just spiritual communion; it is also remembering to take out the trash.

—Joyce Brothers

My advice to you is to get married. If you find a good wife, you'll be happy; if not, you'll become a philosopher.

—Socrates

I love being married. It's so great to find that one special person you want to annoy for the rest of your life.

—Rita Rudner

Sometimes I wonder if men and women really suit each other. Perhaps they should live next door and just visit now and then.

—Katharine Hepburn

Never go to bed mad. Stay up and fight.

—Phyllis Diller

Love: a temporary insanity curable by marriage.

—Ambrose Bierce

Do you know what it means to come home at night to a woman who'll give you a little love, a little affection, a little tenderness? It means you're in the wrong house, that's what it means.

—Henny Youngman

I never married, because there was no need. I have three pets at home which answer the same purpose as a husband. I have a dog which growls every morning, a parrot which swears all afternoon, and a cat that comes home late at night.

—Marie Corelli

And finally, to the 98 percent of my fans who voted to get Jack and Gladdy married:

Come, let's be a comfortable couple and take care of each other! How glad we shall be, that we have somebody we are fond of always, to talk to and sit with.

—Charles Dickens

Maybe they will. And maybe they won't.

Rita Lakin

Introduction
to Our Characters

GLADDY AND HER GLADIATORS

Gladys (Gladdy) Gold, 75   Our heroine and her funny,
adorable, sometimes impossible partners:

Evelyn (Evvie) Markowitz, 73   Gladdy's sister. Logical,
a regular Sherlock Holmes

Ida Franz, 71   Stubborn, mean, great for an in-your-
face confrontation

Bella Fox, 83   The "shadow." She's so forgettable,
she's perfect for surveillance, but smarter than you
think

Sophie Meyerbeer, 80   Master of disguises, she lives for
color coordination

YENTAS, KIBITZERS, SUFFERERS: THE INHABITANTS OF

PHASE TWO

Hy Binder, 88   A man of a thousand jokes, all of them
tasteless

Lola Binder, 78   His wife, who hasn't a thought in her
head that he hasn't put there

Enya Slovak, 84   Survivor of "the camps" but never
survived

Tessie Spankowitz, 56   Chubby, newly married to Sol

Millie Weiss, 85   Suffering with Alzheimer's

Irving Weiss, 86   Suffering because she's suffering

Mary Mueller, 60   Neighbor whose husband left her;
nurse

Joe Markowitz, 75   Evvie's ex-husband

ODDBALLS AND FRUITCAKES

Sol Spankowitz, 79   Now married to Tessie

THE COP AND THE COP'S POP

Morgan (Morrie) Langford, 35   Tall, lanky, sweet, and
   smart
Jack Langford, 75   Handsome and romantic, Gladdy's
   boyfriend

OTHER TENANTS

Barbi Stevens, 20-ish, and *Casey Wright, 30-ish*
   Cousins who moved from California
Pat "Nancy" Drew, 60
Linda Rutledge, 72
Arlene Simon, 80
Merrill Grant, 77

Prologue

PARIS NOIR

"Mon Dieu," *Pierre growls at his business partner, his rotund belly heaving with agitation.* "For what possible reason do you call us to Paris at this late hour?"

"To this foul excuse for a café?" *Oswald adds, his skinny arms waving about as he points to the sign reading* "Café du Canard Mort"—*a sign badly in need of paint.* "To drink this vile vin de table reeking of vinegar?"

"Comme c'est bizarre! *Meeting here in the ninth arrondissement, where there are more houses of ill repute than patisseries!*" *huffs Hortense, overly rouged and heavily corseted, as she puffs away on her Gauloise.*

"And told to wear dark clothes?" *Pierre adds as*

he pushes up his fog-colored beret from his brow.
"What is this Georges Simenon cheap mystery
nonsense? Ridicule!"

Gaston listens impatiently to the continuing list
of annoyances and complaints from his two part-
ners and a partner's wife as they balance uncom-
fortably on spindly unmatched chairs at a
minuscule cigarette-scarred wooden table with
wrought-iron legs.

Let them release their streams of vitriol, he
thinks. In moments he will give them something
real to whine about.

He reaches into a huge basket at his side and
pulls out his own bottle of wine, a corkscrew, four
glasses, and a covered plate. He opens the wine and
says, "I have brought from our own winery our
legendary Pouilly-Fuissé. Voilà," as he fills the new
glasses. He then reveals a platter of foie gras and
crusty bread. "With permission of the esteemed
management," he adds, indicating a stony-faced,
stained-aproned owner glaring at them from the
doorway.

He snaps his fingers and the taciturn man re-
moves the offending carafe of house wine.

Gaston watches them greedily dig in. For a
moment, his partners are appeased by swishing,
sniffing, gargling, and finally sipping their famous
winery's award-winning vintage with sighs of satis-
faction.

To any outsider they would seem like three drab men of an indeterminate age and a woman who would rather die than admit hers.

He gives them a moment for savoring their meal before he drops his guillotine. "A disaster is soon to come upon us."

They look up. Pierre wipes goose liver from his lips. Hortense squeezes her husband Oswald's arm. Oswald blinks rapidly.

Gaston reaches down into his basket again and pulls out a book. He slams it on the table. "Regardez le visage de la diablesse—Look into the face of the she-devil!"

All three stare down at the image of a glamorous redheaded woman in a shimmering gold lamé evening gown. Below her décolleté is the name Michelle duBois. Above her diamond tiara is a title: "Bonbon, Non Non!" And in smaller letters, "Un Crime du Chocolat!" They are puzzled.

"So?" Oswald peers down to look closer.

Pierre asks, "So?" as he returns to his delicacies.

Hortense raises an eyebrow. "She looks familiar."

Gaston sneers. "She ought to. She spent three months thriving on our generosity."

Pierre snarls. "And where was I? I never met such a woman."

Gaston pokes his finger again and again at the visage on the cover. "Take away the gorgeous red curls. Substitute brown hair the color of pigpen mud."

Oswald is annoyed. "Get to your point already."

Gaston smiles nastily. "Remove those drop-dead gorgeous green eyes that dazzle and replace them with dull brown contacts and large ugly horn-rimmed glasses. Ignore jewels we never saw. Think tacky, badly fitted clothes from off the rack."

Hortense begins to comprehend. "It can't be!"

It finally dawns on all of them. "Mademoiselle Angelique—whose grand-père left her a vineyard in Provence," remembers Pierre. "Who came to us and begged us to teach her the business."

Hortense says ominously, "That is not the name on this book—and why is she writing a book, and what is it about?"

Gaston faces his partners. "Michelle duBois is a famous writer who publishes her filth all over the world. As they say in Les Etats Unis, she is a ringer of bells, a whistle-blower! She inserts herself into businesses and digs up their dirty little secrets and then she exposes them, ruins the owners, and becomes rich doing this." He turns the offensive book over and his long fingers point to the list on the back cover. "This exposé is about a renowned chocolate factory in Belgium. Before that was her celebrated bestseller, which exposed La Vache Qui Pleurait. The Cow Who Cried."

His partners gasp in horror at that well-known scandal involving fromage *in Brittany.*

Gaston administers the coup de grâce: "And before that a fatal attack on an olive grove in Tuscany with the horrible American title, It's the Pits!"

"Disgusting," says Oswald.

Pierre's head shakes from side to side as if to dislodge this bad news from his mind.

Hortense lights another Gauloise, puffing madly.

Oswald grabs the book, skims a paragraph. "They put sawdust in the Belgian chocolates? Who could imagine?"

Hortense reads over his shoulder. "The Bretons outsourced their Brie from China? Making people sick to their stomachs?"

Gaston pulls the book away from them and pounds his hands on the table, finally allowing his rage to boil over. "Never mind them! Think about what she found out about us. We are doomed and the fault is yours!" Gaston pokes Pierre in his fat belly. "You son of a gluttonous goat. You brought her to us. You believed her lascivious lies."

"Not my fault, yours," Pierre spits back at him as his fingers beat a tattoo along the outside of his knee. "It was you who agreed to let her in. She fluttered those long eyelashes and you dissolved into a pool of melted beurre!"

"Her fault," hisses skin-and-bones Oswald as

the traitor pinches his wife in her flabby neck. "Hortense said she was to be trusted."

Hortense blows cigarette smoke up her husband's nose. "You were to check up on her but it was her fluffy curls and sprightly bosom you inspected, you lust-crazed cochon.*"*

It is long past midnight and the café is empty. Now all the waiters fuss and hover to the side, flapping their unstarched and deplorably ragged white aprons, signaling their desire to close up and go home.

"Assez!" shouts Gaston, half standing, as his liver-stained serviette falls onto the ground. One of the many cats from the nearby alley rushes to claim the tasty crumbs. "Enough of the accusations. Now that we know who she really is, the question is what to do!"

All four once again glower at the author's glamorous photo on the cover, as if their looks could burn her image away. "And we are next!" pleads Gaston. "Our turn to be skewered. On the back page she hints that she will announce her new exposé at some cursed book conference she is attending in Florida. And it is about wine!"

Oswald pulls at his frizzy hair in fear. "She wormed her way in and we talked and talked and talked . . ."

Pierre nervously pops another bit of foie gras down his gullet, oddly resembling a gulping goose eating its young. "Now the entire world will know the truth about how we make our wine."

"Not if we stop her." *The look on Gaston's face is crafty. The others turn to him.*

Hortense shakes her head mournfully. "La chienne, *she will be merciless. Relentless. And worse"*—she sighs—*"impossible to bribe."*

Gaston's voice drops a few decibels as he leans in closer to all. "That is why I called our little meeting. I have something in mind. So that she will never blow her whistle again. Something of a more permanent solution."

Hortense rears back in horror. "You don't mean—"

Gaston straightens the excited woman's chair before it topples over. "I do mean..."

"How?" *gasps Oswald as he tries to grab his wife's hand.*

"Traitor!" *She shoves him away.*

"I do not know the how, but I know the who," *says Gaston.*

"Who is the who?" *asks Pierre with great curiosity.*

"None else. Mon oncle *twice removed from my aunt's sister on my father's side of the family.*"

"Non!" *gasps Hortense.*

"Oui," *insists Gaston proudly.* "That *assassin* du monde, *the one they call The Snake!*"

The three pull back in shock, their minds assessing, conjuring. Dare they hope?

Finally Oswald asks, "Would he do it? I heard he was retired."

Pierre is puzzled. "That was thirty years ago."

"And never caught. Not once. An impeccable record," Gaston states proudly. "Now living on his yacht somewhere off the coast of Monaco."

"But he must be in his nineties by now," comments Oswald.

"And from what I hear from my tante Evangeline, he's still in the pink," Gaston boasts.

"Surely he would not help us?"

"But of course he will. It is a matter of family honor. He cannot refuse."

There is silence for a few moments. Gaston looks to each of them. "Are we all agreed?"

Hortense fans herself with her serviette in one hand as she grabs Gaston's wrist with the other. "Make the call."

Gaston smiles. "I already have. Fini. He is, even as we speak, on his way to the Fort of Lauderdale and once and for all, the world will be rid of la belle dame sans merci.*"*

1

OOOH LÀ LÀ

Jack is behaving very secretively this evening.
First, he tells me to dress up for a special
evening event. He has something important to say
to me.

Well, as dressed up as one ever gets in T-shirt
land—that is, our senior citizen condo, Lanai Gardens in Fort Lauderdale, Florida, in case anybody
doesn't know. And also, if you're behind the times,
Jack has been living with me since the horrendous
hurricane destroyed his building in Phase Six, two
months ago.

I dig out a peach organza cocktail dress I wore
once, for my daughter Emily's wedding, and
matching high heels. I'm even wearing makeup and
perfume for the occasion.

Jack is in a charcoal pin-striped suit with a cherry red tie and a jaunty white carnation in the lapel buttonhole. I must admit this fiancé of mine is very handsome. As we used to say way back when—tall, dark, and handsome. Even at seventy-five, that description fits him, though his hair, like mine, is mostly gray. On him, gray is dashing. On me, it's the color of wet cement. Ah, when he smiles at me, I get wobbly in my arthritic knees. When his blue eyes crinkle with adjoining laugh lines, I melt.

Even while getting dressed for tonight, what with our traveling back and forth from bathroom to bedroom, he still won't give anything away. Despite my obvious curiosity. I note that he seems serious about his evening's plans.

To make me even more suspicious my sister, Evvie, was not invited, nor were the other of my "girls." Yes, though we're all in our seventies and eighties, they will always be my girls: Evvie, my sister, loyal and loving, though a tad jealous that Jack has come into our lives and scrambled things around. Ida, she of the ramrod back, the coiled gray bun, mistress of negativity. Sophie and Bella, my Bobbsey twins; zaftig Sophie gets half-baked ideas and petite Bella takes them out of the oven when done. One might believe they invented the term second childhood.

Since Jack and I are everyone's designated drivers, Bella and Sophie had visions of pot roast or rigatoni tonight. They wanted to be chauffeured to an early-bird dinner at Nona's restaurant. Naturally they forgot that I told them, twice, that Jack and I have something private planned. So now they are stuck at home, each in her own apartment, improvising dull individual dinners instead. And as we start off, I can see them sneaking glances out their windows, scowling.

They are not the only onlookers. As Jack and I step out of the elevator and head across the parking area to Jack's car, I feel other eyes peering out. Calico curtains part. Venetian blinds lift. The yenta patrol, always on the job. Especially when it comes to us. Especially now. Phase Two has been a hotbed of overwrought schemes since word got out that wedding bells are to ring shortly. A date will be set, a hundred nosy minds wanting to offer us bad advice. I can hardly wait.

How can I resist? I swing my arm out the car window and send a jaunty wave to the curious watchers.

So here we are, Jack and I, at a delightful little French bistro in Margate, sitting outdoors, sipping champagne. It's a wonderful balmy evening, so clear with the stars swarming the sky with their glistening light. I feel as if I've been transported to Van Gogh's painting "Starry Night."

My high heels are now kicked under the table. They were uncomfortable to walk in. I miss my everyday sneakers. From our tiny, rickety, scarred wooden table, I can see inside the restaurant where the walls are covered with watercolors of famous landmarks. There's the Eiffel Tower, of course. The Champs-Elysées, the Louvre, Notre Dame Cathedral, and the Arc de Triomphe. Would that we were in the real Paris, but this will have to do for tonight.

I'd been to Paris seemingly a hundred years ago with my late husband, also named Jack. It was on our honeymoon. I still remember that minuscule room we had near one of the train stations. Two of us couldn't stand in the room at one time. One had to sit up on the bed while the other moved about. It was heavenly.

Perhaps I'll go again someday with this Jack— for another honeymoon?

I'm still waiting for him to explain what's on his mind tonight. He leans over and stares into my eyes. Aha, I think, he's ready to reveal all.

"Take off your ring, please," he says with his hands fluttering toward mine.

Startled, I fold my hands together. "Why?"

"Humor me."

He is not smiling. For a brief moment, I think of the many books I've read and movies I've seen when the guy takes the gal to some very expensive restaurant, and after he's wined and dined her, he tells her he's fallen in love with somebody else. Usually it's someone much younger and cuter. Usually he drops the bombshell before dessert, so he doesn't have to spend more money on a losing proposition. I can't believe I'm thinking these ridiculous thoughts. Talk about insecurity.

Jack is still wagging his fingers.

"I'm trying, I'm trying," I say, as I tug at my garnet engagement ring. Hoping I can't get it off.

He reaches over and gently turns the ring around and around until it loosens and lands in his palm. He holds it as I rub my finger where my precious ring sat only seconds ago. He may be holding my ring, but what I'm holding is my breath. "So, now what?" I make a pathetic joke. "Does it need to be polished, or what?"

"Tonight," he announces, leaning over to kiss the tip of my nose, "is the official new beginning of our formal engagement."

I exhale a huge sigh of relief. Trying to pretend I wasn't the least bit nervous, I say, "Hmmm, I thought we got engaged a month ago."

"You call that a romantic engagement? First we got hit with that frightening hurricane that nearly wrecked Lanai Gardens. Then we had to cope with major damage to my building. All those displaced people needing to find new homes. Especially me. How lucky I was to be invited to move in with you." He grins, very amused, remembering how he talked his way into moving in with me.

I also smile, remembering how I fought that idea at the beginning. Two unmarried people living together! A *shanda,* my mother would have said. But she didn't know Jack. How wonderful it's turned out.

"And then Enya's nightmarish experience, which almost destroyed her. And our disbelief that something so horrendous could happen in our little condo. For a while I was afraid none of us would ever survive that."

I shudder, remembering the terrifying events leading up to saving Enya's life. It's probably the biggest and most harrowing case the Gladdy Gold Detective Agency will ever have to solve. But happily, the result was that Enya has finally come out of her shell. She's in Israel now, looking up a long-lost relative.

"So," Jack says, "we haven't had a peaceful moment to enjoy our new couple state."

"I agree, but the good news is—no private eye cases right now. People are too busy trying to put our city back together. I'm looking forward to a lot of quality time alone with you. Two peas in a pod. Lots of time to do stuff we keep putting off. Maybe some nice small trips away together. Maybe another trip to New York to visit our families. Or just plain laziness."

"You name it, you've got it. I won't leave your side for anything."

"Okay," I say. "Does this mean you're going to get down on your knees and propose again?"

He drops my ring into his jacket pocket. "Only if you have a forklift to pull me up. I've got something more entertaining in mind."

"I have one question," I say, looking around. "What's with this French motif?"

"*Chérie,*" he says with a pathetic attempt at a French accent, "because the French are known to be *très* romantic. And I want to shower upon you the most amorous evening you could possibly imagine."

We finish our luscious bouillabaisse in time to get to a theater featuring a retrospective of the greatest French romantic movies ever made.

Jack informs me, "When the screen actors kiss, so shall we and I shall slip the ring on your finger once again, never to be removed."

I perk up. This sounds good. Too bad Evvie isn't with us. My sister would rather watch a movie than eat. Any movie. "What are we seeing?"

"Claude Lelouch's *A Man and a Woman.*"

I smile. One of my all-time favorites.

We sit in the nearly empty balcony so we can cuddle and behave like kids. We pass the red-and-white-striped paper bag of popcorn back and forth. Small size after our huge dinner. Yum.

Anouk Aimée and Jean-Louis Trintignant are just as sexy as ever. And the famous music score by Frances Lai is still soaring and melodious. Our hero drives his race car, our heroine deals with her adorable child, and finally we are approaching their first big smooch.

"Get ready," Jack informs me. "Dig out the ring."

I'm puzzled. "Me? But it's in your pocket. I saw you put it there."

"Not anymore. I dropped it into the popcorn for the fun of it. You know, like we used to get prizes in Cracker Jack and stuff."

"You didn't!" I gasp.

"I did." He looks alarmed. "You didn't swallow it?"

I start digging through the kernels, spilling them all over the seat and floor, and not finding anything. Oh, no.

He looks chagrined, and then he laughs out loud. He holds up a small candy box. "Kidding. I put it in the Junior Mints."

I take what's left of the popcorn and throw it at him.

He upends the mints and digs out my engagement ring, licking off the chocolate as he ducks the popcorn bits.

I shake my head, trying not to grin. "And just when do you plan to grow up?"

"Never. We did our share of being responsible all the years we worked and took care of our families. We don't have to do that anymore. Remember that great line: You don't stop laughing when you grow old. You grow old when you stop laughing. As far as I'm concerned, silliness trumps seriousness."

Oh, how I agree with that.

He suddenly grabs me. "Jean-Louis is leaning in for the big kiss. Anouk is ready. I'm ready. Are you?" He pulls me toward him and all four of us are kissing with sweet passion. I can feel Jack slip my engagement ring back on my finger.

He pulls away and looks deep into my eyes. "Now we're correctly engaged."

"*Ooh là là,*" I say. What a guy.

I am so lucky.

2

CROISSANTS

Jack and I, still in our bathrobes, are happily buttering the croissants we brought home from last night's restaurant bake shop when the doorbell rings. No surprise, it's the girls. Eight A.M. sharp and they're ready for our morning exercises. Since I haven't appeared outside my door per our usual schedule, they've come looking for me. Lazy me, I'm still not in my walking clothes. Jack and I stayed up very late after we got home from our romantic evening out. Need I say more?

"Door's open," I call out. And in they troop. But what's this? Evvie and Ida have their sweats on, but Bella and Sophie are dressed for going out. They are in matching baby blue pantsuits, frilly baby blue blouses, and flowery hats! Hats? When do we wear fancy hats around here? Is there a garden party happening that I don't remember?

In his chair at the dining room table, Jack stretches languidly. He greets the girls and vice versa. The girls are still a little wary of Jack. Not that they don't like him; what lingers on each of their minds, I would bet, is how this relationship is going to affect them.

Evvie reaches over to the bread basket, then stops. "What's with the croissants? Where's the bagels?"

"Goodies brought home last night. Don't be so picky. Never mind that." I turn to Bella and Sophie. "Where are you two off to?"

Ida answers for them. "They want to go to a book fair." She flops down on a dining room chair next to Evvie and does hand and wrist exercises.

Evvie, slathering strawberry jam on a croissant, says, "They need you to drive them."

Ida continues, "I'm not going. I have better things to do with my time."

Evvie agrees, "Me, neither. Joe and I are busy today."

I notice Evvie doesn't inform us where or doing what. She and her ex-husband Joe, who once again is a fixture in her life after so many angry years, are always on mysterious trips. She has a secret no one else knows but me and I'm sworn not to tell.

Sophie puts her hands on her ample hips. "Can we get a word in here?"

Ida now raises and lowers her arms and does waist bends from her chair. "As long as it's no more than two words. We've been hearing about this book fair ad nauseam."

"It only happens once every five years and a lot of famous romance writers will be there," says Sophie grandly. "I read that in the paper."

"It will be so exciting! Danielle Steel and Kresley Cole and Heather Graham!" Bella adds excitedly.

Jack glances across the table at me and shrugs. He certainly knows nothing about the women who write romance novels. And neither do I, since mysteries are my passion.

Bella, fluffing the frills in her blouse, chimes in again. "We'll be able to meet our favorite romance writers up close. Maybe even get autographs and free books."

Sophie continues, "Everybody who's anybody will be there."

"Won't it be expensive?" I ask.

Bella shakes her head. "We can get a day pass and that's not too much."

Sophie takes out her compact and powders her nose. "And it will be worth every penny. This is big time!"

Bella begs, "Please. Pretty please just drop us down there. It's not far. The Mariner Club Hotel, right on the beach. And we can always call you to pick us up again later."

That's what I get for being the only one of us girls who still drives—I'm their designated driver 24/7. What a privilege. And, of course, since Jack also drives, he is on the available-to-be-annoyed list as well.

Bella pleads, "Come on, you haven't anything better to do."

Jack laughs and then so do I. He gets up. "We'll be ready in fifteen minutes."

Before he has a chance to change his mind, the two of them scamper out.

Ida shrugs as she, too, reaches for a croissant. "I don't understand why you always give in to them."

The Mariner Club Hotel is packed. Hundreds of people, most of them very well dressed women (and yes, I see lots of frilly hats), are moving about the expensive hotel lobby. It's very elegantly faux-Victorian with its Venetian glass chandeliers and plush dark red couches and club chairs. Some of the fairgoers parade up and down the lavish staircases and escalators; others line up for elevators.

I'm aware of a buzz of excitement as friends greet old friends. Every possible seat in the lounge part of the lobby is taken. Drinks with mini Japanese umbrellas are being served. Cell phones are in use everywhere. Much laughter, much animated conversation. Sophie and Bella are goggle-eyed trying to take it in all at once. They clutch their passes tightly even though they are secured around their necks with lanyards. With her free hand Sophie grips her program as she looks up the next event.

"We'll call you when we're ready to leave," Sophie says to me excitedly. With that, they turn their backs on us and rush into the fray.

Jack and I watch them flow and ebb with the tide of moving women until they are swallowed by the crowd.

"Well, that's our good deed for the day." Jack takes my arm, moving us toward the front doors. "How about we go down to the beach now that we're here? Take off our shoes and walk in the sand."

But I'm not paying attention. I'm reading the program for the convention on a stand-up display board.

I poke him gently in the arm. "Third-floor arcade: fiction, mystery, paranormals nonfiction. Since we're here, I think I'd like to get a pass, also, and see what new mysteries will be coming out in the spring."

He looks at me curiously. "Instead of a romantic walk on the sand?"

"Not when I can get a chance to examine new books."

He looks at me and then at the ever expanding mob. "You're really serious?"

"I actually think it might be fun."

Jack smiles. "I promised to give my darling anything she wanted."

With that he leads me to the registration desk.

I have to admit it's pretty exciting. One publishing company after another exhibiting their latest products. Posters, displays, TV presentations. Booths where authors are signing books. Everyone carrying full-to-the-brim tote bags. I feel like a kid in a candy store. Here's the new Janet Evanovich and her wild New Jersey bounty hunter antics. There's the latest Lee Child. I love how his hero, Jack Reacher, travels with only a toothbrush and a debit card. The mother-son writing team who write under the name of Charles Todd have another post–World War I case for the detective who came home shell-shocked. Elizabeth George has a new Inspector Lynley. Robert B. Parker's next with his Boston tough-guy detective and psychologist girlfriend. Cozies, thrillers, paranormals, police procedurals; every possible mystery genre to choose from. Heady stuff indeed for an avid reader like myself.

"Earth to Gladdy. Earth to Gladdy." Jack leans over my shoulder.

"What?" I ask, my mind still floating through this cornucopia of book treasures.

"May I leave you to your mysteries? Macho guy getting antsy around cozies, will head over to spy thrillers and science fiction. I'll come back in an hour and pick you up."

"Okay," I say, still poring over book titles.

He kisses the back of my neck and takes off.

Jack circumvents the romance section, where he spots Sophie and Bella on a very long book-signing line. They see him and wave happily. He waves back. He passes a sign indicating the nonfiction aisle, with science fiction straight ahead. He continues strolling, glancing now and then at colorful glossy posters with life-size photos of famous authors. He has to admit to himself that it's pretty interesting seeing how publishing companies introduce their new books. Suddenly he stops sharply and backs up. Something has caught his eye.

Someone on a poster. A beautiful woman. A familiar woman.

Jack can't believe what he's seeing. Michelle duBois is winking out at him!

He reads the text below her photo over and over again until his shocked mind can grasp its meaning. It announces the signing for her newest exposé,

Bonbon, Non Non! He feels his heart banging against his chest. It can't be! But it is. The stunning copper redhead he met in Paris eight years ago. His fantasy love. She looks exactly the same. Those piercing emerald eyes. That mysterious smile. That adorable lift of one eyebrow. Those luscious lips.

It all washes over him; that magical month he spent in Paris that Spring. The way they met and fell in love so quickly. He, a clumsy tourist, standing outside a taxi and trying to explain to the cabbie where he wanted to go. Suddenly a young woman, a vision of beauty, is at his side. In rapid, lilting French she acted as interpreter, rescuing him, at the same time dazzling him with her perfect English. She finally got in the cab with him and directed the driver to the out-of-the way museum. By the time they arrived, Michelle duBois had offered to continue as his guide in the museum. Jack knew he was in love with her the first moment she smiled at him.

Jack stands in the aisle of the book fair, mesmerized by the poster and his recollections. The Paris days flew by with her guiding him through the city she knew and loved. The memories of their torrid affair keep unrolling in his head. Running in the rain together, kissing and laughing. The unforgettable nights spent together in her glamorous apartment in Vichy. How, with her, he became younger and desired. The movies they saw together that made him pretend, for a few weeks, that he was living in a romantic Claude Lelouch film.

Oh, God! Last night he'd taken Gladdy to the movie he'd seen with Michelle in France! How could he not have remembered that?

Michelle had been an investigative reporter for a French newspaper. When he left Paris, she'd just had her first book published, an exposé about the private life of one of the most famous actors in France. Jack read later that her book made the bestseller list, turning her into an instant success all over the world.

He remembers also how and why he finally fled from her.

Panic sets in. He must get out of here. Now. Michelle mustn't see him! No, not ever. As he hurries back to where he left Gladdy, sweat pours down his face even as the air-conditioning chills him.

He can't believe how out of control he feels. He tries not to run, but his legs disobey. People are staring. Why would anyone be running?

He hears footsteps behind him. He turns, terrified. But it's only Bella and Sophie, tote bags already full, hurrying after him.

"Where's the fire?" Sophie calls, puffing, her arms and legs churning to catch up.

"No fire." Jack slows down. Everything around him is a blur now. Is it possible he's having a heart attack? *No,* he thinks grimly. *This is an anxiety attack.*

"Wait for me," Bella says, gasping.

Finally the three of them are moving at the same pace.

"You look like you saw a ghost," Sophie says, juggling her bags to balance their weight.

Jack groans inwardly. If she only knew.

They make their way through the crowds. Jack is trying to come up with an excuse to leave. There's Gladdy straight ahead, watching a video— an interview with some famous mystery writer. He doesn't know the writer's name.

"Gladdy!" Sophie calls.

I turn when I hear my name, and immediately become concerned. Why are the three of them hurrying toward me? What's wrong? Sophie and Bella seem worried. Jack looks pale. I leave the video and hurry to them. Sophie pushes Jack down on a nearby swivel chair. He jumps back up again.

I reach for his forehead. He seems terribly warm. Sweating as well.

"What's wrong?" I ask, pulling a clean tissue from my purse to wipe his forehead.

"Nothing. I just need to go home and rest."

"All right," I say. "We'll all go home now."

"Okay with me," says Bella. "I can't hold any

more books anyway. And besides, they stamped our hand so we can come back later."

"No," Jack says. "You stay. I don't want to spoil your day."

I can sense him trying to calm himself down. "Nonsense." I fold his arm into mine. "If you're coming down with something, I don't want you driving."

The four of us head for the escalator. Jack keeps his head down. He pulls a Marlins cap out of his back pocket and wears it so low it covers his eyes. "Hurry," he says.

There's actually a line for the escalator. People are scurrying out to lunch, I assume. We wait our turn to get on.

A group gets off at the top. And suddenly one of the women is surrounded by fans. They wave autographed books at her, chattering excitedly.

"Who is she?" Bella whispers to me.

"I don't know. But she must be someone famous."

"She sure is gorgeous with that flaming red hair," Sophie comments. "Is she talking French?"

With that, I'm aware that Jack's eyes widen and he groans. He tries to get the down escalator queue to move but it doesn't budge.

And at the same moment I see the redhead stare at Jack.

She immediately takes leave of her fans. To my

amazement, she hurries over to us. She practically pulls Jack out of the line just as it starts to move. Instinctively, I get off, too. Sophie and Bella are now pushed forward by the crowd. The escalator is finally moving and they are heading downstairs to the lobby. They look back and they are as astonished as I am to see this incredibly gorgeous woman throw her arms around my guy and kiss him. A very long kiss, I might add.

"Jacques!" she says in a musical French accent. "*Mon cher,* I cannot believe it. Is it really you?"

Mon cher? Is that what she called him? I don't remember much of my high school French, but I know enough to worry. Her darling?

Oy.

3

THE PAST IS PRESENT

I am aware of a number of things in a nanosecond. Jack's face is the color of overcooked beets. His arms dangle stiffly at his sides. The redhead is smiling broadly. And looking him up and down like he's some luscious chunk of Brie ready to be devoured. Wow! Even I'm blushing. Jack's redhead is wearing a rather low-cut pale cream silk blouse and skirt with a waist small enough to anger every woman over size five in the crowd. And gasp, with matching stiletto heels! I am guessing she's about forty, but she looks thirty and is probably fifty. I am also guessing Jack somehow found out this woman was here at this fair and that's why he was rushing to get out. To avoid what is happening now.

A mob is forming, with much grinning, much

whispering. Cameras and cell phones are snapping merrily away. To end up somewhere on YouTube, something I've heard about but never seen. Our little happening is being turned into a media event.

There is another redhead in the group who looks very much like the famous author, only younger, probably a relative. She whispers in the woman's ear. The woman whispers something back and the younger one smiles knowingly.

Knowing what, I'm afraid to guess, but I sure can imagine.

I see Sophie and Bella get off at the lobby level and immediately ride the escalator back up. They can't take their eyes off Jack and the woman. And neither can I.

I also notice Jack is frozen, unable to either speak or look at me. I move closer to him. The redhead reads me correctly. I lift his seemingly paralyzed arm and put it through mine. We are together, this movement announces.

She smiles at me, looks down at my ring finger.

"The *fiancée*?" she asks with a voice like velvet.

As a matter of fact, once again, officially as of last night. "Yes," I manage to whisper. When is Jack going to say something?

"It was eight years ago when Jacques and I met in Paris," she informs me and about fifty or so others eagerly standing around. There is a long group sigh. I wonder how many of the wannabe romance writers out there are taking notes.

The redhead gestures lavishly. "How do you call it *en anglais*? A romance of the summer?"

More moans from the onlookers.

I've had it. I nudge Jack to say something.

He looks toward me but he is staring blindly at some point over my head. "Gladdy, this is Michelle, I mean, Michelle duBois." His voice is a croak. You know, the way adolescent boys sound when they first get those raging hormones.

"Michelle, Gladdy Gold..."

I manage a polite nod.

Now Sophie pokes Jack and says, "And her very closest friends, Sophie and Bella." The girls preen. They are having the time of their lives. I am having a reflux choking up of the throat.

Michelle inclines her head toward the woman next to her. "My niece, Colette Marie."

Colette adds, "Named after the famous writer."

Michelle smiles. "She is also my assistant, my PR person, and—how you say—my Jill of all trades." The younger woman bows politely. "Come away to someplace more *privé*," Michelle suggests, motioning to us.

Without waiting for me to agree, she strolls away from the crowd to the nearest room, expecting us to follow. And we do. This woman is used to having her way.

There is another collective sigh, now that the French farce is over, and the onlookers disperse to continue on their merry way.

Michelle uses a key card to open a door marked VIP Lounge. Empty. And now we are inside. Colette immediately gives Michelle a water bottle from her large bulging carryall.

The girls quickly sit together on a floral love seat, their eyes like saucers.

Jack finally manages to come to himself. "Michelle, it's very good to see you again."

"And for me, too. I hoped we might meet, but this city is rather large, *n'est-ce pas*? Such a wonderful coincidence." She makes a small moue with her lips. "Even though I should not be kind to you—the way you left me so abruptly."

Jack jumps in, I assume to stop her from saying anything too personal. "Congratulations on your book. When I met you, your first book was about to be published. And now, I see, this is your fifth. You must be very proud of your success."

Colette speaks for her. "And she leads a very exciting life because of it."

It's obvious the niece is very proud of her aunt and Michelle is content to let the young woman extol her successes. Michelle puts her arms lovingly around her niece, but Colette suddenly blurts, "And because of what she writes, her life is very dangerous, too."

Michelle interrupts. "Now now, we'll have none of that."

"But you have so many enemies!" Colette insists.

Michelle pats the young woman on the head. "My niece worries too much."

Jack, finally in his element, lets the cop in him come out. "Has something been happening to make you fearful?"

"There have been incidents..." Michelle admits.

"More than just incidents. Threats—" Colette inserts.

Michelle puts her hand gently on Colette's lips. "I am not afraid." But her eyes belie her words. Jack catches it as well. This woman is frightened and trying to hide it.

Michelle looks at her thin diamond wristwatch. "*Ma petite*," she says to her niece, "you should have been paying attention." She starts to move to the door. "We are expected at my publisher's booth on the third floor. *Au revoir*, Jacques." She takes his hand in hers and as far as I'm concerned, she holds on too long. And Jack takes too long to remove his hand from hers.

She turns to me with a lovely practiced smile. "It was *très* pleasant meeting you, Mme. Gold. And your friends. I will be here this week. Perhaps we might have tea one afternoon."

"That sounds lovely," I answer equally politely,

knowing that isn't going to happen. The girls' heads swing up and down in their excitement. I smile up at Jack. "Don't you agree?"

He manages a half nod. As we leave the room he glances back. Michelle looks as worried as Colette.

Walking through the parking lot, Jack, who hasn't said a word since we left the hotel, suddenly hands me his car keys. "You go on home," he tells me. "I'll grab a cab later."

"Where are you going?" But I know what he's going to say.

"They're frightened. I think I ought to find out more. They may need police protection."

I am too stunned to protest. Bella, Sophie, and I pile into his car and drive off. By the time I search for him in my rearview mirror, he's already gone. I'm fuming.

Sophie, in the front passenger seat, kicks off her high heels. "So, what's he gonna do now?"

"Quiet!" The girls are dying to talk about it, but I nip them in the bud. "Not a word. You hear? I do not want any discussion."

They cower in the face of my anger. I can't deal with this right now. In fact, I don't want to think about anything now. I want utter silence. My mind wants to shut down until I can be alone and figure out what really just happened and how it might possibly affect my life.

Police protection indeed. And then I remember

she just happened to mention what floor she'd be on. Red flag! She knew he would come back.

Making his way through the hotel, Jack wonders how he will find Michelle again in this crowd. Then he recalls she had a meeting at her publisher's. Third floor. Right. He follows in the direction she was heading. Old cop abilities, like a good memory for details, die hard. He also remembers the publisher's name from the poster.

A decorative gate made of wicker and covered with a trellis of shiny fake leaves leads him to PIP—Paris International Publishing, Ltd. Jack suddenly finds himself in a contained area intended to remind one of France. The partitions are covered with photos of French scenery. Large posters with author photos and book titles are spread about the area. There are small booths for meetings. And young people, dressed in waiter apparel, hand out champagne.

The two redheads are easy to spot. Michelle and Colette are standing with a woman who reminds him of pictures he's seen of Edith Piaf, the famous French singer of sad songs—tiny, dark, intense, dressed all in black. Everyone is speaking in rapid-fire French.

Colette spots him and pokes Michelle. Michelle

waves. She says a few hurried words to the Piaf-like woman. They kiss cheek to cheek and Michelle takes her leave.

She hurries over to Jack. "I was hoping you would return."

"Are you busy? I could come back later."

"For you, *mon cher,* I am not busy. I have completed my editor's *petite* meeting."

His heart is pounding again. He wonders if it's excitement about seeing her, or guilt. What must Gladdy be thinking? He's behaving like a schoolboy. He remembers how often Michelle made him feel this way. Awkward. Fearful of making mistakes. *Was I ever as comfortable with her as I am with Gladdy?*

Her loveliness makes him catch his breath. But then, any man would react to her beauty. He gives her a quick hug. She hugs back. He pulls away first.

"It is such a lucky coincidence seeing you at this book fair. What about a brief stroll around the nearby shops, that would be nice. It's a beautiful day. Away from the crowds, *n'est-ce pas?*"

"Much better," Jack says.

"And we shall find a café and we'll chat. And you will tell me how you have managed to live so long without me." She laughs out loud, enjoying Jack's discomfort at her teasing. "Colette," she calls out, dismissing her. *"À bientôt."*

They stroll along the beach-cluttered T-shirt

tourist avenue. "Not quite Montmartre," he comments.

"Ah, you are remembering our many strolls around my city."

"How could I forget? It was a magical time."

"Real for me. Fantasy for you?" Her eyebrows rise.

"I didn't want to hurt you. But I did anyway."

"That is, how shall I say it—water under *le pont*." She smiles. "I did think to look you up when I arrived, but I wished to avoid another rejection."

Jack reddens. Guilty.

She puts her arm through his and leans into him. "But we found each other again. Perhaps fate meant us to meet again."

Uh-oh. What has he gotten himself into? he wonders.

They reach a coffee shop and Jack suggests they go in. When they are seated, he changes the subject. "Tell me about the threats. And don't make light of this."

"*Alors*. My worrywart little niece. Something to shrug off."

"Details. Come on."

"There were letters. Telling me to stop writing my books. If I do not, I will be killed."

"And you don't think that's serious?"

She shrugs. "Over these years, after each book there have been many...complainers. Threats about lawsuits. Getting even with me—like that. Much name-calling. How you say—it goes with the territory."

"I don't suppose you kept the letters?"

She shakes her head. "No."

"Colette seems particularly frightened. Why?"

"She feels that someone is stalking us. She thinks she saw a quick glimpse of the same man. But I look and I see no one. I am much too busy to believe this nonsense."

"I have advice for you and you are going to listen to me. Say you will."

Again that very French shrug and lifting of eyebrows.

"Say it."

"I will do anything you say, *mon cher*. Anything."

Jack busies himself with his cup of coffee. As long as he doesn't look at her, he can talk—like a cop. Like a friend.

4

MYSTERIOUS WOMAN

When we arrive back at Lanai Gardens, we see Ida, Evvie, Joe, and a group of our neighbors standing in a large circle on the expansive lawn of Phase Two. Joe looks pale, which means he must have had his chemo treatment today. His clothes seem looser to me. But I'm the only one Evvie has told of his illness and his valiant fight to survive. If the girls suspect, they say nothing. Nor will they, until they are officially informed.

Hy and Lola are there, as are Tessie and Sol. The two couples, leaders of the gossip brigade, are quiet for a change. Hy raises himself to his full five feet. Lola looks terrified. Tessie manages to munch on a sandwich with her free hand. Sol winks at Hy as if to show pleasure in this manly stuff. They stare rapt with attention. They, along with the half dozen others, have their legs apart, knees bent, each grasping a walking cane tightly with its point thrust outward.

Merrill Grant, who lives in Phase Four, stands in the center of the group with his cane. In front of him there is some sort of stuffed rag dummy tied to a large pole. What's with canes all of a sudden? Especially since not one of these people needs one.

Sophie and Bella rush to the circle. They are bursting to reveal today's drama at the book fair. I hurry after them, knowing I need to attach myself to them for damage control.

I hear Merrill shout out, demonstrating on the dummy. As he does, his group repeats in cadence with him, "Swing hard. Hard as you can! Sound off. One two, stab into the neck. Three four, push down in the groin. Five six, on top of the head. Seven eight, get him in the gut. Hit him high. Hit him low. Whatever you do, don't let go!"

Merrill was a marine in World War II. To this day, he still wears what's left of his hair in a regulation buzz cut.

The canes are swung at these imagined body parts. My neighbors are puffing away, sweat running down their faces as they shout along with Merrill. They grimace to show their anger at their imaginary enemies. With each thrust they shout "Ugh!"

I join Bella and Sophie, who are standing behind the circle as they try to get Evvie's and Ida's attention. "What's going on here?" I ask.

Sophie answers me as Ida waves back. "A lot of the retirement homes are doing it. It's the latest craze. Old people need to protect themselves, don't they?"

Bella says, "It's called Chop Suey."

Sophie shakes her head. "I already told you six times."

"Well, it's hard to remember." She tries again. "Kung Fooey?"

Sophie corrects her. "This is Cane Fu. Merrill saw it on TV and also in the papers. He decided he should start a group of our own. We would have been here if we hadn't gone to the fair." She giggles as she is undoubtedly thinking about what happened today. "We had more fun with you, Gladdy."

Yeah, hilarious, I think.

Evvie sees us and points to her wrist, then lifts five fingers, indicating to us they are almost done.

I watch in hideous fascination. "Since when do any of you own canes?"

Bella contributes, "Merrill got them for us wholesale bulk rate at a medical equipment store. I'm gonna paint mine pink."

Finally the group disbands with a last loud group "Ugh!" And then, "*Olé!*"

Or is it *oy vey*?

"But what about people who really need their canes to stand up?"

Ida reaches us, panting. She's heard my comment. "That's a different class. Merrill shows them how to fall down and attack from the ground."

If they don't get killed first or die of a heart attack, I think.

Sophie and Bella grab Ida and Evvie. Naturally Joe is right at Evvie's side. "Invigorating!" Ida says. "I think I might get arm muscles out of this."

We head for a patio table where the girls left snacks, lemonade, and towels. They flop down, dropping their canes, exhausted. "That was some workout," Joe says.

Evvie adds, "Beats our boring calisthenics."

I can't get over this craziness. "What if the attacker gets the cane away from you? He'll be like fifteen, tough, in perfect condition, armed and unafraid. You'll be shaking and terrified and won't have a chance in hell to overcome him. What then?"

Hy, passing by, calls out, "Then you kiss your ass good-bye." He grins and pats Lola on her rear. I have a feeling all this macho physical activity is turning him on and she'll be led to their bed as soon as they hit their apartment. Ugh, indeed.

Sophie and Bella grab seats and start blabbing.

As if I could stop them. I pull a chair away from the table and sit there with my head in my hands.

Sophie says, "You ain't gonna believe what happened to Gladdy this morning."

"What? What are you so excited about?" Evvie downs a large glass of lemonade.

Bella blurts, "Jack met his French girlfriend."

This gets everyone's attention.

"What French girlfriend?" Ida asks.

I say in desperation, "At least keep your voices down. This is no one's business but mine." Why am I kidding myself? Juicy news like this will spread like applesauce on a latke within an hour.

Joe is leaning so close, he's almost in my lap. "Wow!"

Sophie stage-whispers at a fast pace, "She's a redhead and she's way younger than us and she's gorgeous."

"Talk slower," Evvie says. "Take a breath."

"Andshe'safamouswriter," Bella adds, unable to slow herself down.

"And she kissed Jack. In front of a thousand people!" Sophie is ecstatic.

"Maybe twenty... or fifty," I say with a dollop of sarcasm.

"And she called him 'moan chair,' whatever that means." Bella looks to me for help.

"*Mon cher*," I correct. Why did I do that? It's like tightening the noose at my own execution.

Bella fairly jumps up and down. "That's it, whatever. It means she was madly in love with him." Bella adds, "Her name is Michelle. Isn't that sexy?"

"And they met in Paris." Sophie jumps in as she reaches for the guacamole dip and Doritos on the table. "And Jack was so embarrassed."

Evvie suddenly realizes he is missing. "Where *is* Jack?"

What can I say? My little family group looks to me for answers.

"Is he back in your apartment?" Evvie asks.

All the chairs are moved closer in, sort of reminding me of the early settlers seated around their campfire inside the wagon train. "I don't know what to tell you except that Jack seemed very surprised at seeing the woman. He knew her in Paris eight years ago."

Sophie is fanning herself nervously with a napkin. "He sure was flustered. That must have been some hotsy-totsy romance. Does this mean the wedding is off?"

Ida throws her a dirty look—Sophie, subtle as usual. "Don't be in such a hurry to throw the baby out with the bathwater."

Bella, holding a Dorito aloft, looks around perplexed. "What baby? Where is a baby taking a bath?"

Ida shakes her head. "It's just an expression. It means don't jump to conclusions."

"Oh." Satisfied, Bella delicately dips her chip in the dish of guacamole.

"Girls. And Joe," I say. "I really don't feel comfortable talking behind Jack's back."

"Yeah, men hate that stuff." So says Joe, spokesperson for the entire male sex.

"Well," Ida says, looking back toward the building. "You won't have to do that anymore. You can do it to his face." Ida's chin nods to the twosome coming our way.

Surprisingly, Lola, who is never without her Hy, is heading toward us with Jack in tow. He clearly isn't happy about it, but she's holding firm to his left arm.

"Not a word," I whisper. "Act natural."

"Be careful," Evvie warns. "Watch every word you say. What goes in Lola's ear will eventually come out of Hy's mouth."

Lola is very pleased with herself. "Look who I found just about to go upstairs. I told him you weren't up there."

Jack waves feebly with his free arm.

What I'm thinking is that my mind is a clock. It's an hour and ten minutes since I got home. What has he been doing?

Sophie and Bella suddenly pretend great interest in pouring themselves another drink. Ida taps her fingers on the table, looking hither and yon. Evvie is busily examining her nails and giving them a little buffing with a nail file. Joe's nose buries itself in his newspaper. Upside down.

So much for acting natural.

Lola awards me a toothy smile. "Now that I have you and Jack together, I have good news for you. I found you a wedding planner. She comes with great recommendations. You are very lucky she has a spot available right now."

With that, Lola places a small card in my hand. "Call her. You'll love her."

As she turns, she adds, "Her name is Trixie Tryhard." She grins. "I think it's her professional name. I hope." And she scampers off.

Everyone gets up all at once and begins moving away, excuses given on the run.

Evvie says, "Joe, come on. We have to check on your calf's liver." She pulls him along.

Sophie drags Bella with her. "We have to go, too. We're cooking together tonight. Salmon croquettes."

Bella embellishes, "She cooks. I wash up."

Ida just gathers up her things and tosses a casual wave over her shoulder as she leaves.

After they scamper off, Jack says, "Let me guess. I was the prime subject of the conversation."

"You got it."

He sits down next to me and pours some lemonade for both of us. "I have to apologize for my behavior back there. I was so taken by surprise—I mean I never thought I'd see Michelle again and suddenly, there she was." He shrugs, and smiles wryly. "I'm afraid I didn't handle it well. I suppose you want a full report."

I smile back at him, amused. I reach out and touch his cheek. "Honey, I would expect that you knew other women in your life before me. Granted I was a little taken aback that there was someone so much younger."

"I was pretty amazed myself at the time. That's why it didn't work out for me—the age difference."

"Did it matter to her?"

"She said not." He shakes his head. "All I kept thinking at the time was that twenty-five years' difference would matter fairly quickly."

I want to say reassuring things like, To me you're not old, and other well-meaning comments, but I know it's better to let him talk. I try to imagine myself in such a situation, being much older than someone I loved. I suppose it would have bothered me, too. But to give up happiness for that reason?

It's as if he hears my question. "It was wonderful while I was thousands of miles away. But what would happen when I came home? I played all the scenarios in my head. Being embarrassed to introduce her to my children. Or my friends. They might have laughed at me or thought me a doddering old fool. So I took the coward's way out. Took her to an expensive restaurant and then I broke the news to her. That I was leaving without her."

"Before dessert, I'll bet," I blurt and immediately wish I could take the words back. I think of the little scene I played for myself last night about men dumping their girlfriends at expensive restaurants. Then it hits me all at once. Was that Jack's unconscious mind at work? Having a "French" evening to become engaged because it would be romantic? Oh, my!

He stares at me, startled. "How did you know?"

I cover quickly. "Saw it in a movie once." *Don't pry,* I tell myself. *You don't want to know too much. The less to worry about.*

He takes my hand in his. "But that was in the past. You know I'm totally devoted to you."

Tessie and Sol walk by, towels in hands, having just come from the pool. They start toward us, I suppose to chat. But I shake my head and Tessie gets the message. Private stuff. She steers Sol away.

I want to change the conversation, hopefully from personal to . . . what? Something less emotionally charged? "So you found her when you went back to the hotel?" I say. Do I want those details or not? I don't know which is worse, knowing or not knowing.

He's relieved. "Yes. She told me she was heading

toward a small shopping area and invited me to walk with her."

Good. At least she didn't invite him to her hotel room. To see her advance reading copies? I breathe a small sigh of relief. How much is he really telling me and how much has been abbreviated to protect the innocent? Why is all of this making me uncomfortable?

"Gladdy, she really does have a problem. There might be someone stalking her. She gets notes threatening to kill her if she doesn't stop writing her books. Unfortunately she threw the notes away. But she refuses to take it seriously. For example, I told her she shouldn't be walking around alone. Not that she couldn't be targeted in a crowd, but it lessens the odds. She promised me she'd report it to the security office. I think I'm going to phone Morrie and see what he suggests."

Yes, let Morrie take over and you stay away. I wonder if his policeman son knows all about Dad's hot love affair.

Hopeful me says, "So, that's it. You don't have to see her again."

He hesitates. Face turning a bit red again.

"Well, she did invite me to her book signing tonight." He pauses. "And of course, she said for me to bring you."

Oops. Spoke too soon. The pause gave him away. Not out of the prickly woods yet.

I pick up the now empty lemonade pitcher. Jack takes his clue from me and discards the empty paper cups and napkins in the trash bin.

I start on the cobblestone path toward my apartment, mind whirling. I feel insecure. I was so sure of Jack's love. Not anymore.

Jack follows behind me. "I'd like it if you came with me," he says to my back.

"I don't think so. Thanks anyway for asking."

"You'd probably enjoy it."

He's being too eager. Trying too hard to amuse me. His tone is insincere. I should go. Just to watch the body language between the two of them. But I don't really want to see it. Right now I can't even look in his eyes for fear I'll see a lie there.

We walk up the stairs, my posture still stiff and aloof. But I can't keep my back to him forever. I'll have to face him and my eyes will reveal my fears.

We reach the apartment door and he turns me around. "Tell me what you're thinking."

I take a deep breath. "I was thinking that with you away I could do my nails...and wash my hair." I pause. "Honest."

He looks at me, but I hold precariously on to my blank expression. He nods once. "I promise not to be too long." He pauses. "Honest."

Now his back is to me as he opens our door.

5

THE BOOK SIGNING

Jack hovers over me as I cook. He tries to help me get done quickly, so of course that slows me down. He sets the table fast and clumsily. Grabs plates, silverware, napkins, scurrying back and forth from kitchen to dining room, knocking into me, as if he were running a marathon. I try to keep out of his way. I don't comment on his behavior.

When dinner is finally ready, he gobbles it down. I doubt if he even knows what he ate. No leisurely conversation at this meal.

He scrapes his chair getting up, almost overturning it, and apologizes sheepishly. "I really shouldn't be late."

As he grabs his jacket off the couch I see a tie sticking out of its pocket. A tie to go to a book signing? "I hope you don't mind doing the cleanup?" he says.

"Not a problem."

"I was told it starts on time. First a speech and then the signing." He makes a last dash for the bathroom. In moments he comes out and his hair has been wetly combed and he smells of aftershave. After giving me a quick kiss on the cheek he heads out the door.

Then he hurries back to where I still sit, unmoving, at the table. He asks, "Are you sure you won't come?"

Since I'm in shorts and a T-shirt and barefoot, obviously it would take me time to get ready and if I said yes, he'd be stumbling all around me, anxiously hurrying me. "No, thanks. On your way now and make sure you buy a copy. I'm very interested in reading her book." *And I hope she's an awful writer,* I think meanly.

"Thanks, honey, I will." And he is gone. In a flash.

I sit there and sip my chardonnay. Well, that was fun. I address Jack's empty chair. "And how did you enjoy your dinner, dear? Yes, delicious, wasn't it? Read any good books lately?" No, that's not a good topic at this time. So now I know what it might be like to be married thirty years. Boring life. Boring wife. Hubby off to some adventure somewhere else. Hopefully, just an adventure, not an affair. What is he thinking? I'd really love to know. Is it the excitement of seeing someone he once cared for? Maybe it's more like unfinished business. Hopefully it's not testosterone. Now I interrogate myself. *And how do you feel, Gladdy Gold, about being dismissed?* I lift up my uneaten plate of vegetable stir-fry, which is starting to congeal by now. Like this sodden mess, that's how.

The doorbell rings. For a second I think Jack's changed his mind and come back. But, no, he'd use his key. It's got to be Evvie.

I know my sister. She walks right into the dining area and heads for the bottle of wine on the table and helps herself to a glass. "I saw Jack leave."

"Spying out your window, were you?"

"Better than watching Joe maul our dinner. Now where's he going?" She plops herself down at the table and pulls off a chunk of rye bread.

"Book signing. Of course he asked me to go with him, but I said no. And he was relieved."

"That was the right thing to do. Don't want him to feel trapped." She butters the bread.

"Didn't you eat?" I move dishes around to make room for her.

"Sort of. It's Joe's turn to cook. He makes the worst liver and onions ever. Have you ever tasted gray cardboard and unidentifiable shrunken charcoal? Yuk."

"So why do you let him cook?"

"Because I don't want him to get into his old habit of taking me for granted. My poor stomach. Got any Tums?"

She gets up and goes into my kitchen. "Never mind, I know where you keep them. Maybe on his cooking nights we should go out to eat. No, let him work. So, I'll suffer."

I start clearing the table. Evvie helps me. "What do you think? Should I be jealous?"

Evvie considers this. "Not yet. It's just the newness of the situation. Do you trust him, Glad?"

"I think so. Rather, I thought so. Never in my wildest imagination would I have expected this. Competition? Ridiculous! At our age?"

"No ring on her finger, huh?"

"Nope. Lots of expensive jewelry. No wedding ring."

"Try not to worry. It'll work out." But I see her cross her fingers like we did when we were kids and were lying.

At the sink, I scrape the hardly eaten food from the plates. "She's much younger. She's gorgeous. She's obviously rich. Probably very talented and travels in high literary circles. And they were once in love with one another. Now he's running around like a chicken without its head. Should I worry?"

Evvie stands near the stove nibbling at the stir-fry out of my wok.

"You're taking too long to answer me," I admonish her from where I'm stacking the dishes in the dishwasher.

Evvie laughs. "Remember that famous hysterically funny line from an old Jack Benny radio show? When this robber holds him up with a gun and says, 'Your money or your life.' And cheap Jack Benny says..."

I join in the punch line with her:

" 'I'm thinking. I'm thinking.' "

Evvie and I hug each other. What would I do without my sister?

Jack listens to Colette explain that it's almost closing time in the book room. "During the day," she tells him, "this room is packed. Booksellers from all over Florida and adjoining states are selling books by the attending writers. There are only a few people making last-minute buys right now, so you can imagine what this room is like when these booths are jammed with readers."

He straightens his tie as he watches Michelle and Colette retrieve copies of *Bonbon, Non Non!* from a tall bookshelf. Michelle stands on the ladder and hands books down to her niece. Jack, wanting to help, stacks the cart with the books Colette hands to him.

"I'd be happy to change places with you," he offers Michelle.

Michelle smiles down at him. "Thank you, but it is not necessary. I am used to rickety ladders all over the world."

Colette shakes her head in dismay. "What I never get used to is my controlling aunt who has to do everything herself. Does it make sense that she should climb the ladder, when it's obvious that a much younger, more agile me should be doing this silly job? And even more preposterous when a very able male like you could do it easier. A handsome man with whom she could be relaxing and having a cocktail instead."

Michelle laughs, and with a tingle, Jack remembers how that throaty, sexy sound turned him on years ago.

"She's right, you know," he says.

Michelle steps down and rearranges the books on the cart to her satisfaction. "I am a businesswoman, and to run a successful business, I make sure I know everything is done exactly the way I want it."

Colette shrugs. "And drives her publishers crazy. She doesn't know how to delegate, even though I am her only assistant and PR person and vice president of her company."

Michelle hugs her and says deprecatingly, "*Ma petite*, you exaggerate. Come, let us set up before my eager fans arrive."

Colette addresses Jack. "Tell me, how am I to learn the business when all she does is keep secrets from me? Have you ever heard of an author who never lets her closest in command even see her manuscript as she writes it? Not a word said, not a clue. Not even a charming sentence to whet the appetite. All locked up in her laptop and not one word seen until finished." She points to the small briefcase hanging from Michelle's shoulders. "And I might add, a laptop that never leaves her side for a moment."

Jack doesn't want to get between these two. He shrugs and takes a wild guess. "Maybe Michelle finds it necessary not to ruin her concentration when she writes."

Michelle shifts her shoulder strap and puts her arm through Jack's. "You see," she says to Colette, "he understands the author's need to keep solely in touch with her muse."

Colette pouts. "Sometimes I think she should write spy novels. She has the paranoid mind for it."

Michelle moves past the book cart and indicates it to Colette. "I am giving over control to you. Right now. You can wheel the cart all by yourself." They all laugh.

"And so, after three months of living with the Marais brothers in Ghent, I had enough material for this exposé. And now here it is." Michelle hefts the book. "And here I am. And soon the brothers will be eating jailhouse food. No more *chocolat* for them. Not even their own scandalous marzipan. I thank you very much for attending."

Jack, sitting next to Colette in the front row, watches proudly as the small meeting room erupts with applause from the audience.

The questions begin.

A voice in back calls out, "How did the brothers not know it was you, madame? You are famous everywhere."

Michelle smiles. *"Voilà!"* She waves her bracelet-filled arms. "Not the way I come to them. No jewelry. Poorly bleached hair of an unattractive color. Cheap clothes. A poignant, made-up story which flatters men into revealing their secrets. Nerves of steel. And, last but not least, professional acting lessons."

The audience loves her. And the questions continue on. Colette whispers to Jack, "This happens everywhere we go. If she let them, they'd keep her here for hours."

Jack surreptitiously looks at his watch.

Fortunately, Michelle wraps up the Q&A and signing in an hour. As the last fan leaves, Jack attempts to wheel the cart, but this time Colette insists she is capable of returning the few unsold books back to the book room without his help. Taking it from him, off she goes, calling over her back, "Your dinner is waiting."

Michelle admits to starvation and thirst. She tells Jack she can never eat before a lecture. Jack walks her to the elevator. He's about to take leave of her when she says, "A nightcap? For a few minutes. Besides, I like having company when I eat."

Jack hesitates, then agrees. "All right, a nightcap for just that—a few minutes. I'd like to discuss your safety one more time."

When they reach the top floor Jack looks around Michelle's luxurious Mediterranean-style suite. A tray is set, waiting for her on the large white coffee table with its seashell border. Sandwiches, fruit, cheese, and wine, ordered earlier by the efficient Colette, Michelle informs him.

No doubt she is considered a star to rate this, thinks Jack as he looks around.

"Care to join me?" she asks.

"No, thanks, I had a big meal before I came."

"At least some wine?"

"I shouldn't. I have to drive home."

She smiles, looking at the label of the bottle. "Good, this is from a fine French winery. Not the one I intend to destroy in my next exposé."

Michelle kicks her high heels off. She tosses her briefcase on the desk, then removes her jacket and plops down on the couch, tucking her legs in under her. Her low-cut silk blouse flutters with the movement. She starts to laugh as she reaches for some Camembert and a small sesame thin wafer.

"What?" Jack sits down near her and pours himself a drink from a carafe of water.

"I was remembering a night when it was I who drank too much wine and you had to drive us home. Remember?"

He smiles. He realizes he remembers every detail of that month he spent with her. "How could I forget?"

"You had to drive my car and you weren't familiar with the controls and it was very dark. You were swerving as you had trouble with the stick shift."

Jack, caught up in her story, absently pours himself some wine. "And the *gendarme* on the motorcycle pulled us over."

"And he repeatedly shouted at you and all you could say was *Je ne parle français*."

"I remember poking you to help me out, but you pretended to be asleep."

"And the policeman got angrier and angrier and more frustrated."

They are both laughing hard now. "I was so irritated that you didn't help me out. Until you told me later all the horrible things the cop was saying."

"He called you an idiot and insulted you because you were an American and because you didn't have the decency to learn our language. And he accused you of being drunk because you were wobbling across the highway. And he wanted you to follow him to the police station. He finally gave up and called you stupid and drove off."

"You were so right not to let him know you understood him. You saved me from a long night of explanations that wouldn't be believed."

"You would not have liked French jails."

The laughter stops.

"About Colettte's comment. I must defend myself," Michelle says, reaching across him to take the wine bottle out of his hand. Jack suddenly feels he is too close to her. Her perfume reaches his nostrils. Her bodice is too revealing.

Michelle, seemingly unaware, says, "Colette was too harsh. I keep my manuscript well hidden for safety, because there are too many people who would like to know who my poisoned pen will destroy next. If any pages were left around, they would invariably find themselves in the wrong hands. Someone who will sell them in advance to some magazine or the Internet. For example, my next manuscript contains information that will destroy a winery in Bordeaux. Information has probably leaked out already, but if the vineyard owners ever saw what I wrote, they'd be at the lawyers immediately, trying to stop the publication. What could be worse?"

Jack shakes his head. "What would be much worse is that someone might kill you to be rid of you for what you write in your books. You are more protective of your work than your life."

She shrugs. "What am I to do? Hire bodyguards and have no privacy in my life?"

"You take too many risks."

She reaches closer to him and refills her empty glass. "And what life isn't filled with risks?" She shifts slightly; her body leans against his chest. Her voice softens. "Ah, Jacques, I have missed you."

Jack leaps up, afraid he's not thinking clearly. "I must go. It's late."

"I'm sorry. I should not have said that."

He watches her gracefully unravel herself and rise, too, reminding him of a satisfied, well-fed Siamese cat. "Of course you must," she agrees smiling, knowing how she affects him.

At the open door, he feels clumsy and tongue-tied. "Please be careful. Use all the locks and bolts. You have my card. If you need any help, call me."

She gives him a delicate kiss on his forehead. "Your wish is my command." Then she tilts her head. "Wait," she says, turning and hurrying to her briefcase. She takes out a copy of her book. "This is for you. I hope you find it interesting."

Jack takes the book, thanks her, and practically dashes to the elevator. What a clod he is! How badly he's handling this situation. And he doesn't understand why.

The Snake waits patiently. He feels it is his finest attribute. He never tires. Although he complains to himself, wondering why he agreed to this silly job. But family is family. And to tell the truth, he's enjoying this petite *vacation from retirement. Like riding on the bike, he thinks as he smiles, one never forgets.*

Aha! His virtue is rewarded. He sees the top of that lovely mane of red from the light in the hallway as his mark unlocks the door and pushes the book cart into the room. Her head is bent down, engrossed in reading a book as she walks. She is startled when she attempts to turn on the lights and they don't go on. She clicks the switch a few more times. Then she slides into the dark room anyway. He can almost read her mind as she stands in the aisle between the booths. Should she go back outside and find someone on staff to help her? There is a little light from the hallway and she has so few books, so she chooses to just drop off the books quickly and leave.

Exactly what he expected she would do. He stands watching as she makes her way to the shelves. Little did she know that he'd been in the book room watching her remove the books before her reading. Had hidden so as to make sure he'd be locked in. He knew she'd return.

The Snake is pleased with himself. Had he not chosen to get rich as a thief, he believes he would have made a fine psychologist. He reads his victims so well. He pictures his yacht docked on the Riviera, waiting for him, the small refrigerator stocked with his favorite champagne. If all goes well, he'll be on his way home in two days. This boring Florida coast is nothing compared to the beauty of the south of France.

But what's this? He no longer hears the clicking of her heels. She's stopped.

"Hello, is someone here?" the woman calls out and he can hear the tremor of fear in her voice. She waits. Of course there is no answer.

The Snake hardly breathes. She must come to the high bookshelf. His plan depends on it.

"Please. I beg you. Is someone here?"

The Snake is poised to go after her should she try to run. But no, she seems to have calmed down. He hears the heels clicking again.

As quickly as she can, she climbs the ladder with her few books in one hand. She thrusts them on the shelf and starts to step down.

Now! The Snake leans from his hiding place behind the bookcase and pushes. He hears the redhead gasp as she feels the bookcase vibrating. She tries to steady it, but she realizes someone is there, pushing it toward her. She tries to hurry back down the ladder. But The Snake gives her no chance as she suddenly feels herself tilting backwards. Both arms go out instinctively to stop the now quickly falling bookcase with all its books tumbling out.

The Snake imagines the look of helpless horror on her face as the bookcase slams his victim to the ground. Her screams die inside her. The job is done.

6

AFTERMATH

"Gladdy, are you sure I should leave?" Evvie hesitates at my door.

"It's all right. The babysitter may go home now. Thank you for playing ten endless rounds of Spite and Malice to keep me company."

"Thank you for letting me win. Not because you played the cards badly, but because you weren't concentrating. As if I didn't know where your mind was."

How right she is. All I can think about is why Jack isn't home yet. How long can a signing take? I gently push her out the door.

"All right. I get the hint. See you in the morning. And don't worry."

After Evvie leaves, I curl up on the couch and

watch another rerun of *Lost*. My favorite show. I admit I'm still hooked on the adventures of the once-stranded islanders. But this time it doesn't distract me. Not even the sexy Sawyer or Sayid hold my attention. I can't stop myself from looking at my wall clock every few minutes. I give up. I'm going to bed.

I turn all the lights off in the apartment except for a night-light. When Jack finally arrives home all is silent except for the dishwasher in its last rinse cycle. I listen to him tiptoe into the dark bedroom so as not to wake me. But I am up. Believe me, I would have waited all night, if necessary, for his return.

I'm turned on my side, pretending to be asleep. I don't want to talk to him right now. He probably knows I'm faking it and he's undoubtedly thankful. I hear the rustling of material as he takes off his clothes. Then he is in the bathroom. Naturally, I'm curious about what happened and why he is late. But I'm afraid if I discuss it now, I might handle it badly and maybe say all the wrong things. Better to sleep on it.

Jack climbs into bed behind me and snuggles his naked body close to mine, reaching his arm around my waist. Our favorite sleeping position. Do I smell perfume on him? I'm not sure. I don't want to know. In moments I hear him snoring lightly.

Now that my ship is back safely in its harbor, I can sleep as well.

But it seems I've only just drifted off when the phone rings. We both stir.

"Please, you answer it," I tell Jack in my barely awake state. One open eye glances at the clock; it's only five A.M. Then I become more alert. No one phones at this time of night unless it's bad news. Oh, my God, has something happened to one of our children?

I hear Jack's voice, full of tension. "When? Where? Yes, of course I'll come right away."

He jumps out of the bed and hurries to the closet he shares with me.

It couldn't be family. All of our clan are up north in New York. It's someone close by. Oh, no . . . one of the girls . . . ?

"What's wrong?" I'm definitely awake now. "Who's in trouble . . . ?"

Jack struggles into his clothes. "It's Michelle. Her niece Colette has been very badly hurt. She's unconscious. Michelle is afraid she might die." As he runs out the door, he calls back to me. "I'll call as soon as I know more."

Great. No way I can fall back to sleep now.

Jack stands in the hallway outside Colette's cubicle in ICU watching Michelle, who is sitting at her niece's bedside and softly crying. It is very quiet in the hospital. Patients are still asleep. The only person around is a slightly built older man in a white jacket dusting the floorboards along the corridor. Nurses are preparing medication doses. Breakfast will follow soon after. Doctors will make their rounds. After that, there will be a lot of activity. Another nurse comes by with a bouquet of flowers for one of her patients. The old man sneezes. Three times. Jack turns and says, "Gesundheit."

He spots his son, Morrie, coming toward him down the hallway. The old man is still sneezing.

"What did you find out from her doctor?" Jack asks as Morrie reaches him. Detective Morgan Langford. Jack can't help thinking with pride about his son who followed in his footsteps.

"They don't know yet. She has a serious concussion, cracked ribs, and a fractured leg."

"Is it possible this was an accident? Could she have pulled the shelves down on herself?"

"I went with hotel personnel to inspect the bookcase. It seems like a bolt had come out of the wall. Though they can't understand how that could happen. They swear everything was up to code. They probably fear a lawsuit out of this."

"Maybe she grabbed at the shelves trying to steady herself on the ladder and accidentally loosened them even further."

"No way of knowing until she regains consciousness and tells us. If she comes out. She might remain in a coma." Morrie glances over to Michelle. "So, this is the woman you fell in love with in Paris?"

"You remember me talking about her?"

"How could I forget? You came back a confused and agitated man. You drove us crazy. Should I have married her? Did I do the right thing leaving her? It took you forever to stop agonizing over whether you had made the right decision. She is a beauty, Dad. You weren't exaggerating." Morrie sees Michelle glancing out the door at him. He speaks softer. "So, you were with Gladdy when you ran into her at the book fair?"

"Unfortunately—yes."

"Good luck with this, Dad. I see complications ahead."

Jack sighs. "It's already complicated."

Michelle comes out to join the two men. Jack is pained to see how upset she is. She is beside herself. "It's my fault. I never should have let her go alone."

Jack tries to be comforting. "Don't say that, Michelle. How could you possibly have known?"

Michelle clutches at his arms. "If I had been with her."

Jack shakes his head. "Then possibly both of you would be in hospital beds now."

"I saw how rickety that ladder was. How could

I have been so careless? I should have kept her away from it. Will she be all right?"

Morrie says, "We don't know for sure yet. But the doctor did sound confident."

Michelle looks at Morrie and then at Jack. "You are related?"

"Michelle, this is my son, Morgan."

"Oh, yes, I remember. The policeman. You talked so much about him. It is terrible to meet you like this." Michelle still holds on to Jack as Morrie takes notice and exchanges a meaningful look with his father. "Your father is the only person I know in this country. I feel so alone."

Morrie adds his sympathetic comment. "Well, now you know two people. We'll do all we can to help you."

"Thank you."

"I'm on my way back to the hotel to meet with Security." To Jack, he says, "We'll talk later." With that he nods at Michelle and heads back down the hall. The hospital employee dusting the woodwork scurries out of his way.

Michelle clutches Jack even tighter. "I am so frightened."

"I'm here for you, and my son is very good at what he does."

"I have already called our family back home. They are distraught. They want her home. But there is no way I can move her. She was my responsibility and I failed her."

The tears start to fall again and Jack puts his arm around her.

"Please stay with me for a while? Please?" she begs.

"As long as you need me."

The Snake slithers away, pulling off the white lab coat he stole from a closet, and tossing it and the dust rag into a nearby trashcan. Damn his allergy to flowers. Not that it really mattered. He has always had the ability to seem invisible, to slither in and out of people's lives, allowing them to recognize him only when it was too late and their fate was sealed. No one has ever been able to identify him.

But now he is furious with himself. The woman Michelle is still alive. How could he have been so stupid as to try to kill the wrong person? And he even failed at that! The niece is still alive. The red hair fooled him. No, no, alors! Admit it. He was told he needed glasses, but how can so famous a man as The Snake wear glasses? Absurd!

And now, to discover the woman knows un flic—*a policeman—in this country! It complicates things, but The Snake will prevail. He manages a cruel smile. So far the authorities believe it was an accident. He will have to call his nephew, Gaston,*

back in Paris. But now he has an excuse for his fail-
ure. He can tell the others he injured the niece on
purpose, to separate from the target the one who is
always at her side.

He sneers at a fast-moving nurse who almost col-
lides with him as she hurries into a patient's room.
No, perhaps he won't call Gaston yet. He will do
the job right next time. He will not miss again.

I'm warming up for our morning exercise downstairs next to our usual patio table before the girls
arrive. Why? Because I don't want them to find an
excuse to come into my apartment. Otherwise
they'll ask where Jack is and where he went so
early in the morning. Since I won't lie and say he's
still sleeping, it will open a can of peas I don't want
to open. All right. It's not as if he didn't check in
and call me from the hospital, but there was no
mention of when he'd be home. It is very small-
minded of me to feel distress about Jack being there
to help Michelle. And now Morrie's showed up. I'll
bet he heard about Michelle years ago. Pretty soon
my entire world, meaning all of Phase Two, will be
sticking their noses into my business to find out
about the mysterious gorgeous Frenchwoman who
may or may not be taking Jack away from me. I
love living here, but somehow privacy is not a
word in anyone's dictionary.

"You're talking to yourself, did you know?" Evvie briskly jogs over to me as part of her warm-up. She's wearing bright orange shorts and a green T-shirt.

"I know."

"You're here before Ida and Bella. The three of you always come downstairs together. Change of pattern means something's happened."

Here we go. I have to tell Evvie, so how can I keep it from the other girls? "Michelle's niece Colette had a horrible accident last night."

"Tell me."

"Might as well wait for the others, so I don't have to repeat it."

"So I gather Jack is with her at the hospital."

"Right on. Since five A.M."

"Fate." Evvie leans her hands against a building wall and does arm and leg stretches. "If you hadn't gone to that book fair, you and Jack would never have run into her. And this wouldn't be happening."

"And your point is?"

"No good deed goes unpunished. You shouldn't have driven the girls to the hotel."

"So, you think this was meant to happen? Miss Philosopher?"

Now Evvie is doing knee bends. *"Que será, será."*

Bella and Sophie, in color-coordinated sweat

suits, Sophie in yellow, Bella in pink, trot over in their imitation of jogging. Teeny tiptoe steps at a snail's pace. Sophie stops and jogs in place. "We're here."

Bella immediately sits down at the nearest patio table. *Her* philosophy is why stand when you can sit.

Ida, in her usual grungy-looking gray sweats, arrives. "What's going on? Since when do we do warm-ups downstairs?"

I fill them in, giving the same useless warning: Keep it to yourselves. I know they'll try, but I also know they'll slip up.

"Wow," says Sophie.

"Me, too, wow," says Bella.

"That's what you get for driving them to the book fair." Ida bends, touching her toes.

Evvie shrugs. "I rest my case."

I hear a "Yoo-hoo, Gladdy," coming from behind and we all look around. There's Lola heading toward us with a woman in tow. Since when is she without Hy? And who is this strange apparition bearing down upon us? She's about five ten and very hefty. I thought Evvie was the queen of colorful, but this babe puts her to shame. She is every color of the spectrum and that includes her hair. I can't even describe the hairdo. It's kind of fifties retro with a bubble top and bangs that nearly cover her face. Her dress seems like a muumuu, but isn't.

It's just large and bright. And she wears matching high-heeled shoes. Which seem too tight for her, since she's wobbling on them. She carries an elephant-size purse over her shoulder. Ditto same colors. And a huge sun hat hanging from a string on her arm. Think of a very large walking rainbow.

Everyone stares.

I have a sinking feeling that this is Lola's suggested wedding planner.

Lola plays Perle Mesta, the once-famous hostess. "Everybody, meet Trixie Tryhard, Florida's most famous wedding planner."

Say it isn't so.

Trixie lunges toward each of us for a hearty handshake as Lola states our names.

"Hello. Hello. Hello. Hello. Hello."

"And hello back," says Bella. Miss Charm. I'm surprised she didn't curtsy.

Lola beams. "Trixie was in the neighborhood and dropped by, hoping you had a few minutes to get acquainted."

"I suppose so," I say warily.

Evvie pushes me forward. "You could use the distraction." She turns to the girls. "Come on, let's hoof it."

The girls follow her, high-stepping in imitation.

Just then we hear Hy calling Lola. Her master's voice. And off she goes.

Now I'm left alone with the overwhelming Ms. Tryhard. What a name.

"Just call me Trix," she says as she unloads a pile of stuff from her massive bag onto the patio table. "Isn't this the loveliest day?"

I sit down slowly at the edge of a chair in case I need to make a fast getaway.

First she puts on her huge sun hat. "Don't want too much sun, do we?"

She reaches for an oversized three-ring binder notebook. And whips out a pen. As she does, she takes a handful of pens out and rolls them toward me. I read the writing on their sides. *Call Trix for your wedding fix.* "Take some and pass them around to your friends."

I start. "Ms. Tryhard..." Trix shoots me a look which says, Didn't you hear me? "Trix, I mean. I'm not really sure we need a wedding planner."

She is horrified. "Not need? No problem. Just hear me out and you'll know this is the direction you want to take. Names!"

"Excuse me?"

"The name of the happy couple. You are Gladys Gold. Who's the lucky guy?"

"Jack Langford. But I'm not sure..."

"Jack Langford." She writes slowly with one of her pens, her tongue licking the side of her lip as she does so.

I try again. "Look, I don't want to waste your time—"

Trix puts her large right paw on my arm. "Just hear me out. Advice is free. After you hear, and I demonstrate what I can do for you, you will be thrilled to write me my itsy-bitsy checkee."

Checkee? Oh, no...I have the feeling if I try to get away she'll sit on my lap and smother me. Oh, well. Evvie's right. I'm already distracted.

"First things first. When is the wedding date?"

"We were talking about the first of the year. Maybe even earlier. We're flexible."

Trix is horrified. "That's impossible! We usually expect six to twelve months to prepare!"

I start to get up. "Well, that's that. We'll just have to manage—"

That large paw pushes me right back down again. "That's a very good word—manage. That's what we'll do." She sighs. "It might not be as grandiose."

I equal her sigh. "Grandiose is what we don't want. Simple, that's the operative word."

Trix laboriously writes the word in her notebook. It's obviously not a word she likes. "We'll just have to work speedo."

Speedo? I hate to think what that means.

Trix pushes brochures at me. That purse must be bottomless.

As she mentions a name, she slaps down a

brochure to match. "Here's our checklist: Decide on a definite date. Make an appointment with the clergyman. Determine a budget. Compose and set a guest list. Set time, location of ceremony, rehearsal, and reception. Choose photographer or videographer. Shop for wedding gown; several fittings will be necessary. Obtain floral and music estimates. Make appointment for bridal portrait. Register with a gift registry. Select bridesmaids. Pick honeymoon place. Will you need a passport? Are your passports up-to-date? How do you feel about confetti? And don't you love ice sculptures?"

Help! Somebody get me out of this!

By the time I escape from Trix and head off to catch up on my exercises, the girls are off to other activities. Ida is on her way out to her cooking class when she notices Bella and Sophie heading toward the back of their building. They seem fairly dressed up with matching colored walking canes. Ida calls out to them. "Hi. Where are you two going?"

Bella and Sophie look at one another guiltily.

Sophie says, "Going to the post office across the street," and at the same time Bella says, "Just out for a little stroll." They both stop. Sophie throws Bella a dirty look. "Post office, remember!"

Bella looks chagrined. "Yeah, I forgot. Post office. Need any stamps?" she asks Ida.

Ida shakes her head. "If you're gonna lie, try to keep your stories straight. And never mind, I don't care where you're off to."

With that, the two of them scamper away, swinging their canes as they go.

Ida, though, is curious. She follows them, staying well behind. She watches them cross Oakland Park Boulevard, and to her surprise they head for Jerry's Deli, next to the Fort Lauderdale hospital.

Strange, she thinks. Why were they so cagey about going out to breakfast? She turns around and heads to her cooking class.

Meanwhile, Sophie, leading Bella by the hand, enters Jerry's Deli. Jerry, the owner, stands behind the counter with his son, Larry. She sniffs, thinking how these are two of a kind. They sure do look alike, very heavy, swarthy, with identical small moles with a tiny tuft of hair on their chins. They're always noshing at something while they cut meat slices and make sandwiches. Their aprons are always unattractively stained with a variety of foods. Jerry recognizes them and nods his head toward the back. Bella sniffs too, only she is kvelling over the wonderful odor of delicatessen. "Maybe we could eat first?" Sophie yanks her arm. "We can't be late."

They make their way through the restaurant past a few customers who don't look up, totally involved in their food. Sophie agrees that what they are eating smells delicious. Bella slows up, hoping they'll stop to eat, but Sophie pulls her along.

At the far end of the deli there is a large, heavy, russet-colored drape. Sophie pulls it aside; behind it is a door. She looks over her shoulder, sensing someone watching them. She's right. Father and son are staring at them from behind the counter, beady-eyed, their mouths twisted in a knowing grin.

The heck with them. Sophie knocks, and she and Bella walk right in, shutting the door behind them.

The girls enter what Sophie imagines was once a back storeroom. Now it's been cleared out and the room is painted totally white. A number of women are already seated in a semicircle facing a chalkboard at the rear of the room.

Mrs. Jerry—the girls have never known her first name—sits near the entrance behind a small table with a notebook and cash box. Sophie thinks that Mrs. Jerry looks just like her husband and son. At her side are white painted shelves full of what to Sophie seems like a peculiar collection of products. Vitamins. Crystals. Beads. Incense. Energy drinks and energy bars. Photos of their leader posed with very famous, mostly showbiz clients. Dried flowers. Lists of ashrams in India with dates of events. CDs of Indian New Age music. Posters. And much more.

Daunted by the oddness, the girls haven't bought anything on their previous visits.

"Here's my five-dollar entrance fee," Sophie says eagerly.

"Mine too," adds Bella.

Mrs. Jerry hands them each a small ticket and notes their names and amounts in her spiral notebook. Knowing the rules, the girls open the closet adjoining the shelves and place their purses in alongside everyone else's. Mrs. Jerry explained it the first time they attended—there must be nothing to distract in this plain room. They remove their shoes, lining them up with others against the wall. They take seats, and park their canes next to them. They smile at the neighbors they know from the Phase Three building in Lanai Gardens. Sophie glances around, noticing that few of the women are under sixty-five. She waves at Arlene Simon, a neighbor from Phase Four. Arlene waves back. Bella sniffs again and pokes Sophie. She whispers, "I don't like the smell of incense. It makes me want to sneeze. Why couldn't they use pastrami or corned beef?"

The room eventually fills up with about thirty women. While waiting, they study the posters on the wall. "I still don't get them," Bella says. "What's a chakra anyway?" Each poster has a dramatic, multicolored painting with names identifying the different kinds of chakras and their corresponding crystals.

A gong sounds and a door at the side of the room opens and he comes in. Their leader. Their guru. Baba Vishnu. He is tall and very thin and wears a white robe and white turban. Around his neck is a string holding a large crystal.

"Yum," Sophie says, admiring the young man's looks as always. "Such a gorgeous *punim*." Baba Vishnu slides slowly down onto the white pillow on the floor facing the semicircle of his admirers. As he lowers himself he bows his head. Everyone bows back to their guru.

As he reaches the pillow he begins the chant and the women follow. The sound of their group mantra, *om*, slowly builds, filling the room.

Sophie grabs Bella in excitement as the gentle chimes begin to ring. She wonders whose husband will join them today in the Dead Husbands Club.

When Ida gets to her cooking class, she is disappointed. There is a sign on the rec room door saying her class has been canceled. She looks around hoping to find some of her classmates; at least they can talk Thai cooking on their own. But no luck. There's no one around unless she counts the quacking ducks along the walkway. She feels a hunger pang. All she ate before meeting the girls for exercise was toast with orange marmalade and tea. Why not join Sophie and Bella at Jerry's Deli?

Her salivary glands respond instantly to the idea. She hurries to the back of the buildings to take the shortcut across the street again and heads to the deli with visions of a three-decker turkey, swiss cheese, and tomato sandwich on rye urging her on. In five minutes, she's there.

Ida walks in with a smile on her face, which quickly diminishes as she finds no sign of Sophie or Bella. She looks again, booth by booth. That's odd, she thinks. They couldn't have finished eating that quickly. She counts the customers. Three different men in three different booths. A mother and two kids sitting at the counter. That's it. She looks to Jerry and his son, but suddenly they seem very busy chopping onions and don't look at her. A scowling waitress, fortyish and seemingly anorexic, with stringy hair and sallow skin, approaches. She looks suspiciously like the father and son behind the counter. One might guess that's because they *are* her father and brother. Phoebe (her name tag announces), menu in hand, asks, "One?"

But Ida doesn't want to sit there by herself. Annoyed, she leaves the restaurant to go back home and forage in her near-empty fridge.

*　　*　　*

Evvie is watching me pace my apartment, back and forth. "Talk about a cat on a hot tin roof," she says as I unwrap groceries and stack them where they belong. We are listening to the messages Jack left about Colette. It was a terrible accident. A very heavy bookshelf fell on her. She's still in intensive care. They're worried that she might not come out of the coma.

"That poor, poor girl," Evvie says.

I agree. "How could I be so dumb? I get myself all aggravated because he hasn't called me all morning, and then I realize I forgot to turn on the cell phone." I slam the fridge door unnecessarily hard. "And then I get home and there are three more messages on the apartment machine."

"Well, look at the good side. Instead of him being the unfeeling rat you were furious with all day, he did call in as he promised he would."

"And I can't call him back on his cell in the hospital."

"Patience, my darling sis. He'll probably be home any minute now."

I toss a loaf of bread at her and she catches it. "Look who's giving me lectures on patience— Ms. I-want-to-know-now-this-very-second-or-else gal."

She throws the bread back at me, grinning. "I like to think I've matured."

"Ha! That'll be the day."

I rewind the machine again. "Did you notice anything about all the messages—something left out?"

Evvie listens as I play them again. "No, what am I missing?"

"He never mentions Michelle at all. He was with her since about five A.M. and still not home and not a word about her."

"Aren't you overreacting? What do you think he's doing with her? They've probably been at that unfortunate girl's bedside."

"What a terrible person I am. Michelle must be going through hell and all I can think about is being annoyed at Jack for not being home."

"I thought you said you trusted him."

I break off a piece of my dill rye bread and nervously chomp on it. "I don't trust Jack's old girlfriend. She's up to something and I don't know what."

Eventually Evvie leaves to have dinner with Joe. I'm too antsy to eat. When I finally hear the key in the door, the first thing I do is look at the clock. It's nearly ten-thirty. I hurry to open the door. Jack enters, but one look at his ashen face shows his exhaustion.

"Are you all right? Are you hungry? Have you eaten anything all day?" I don't know what to offer him first. I put my arms around him, but he gently shrugs me off.

"Need to sleep. That's all I want. We'll talk later." With that he moves right past me to our bedroom, undressing as he crosses the room.

Not like my Jack, I think. *Not like him at all.*

7

THE SNAKE CHECKS IN

The Snake paces back and forth across his cheap, sleazy motel room. He almost blends in to the decor. His blandness and grayness match the dreariness of his chosen hideout. But he doesn't care. It's close to the fancy hotel where his quarry, Michelle duBois, resides, and near enough to the hospital where the niece, Colette, remains in her comatose state. He is jabbering into a cell phone, but like a jackrabbit, he can't seem to stand still. *Alors,* how many other ninety-year-olds are as amazingly agile as he, and can whip around the room talking rapidly as they pace? He stops a moment to peer out a window but it is too dirty to let him see much. With his elbow he smears a spot of murky light and examines the weather.

He is furious at his cousin Gaston, who rattles away angrily at him from his winery a few kilometers outside of Bordeaux. "You have only five days to accomplish our objective and you waste it attacking the mark's niece? How could you waste our precious time on such foolishness?"

The Snake snarls. "You dare question The Snake's techniques?" He is glad Gaston cannot see the reddish hue of his guilty face. He lies blatantly. "You think The Snake didn't analyze the complexity of the job? The mark is difficult to get to. Her routines are rigid. She is constantly surrounded by many sycophants, especially the niece, Colette, who never leaves her side. This Colette was not supposed to go on this trip, according to your research."

Gaston mutters, "How was I to know she decided at the last minute?"

"And how was it you didn't warn me duBois has friends in the States?" The Snake knows well how to attack on the offensive when he's in the wrong.

"What friends? I know of no friends. She never makes personal calls to the States or gets letters. I tell you we thought we made a thorough investigation!"

"You thought! You thought! You swore to me your information was accurate. And what do I discover? She has friends who are gendarmes!"

"Mon Dieu." *Gaston must be sweating by now. The Snake is sure of it.*

"However, The Snake is not perturbed by your incompetence, so he attacked the niece first. Now the duBois woman will be off balance and upset. His plan is working perfectly. She is lost without the assistant, who is no longer at her side and out of our way forever."

"Brilliant," *Gaston timidly agrees.* "Forgive me for having doubted the brilliant Snake."

"She is at my convenience now."

"C'est merveilleux! *But, cousin, you must not forget the manuscript of the new book. We need to know what she has written about us so that we can be prepared to fight her."*

"Why do you waste my time spouting stupidity? The Snake has not forgotten his secondary goal. That is his very next step, and after the shock of her tremendous loss, there will be nothing left of her resolve. She will be a woman of jelly and putty in his hands."

Gaston sighs. "Someday you must write your memoir. You are magnifique!"

The Snake leers. This old guy hasn't lost his touch yet.

"I will inform the others of your great progress, dear uncle," *Gaston concludes.* "Adieu."

With his usual arrogance, The Snake hangs up without saying good-bye. The ploy reinventing his negligence worked like a charm. He grabs his small, dingy backpack and rushes to the door, then stops, startled, as he realizes he missed the door and has smacked his face hard against the wall instead. "Merde!" he yells in pain. Assez! Enough. It is time to get the eyeglasses!

8

GLADDY DETECTS

I hate to admit it, but the Frenchwoman is a good writer. Her book matches her personality: She is well-organized, concise, tough, and has clearly done her homework. And how cleverly she lets her victims hang themselves with their own words. They probably want to shoot themselves for their careless chatter that leads them easily to prison. Or want to shoot her, more likely. Probably Mme. duBois is right when she says she has many enemies.

She has me so enthralled with her book that I'm still in my robe, with my legs propped up on the kitchen chair next to mine. And on my third cup of coffee at that. I even skipped my early morning exercise with the girls, to their surprise and annoyance. Our daily routine is not to be missed unless the circumstances are dire. None of us especially likes exercise or the pool, so a united group attendance prevents malingerers.

But in deference to what seems to be a problem concerning Jack and "that French hussy" as they call her, they are cutting me some slack these days. Except for Evvie, I don't dare let the girls touch the book. Heaven only knows what their response will be to the inscription Michelle wrote on the title page for Jack. In large, yet delicate handwriting, in pale blue ink, she wrote "*On pardonne tant que l'on aime,*" which she credits to the famous French writer La Rochefoucauld.

Needless to say, I immediately look it up in a huge volume of quotations I own. Fortunately it's there, saving me a trip to the library to do research or asking someone who has a computer, which would take time. It translates to "We pardon to the extent that we love." Who is asking for forgiveness from whom? I'm sure Jack hasn't seen it yet. When he reads it, do I look directly into his eyes to perceive recognition of its meaning? Or do I look away, preferring not to know?

I hear his footsteps and quickly slip the book on the chair next to the window.

"It's nine o'clock already?" Jack makes his way into my kitchen, rubbing the sleep out of his eyes. "I can't believe I slept so late. Why didn't you wake me?" He bends to put a quick kiss on my cheek, then makes his bleary way to the coffeepot.

"You needed your rest, obviously. Would you like some breakfast?" I'm pleased with myself that my voice is steady.

"No, thanks, I'll just put up a piece of toast." He takes a slice of the rye bread from the table and pops it in the toaster.

Not hungry, eh? Had a late dinner last night with Michelle?

Taking butter out of the fridge, he asks, "Where were you yesterday? I tried reaching you all day."

He beat me to it. I was just about to ask him the same question. "Silly me carried my cell phone and forgot to turn it on. How is Colette?"

"When I left she was still unconscious. What a terrible accident."

Jack brings his toast and coffee to the table and sits down next to me.

As I make room for him at the tiny kitchen table, I ask, "So you hung around the hospital all day with Michelle?" Now I hear the quaver in my voice.

"Most of the time. There were forms to fill out and people she needed to call. Morrie came round. More forms. And he questioned her, trying to formulate what might have happened."

All of that must have taken about two hours.

What about the fifteen or so other hours? But I won't ask that question.

Jack suddenly spots Michelle's book. "Oh, you found it. I was going to give it to you this morning."

I say guiltily, "I saw it on the hall table. I hope you don't mind. I was curious."

What I don't tell him is that my imagination kept me awake, thinking of that book with her gorgeous face on it just lying there. So what choice did I have?

"She's a very good writer," I say brightly.

"You finished the whole thing?"

"You know what a quick reader I am." I didn't tell him that I stayed up all night to finish it. "Are you sure I can't make you an omelet?"

"I'm good. Honest."

Are you good, really good, Jack? I'm reminded of ex-President Jimmy Carter's famous line, "I only lust in my heart."

I get some cranberry juice. "I learned quite a bit of fascinating information about Michelle's life. In a section called 'About the Author.' A couple of facts stick in my head. She seems very accident-prone. And very lucky. Her ski broke off on a slope when she skied Chamonix and she shattered her leg. Her Lamborghini rolled over on a dangerous mountain road in Monaco, not far from the castle road where Princess Grace died. While she was flying in a private Cessna to Austria, the plane ran out of gas. Luckily the pilot was able to make a remarkable landing. And there's more."

Jack is surprised. "Never knew any of that before. She really means it when she calls herself a risk taker. She's like a cat with nine lives."

"The risk isn't in going skiing or driving a fast car or flying in a small plane."

Jack looks at me sharply. "Are you saying what I think you are?"

"Colette had even commented about that. Her aunt writes books that expose companies for their illegal business practices, and because of her, either they are ruined or they land in jail. A woman with a collection of many enemies who just might want her dead."

Jack shakes his head, not wanting to believe what I'm saying.

I go on. "Skis tampered with? Car tampered with? Airplane gas tank tampered with? All those 'accidents.'"

"No one's after Michelle. Colette's the one who had the accident."

"Suddenly bolts fall off a heavy bookcase?" I start clearing the table. "Maybe this time the killer got the wrong redhead."

Jack jumps up and paces, upset with my idea. "But they're a different height and weight and

Colette is much younger. No one would mistake one for the other."

"I think this cat of yours has used up yet another life. I hope the next attempt isn't the ninth."

Our conversation peters out shortly after that, and I go and change into my swimsuit. I hurry to catch up with Evvie on her way to the pool. I wave my beach towel at her. She sees me coming and waits for me.

"Oh, good. I'm glad you could join us. Where's Jack?" she asks.

"Getting into his suit."

"Find out what he was doing all day yesterday?"

"Not really." Our pesky ducks quack at us to get out of their way on the cobblestone path. They act like they own the place and maybe they do. "I guess he was keeping Michelle company while she hovered over her niece's bed. By the way, Jack brought home her new book."

"I bet you read it already."

"You know I did. I'm going to give it to you and see what you get out of it. I have a strong theory that Michelle was the target, not Colette. Jack doesn't believe it, or maybe he doesn't want to believe it."

"I can hardly wait. I'll pick it up after our swim."

We reach the pool.

"So, look who's here, late as usual." Hy Binder

has to comment on everything. "And where are your menfolk?"

Evvie glares at him. "And why do you care? You'll see them when you see them." We lather each other with sunscreen. The usual gang is here: Hy with his adoring, clueless wife, Lola, Tessie and Sol, Irving and Mary. Irv's wife, our friend Millie, is still in the Alzheimer's clinic. The cousins from LA, Barbi and Casey, who run the Gossip information business, are there as usual, tapping away at their laptops.

Lola is in the pool, strolling back and forth in the shallow end with Tessie. She calls out to me, "So how did you like Trixie? Isn't she a hoot?"

Hy pokes his nose from out of the day's newspaper. "She's more like a howl. What a nutcase."

Lola is insulted. "You take that back. She's good at what she does."

"Hah!" Hy turns a page without glancing at her. "The way she dresses, I can think of a better occupation for her. Some kind of interesting all-night job."

I ignore him. "I'm not so sure about working with her, Lola. She and I see our wedding plans very differently."

Lola swims over to me, holding onto the edge. "Give her a chance. You'll love the results."

"I don't think it's for me."

She climbs out of the pool and whispers in my

ear. A whisper so loud that everyone hears it.
"Please, don't drop her so fast. She's got a very sick
grandchild in an expensive hospital. She desperately needs to make money."

Swell. Just what I need. A little guilt trip. Before
I can say more, Jack appears. Not in bathing
trunks, but suit, tie, the whole dress-to-go-out-to-
someplace-else.

I look directly at him. "What's happened?"

"Michelle was told Colette just woke up and
Michelle wanted me to be at her side."

Damn, why is he saying this in front of everybody? He should have taken me out of earshot. No
way will I get into a discussion with him with this
group's ears hanging out eagerly. I can't give any
indication of how unhappy this is making me—not
in front of the yenta patrol. Trying to seem disinterested and fooling no one, I say to Jack, "Well,
give me a call later and fill me in."

He gives me a chaste peck on the cheek, waves to
everyone, and takes off.

It's silent as everyone watches him go.

When this pack does "silence," it speaks a thousand words. They are evaluating every glance,
every piece of information gathered, and every nu-
ance. Don't worry, the quiet won't last long. The
comments will fly.

Hy, always the first to chew on a tasty bit of gossip, climbs up on the diving board, calling down to

me. "So who's the sexy Frenchie your fiancé is hanging out with? I hear she's some looker." With that he raises his arms and takes a showy dive.

When he pops up again his pal Sol, of course, takes the next turn. In very bad French, he tries to amuse. "*Voulez-vous coucher avec moi.* That's all I ever learned in French. When I was stationed in France after the war, the guys figured a pair of silk stockings and that line would get them anything."

Tessie gets out of the water and gives her husband a back-of-the-hand smack on his rear. "I don't know what you said, but I bet it was dirty, so you better take it back. What a tacky thing to say. I think."

Our computer whiz, Barbi, without missing a beat as she types, translates. "He was asking some Frenchwoman, any woman, to go to bed with him."

"I knew it!" Tessie smacks Sol again. Sol jumps out of her way.

How do they do it? How do they find out every secret in this entire condo? I lie down on my chaise, put my sun hat over my face, and ignore them.

"Lo, bubbie," Hy says to his wife, "your crazy wedding planner may be out of a job, so you can forget about your finder's fee." Hy gets out of the pool, patting what little hair is left on his mostly bald pate. He calls out to his buddy, Sol. "What odds you wanna give on whether this wedding will ever take place?" He leers. "Unless we all get invites to Paris, France."

Sweet, shy Irving shakes a fist at him. "Enough with that mouth of yours."

In my imagination, I walk across to the other side of the pool and jump on Hy's stomach till he screams in pain.

In reality, I peek out from under my sun hat and watch as Evvie lifts a trash pail and tosses its contents at Hy's body.

There are gasps, sighs, and applause.

My sister, my hero.

Jack pulls up to the hotel entrance and looks for Michelle. He finds her pacing anxiously in the lobby. They see each other at the same time. He gets out of the car and she rushes into his arms. Even without makeup, the woman draws admiring glances from the other men around.

"Thank you, thank you, for coming. I was going to take the taxicab, but I couldn't face this alone. I'm trying not to think of the bad things, like Colette might have amnesia or worse."

They get into his car. Michelle sits beside him. In Gladdy's seat. He feels guilty, but what else can he do? The woman has no one to help her. They leave the hotel and head for the hospital, which is only a short trip away.

He asks Michelle, "Didn't the doctor give you any information at all?"

"He was busy, but he took the time to phone me and tell me that Colette was awake and I should come over. Then he had to run." The tears start to fall. "I'm afraid of bad news."

Jack tries to reassure her. "But that's good news. She's out of the coma."

"But what if she's lost her memory? Or she's not like her old self? I've heard horror stories about brain injuries."

"You don't know that yet. Try to stay hopeful."

She leans in closer to him. "I don't know what I would do without you."

When they pull into the hospital parking lot, it's jammed. But Jack spots a valet parking sign and pulls up next to the curb.

They hurry through the entrance. Jack asks, "Where did the doctor say to meet him?"

"At his office on the third floor, but I want to see my niece. Now. She's out of ICU, finally."

"Patience, Michelle. If he isn't in his office, we'll go straight to her room."

They get into the elevator. Jack watches Michelle's intensity, as if by sheer force of her will she can demand the slow elevator to climb faster.

The doctor is in his office. On the phone. Jack looks him over. He's a man in his fifties. Very fit. From his voice and the medical advice he is giving,

Jack's impression of him is that he cares and he knows what he's doing.

The doctor signals them to sit.

Michelle can't. She stands and fidgets. This is a Michelle that Jack never knew. Her toughness. Her need for instant action when she wants something. How demanding she is of herself and others. When they were together it was all sweetness and light and love. Would they have lasted as a couple?

When the doctor completes his call, Michelle introduces Jack to Dr. Jessup, then listens intently to hear what the doctor will say.

"Here's where we are, Ms. duBois. Colette's awake, but disoriented. She knows who she is, but she doesn't know what happened. This is called retrograde amnesia."

"How bad is that?" Michelle needs to know.

"That term covers a lot of territory. She may start to remember in a few hours. Maybe days, maybe longer. She might see you and it could all come back at once."

"Please, God," Michelle whispers.

"She's had a CT scan, an EEG, and an MRI and we're not seeing any major damage. So this is good news. She's very lucky. It could have been much worse."

He heads for the door and they follow him down a long corridor past the nurse's station. Jessup asks if Colette is on any kind of medication or allergic to any drugs. Michelle assures him she's a healthy young woman and probably takes only vitamins.

Obviously Michelle has ordered a private room. Jack watches her take a deep breath before she enters. She goes directly to Colette, who seems to be asleep. The room is filled with flowers. Michelle tells him they came from her grandparents, their only family back in Paris.

Dr. Jessup checks her chart.

Michelle leans over, almost holding her breath. She whispers. "Colette..."

Jack looks closer. Colette's bruised face is purple and bloated.

"Colette, my dearest. It's me. *Ma petite*, I'm here." Michelle gently runs her fingers down the waxen face.

The young woman wakes up. For a few moments, her eyes seem to roll around in her head, as if she needs to refocus. Then she smiles. "Michelle." Her niece reaches for her, but the effort makes her wince in pain.

"What happened to me? Why am I in a hospital? We are not home? People here speak English."

"Do you remember we came to Florida for a book fair?"

Jack watches her struggle to remember.

"Yes. I do."

"Do you remember going to the book room to return some books after my reading?"

Colette smiles. "You finally give me a little responsibility and..." She stops, confused and frightened. "I don't remember."

Dr. Jessup is encouraging. "Just relax, Colette. It will all come back to you in time." Michelle bends down and softly calls her name over and over, tears falling.

"We had a most lovely time," Colette says. "I especially enjoyed the men on the wire. I dreamed I was at Le Cirque. Was I up there? I remember falling. Did I drop from the wire?"

Jack looks to Michelle. She shakes her head. "She is remembering a trip we took to see Le Cirque du Soleil. That was two years ago. She's confusing time."

The doctor pats Michelle on the shoulder. "Give her time to get past her trauma."

Michelle grabs his arm. "Can I take her home? I can rent a private plane."

Jessup shakes his head. "Not a good idea. Not so soon. There are more tests. We must deal with her fractured leg."

"But she is so alone, except for me."

"Perhaps her family can come here?" The doctor makes notes on her chart.

"We are a very small family now. She's been raised by her grandparents and they are not well enough to travel." She begs. "What can I do?"

"Just wait." He pats her gently on the back and leaves the room.

Jack indicates to Michelle that Colette is falling asleep again.

Michelle bends to kiss her. As she does Colette whispers something in her ear.

Colette drops into sleep. Jack sees the shock on Michelle's face.

"She remembered something?"

"I'm not sure, but I think she said a gray ghost whispered to her. What can that mean? A gray ghost? Who whispered? Is she still thinking in the past?"

Jack immediately thinks of Gladdy's theory. "If that was a true memory, Michelle, then we're no longer talking accident."

Misdirection has always been his best weapon. The Snake sighs happily to himself. He really is tempted to write his autobiography. Though naturally he wouldn't let it be found until after he is gone. He has much to teach those who hope to commit crimes successfully.

As he strolls through an enormous boring mall with the name Sawgrass, looking for the Eye Openers eyeglasses shop, he congratulates himself on how well he uses illusion. It's all about blending into the woodwork, like a chameleon. Look at those dreary old men in their Florida casual male attire. Which by his standards is uglier than dirt. It's not for him to wear red-and-white checked shorts and nonmatching purple Izod tennis shirts. And those baseball caps! This country is mad about these foolish baseball caps with advertisements on their heads, he thinks. He would make products pay him to push their wares. He's counted at least ten caps with the logo "Retired and loving it." If his friends back in Monte Carlo could see this, they'd fall down with laughter. The final touch is the medical equipment they drag along with them around this city. Canes, walkers, golf carts.

For The Snake everything is gray: hair, shoes, clothes—even his grayish skin. Even this infernal pair of glasses will have gray frames. He chuckles. He is a shadow. A cloud. An apparition. Invisible.

He reaches the eyeglasses store. He'll pick out the dullest frames in stock. Naturally they will be gray.

9

AT THE BEACH

Jack and I trudge along the ocean's edge, holding hands. Jack is moving at a brisk pace, half dragging me along, carrying a blanket and picnic basket with his other hand, swinging it in cadence to his walk and talk.

The girls didn't even ask to join us. Not that they would come to any beach at any time. Heaven forbid a grain of sand should ever touch their nice clean floors when they get home. Evvie and Joe might have joined us, but Joe wasn't feeling up to going out. Just as well. I am in no mood for any company.

Jack is chipper and smiling. He takes in expansive breaths of air. As for me? I am a sullen drudge in black slacks and blouse, with sneakers clogging up with muddy sand. I am not in stride with his mood. Not at all. Kicking up sand like some stubborn kid who didn't want to go to the beach and had no choice.

" 'I grow old...I grow old...I shall wear the bottoms of my trousers rolled...and walk upon the beach. I have heard the mermaids singing, each to each.' "

My romantic boyfriend, seemingly impervious to my passive-aggressive behavior, is quoting poetry. Perhaps he even dressed for reciting T. S. Eliot. He wears his pants rolled up, a white T-shirt. He is barefoot. Exuding the sense of a man happy with his world, despite the fact that Eliot's poetry is depressing, remembers this former librarian.

I wonder why he's in such a jolly frame of mind. As if I didn't know. A few days with a romantic long-lost love fawning over him and he's laughing at "I grow old."

"What a glorious day." He finally comes to a stop. Why he's picked this spot I haven't a clue. It looks like every other part of the beach, which is crowded as always "in season." Northeast-coasters and Canadian snowbirds, who come flying down in droves to escape the wretched winter weather, cram the beach with their colorful umbrellas. Their blankets are covered with their melting, lotioned bodies and massive amounts of play gear. Activity galore, as if fun happens only in perpetual motion. Volleyball games every which way I look. Vendors wearing insulated backpacks on their shoulders to carry their ice creams to and fro, calling out their wares. Screeching kids racing in and out of the water. Parents yelling orders that are ignored.

Noise erupts out of all the various boom boxes that carry dozens of musical choices, gorging air space in one big dissonant war. I already have a headache. I am not a happy camper.

Jack spreads our blanket neatly on the sand and sets down the basket. He drops down and beckons me to join him.

I do so and kick my sneakers off to dump out the muck. "Sirens, I say, not mermaids."

Jack looks surprised. "Where are sirens in Eliot's poetry?"

"Actually I'm thinking of Homer's *Odyssey* where the sirens lured the love-struck sailors to sail their boats onto the reefs and die there."

He removes a thermos and pours me a cup of coffee and then one for himself. "Whoa, what's that all about? First day we get a chance to play and you're on a downer."

"Maybe it's because you haven't been around much lately." As each whining word leaves my mouth, I want to take it back.

"Do I guess right when I say you are referring to

Michelle? A siren, not a mermaid?" He actually smiles. He finds it amusing.

"Could be."

"It doesn't matter to me what she is. Michelle was eight years ago. In the past. Over. Done with. It was all about timing. I was lonely after Faye died. I went to Europe and lived a brief fantasy."

"Your fantasy seems to want to take another shot at you."

Jack laughs out loud and hugs me.

"Let's be honest here," he says. "Michelle wasn't really all that interested in me. She was playacting. Probably bored. Let's have fun with the old guy tourist. I realized that when I got home."

"Something is bothering me about her. I can't quite get it yet."

"Come on, eat." He jokes, "The potato salad will get hot." He hands me a plastic container. "You know, we've never had this conversation. Young kids, when they plan to marry, get into that—Should we tell each other about our past affairs? Or not?"

I feel myself tearing up. He's hitting a nerve. I look a few feet away where a young couple, probably in their twenties, lie entangled in each other's arms.

Jack continues. "So, I confess. Before I met Faye, I was randy all right. Lots of girlfriends and good times. I married at an older age than usual. I was forty. But once I settled in with Faye, that was it. I was committed. I'm a simple man. I believe in family and I believe in honesty."

Now my tears are flowing.

Jack takes my plastic dish from me and covers my hands with his. "You're adding salt to your salad and salt's no good for us old folks. Forgive me for being so insensitive. You were widowed at such an early age and in such a tragic way. I just assumed that somewhere over so long a period of time you fell in love with someone else."

I say sadly, "You assumed wrong."

He gently wipes the tears away. "You're a beauty even now. But I've seen photos of you when you were younger. You were a knockout. I can't believe some eligible suitor didn't grab you off the market."

"Yes, of course I dated. But I never met anyone who was as good and as kind and as loving as you are."

Grinning, he pretends to swell his chest and open his arms akimbo. "Here I am. Better late than never."

I lean into him and I'm crying again. "I can't bear losing another man I love."

He rocks me in his arms. "And you actually think Michelle is going to steal me away?"

I nod through my bleary eyes. "Something like that."

"First of all, that can never happen. Second, as soon as Colette is able to travel, they'll be going back to France, probably never to be seen on these shores again. So I won't be spending any more time with her."

I sit up, indignant now. "She was flirting with you."

He smiles. "And I was properly flattered. What red-blooded male wouldn't be?"

"I think she has an agenda. What does she want from you?"

"But our meeting was pure coincidence. Turned out she needed help and there I was. After all, she really didn't know anyone in America. What happened before isn't going to repeat itself."

Now I have an appetite. I chew on my hummus-on-pita-bread sandwich. Even the group dancing salsa, playing their Latin song at ear-piercing decibels, no longer bothers me. "As long as you don't see her again."

Jack is suddenly silent.

"What?" I ask.

"Well, I did promise to take her out to a farewell dinner."

"When?"

"Actually tonight. I was about to tell you."

"Oh, really?"

"Look, I'd rather just say good-bye on the phone, but I don't want to hurt her feelings."

Now I'm silent. Her feelings? What feelings are those? It's his turn to talk himself out of this sticky predicament. Finally his face lights up. "I've got an idea. Come to dinner with us."

"You're kidding."

"No, I'm not. This way you'll see how unintimidated I am by her. No way can she manipulate me."

The dancers are moving away and now I don't have to shout to be heard.

"What are you going to do, just bring me along and say Hi, guess who's come to dinner?"

"No, I'll tell her sweetly in advance that you're joining us."

Boy, I hate the way he refers to the two of them as "us."

The wind is picking up. Without saying a word to each other, we gather up our belongings and start to head back down the beach. Others are doing the same.

"Okay," I say, "I am officially invited." I bet she won't be thrilled to hear that update.

It suddenly comes to me to ask, "I'm sure by now you saw the inscription she wrote to you in her book. 'We pardon to the extent that we love.' What did it mean?"

He shrugs. "I have no idea."

We slog through the sand. I keep thinking. And then I get it. "Jack, you broke off the relationship."

"Yes, and I'm still ashamed of my cowardly behavior. The very next day after that embarrassing dinner, I left her a note and went straight to the airport. I guess maybe the quote means she's forgiving me for dumping her in that unmanly way."

Now I know what that weird expression means—my blood suddenly runs cold. "Jack, maybe I shouldn't go."

"Nah," he says, smiling. "I can't wait to see you gals together."

I doubt there'll be mermaids singing to each other. More like sirens slinging mud.

10

IDA SPIES

Ida stands in the circle, watching Sophie and Bella. She is aware that they are purposely not looking at her. She smells that they are up to something again.

"Okay," Merrill Grant says to his Cane Fu class of twelve, who listen with all eagerness. "This is our final scenario of the day. Pick a partner. One of you is the senior victim, carrying a cane. The other is the bad guy. Bad guys will toss their canes out of the circle."

The participants fumble around, chattering, giggling, and picking partners and positions. Ida knows the players so well. Husbands and wives will stay together. Naturally the husband will insist on the role of attacker and the wife gives in and enters the familiar victim role. The men fling their canes out of the circle. Ida sneers. How easy they are to read.

Merrill lectures on. "The odds are that the guy picking on you knows you are old and assumes you are creaky and an easy mark and doesn't think he'll need a weapon. Victims, hold onto your canes as you were taught."

Sol, Joe, and Hy grin at each other, ready to have fun. Ida smirks again. Any chance to lord it over their women. Tessie, Evvie, and Lola give each other the eye. They are prepared to play hardball.

Sophie and Bella partner up. Ida partners with a friend from her cooking class, Patricia Drew. Her nickname is Pat "Nancy" Drew because she loves mysteries the way Gladdy does.

"Everybody ready?" Nods and yeahs. Merrill aims his next words at the married couples. "Since this is a practice and not reality, please do not take any aggression out on the person you live with. I know you'll be tempted. All attacks are pretend."

Hy can't resist. "Spoilsport."

Lola, who thinks every word out of her hubby's mouth is a pearl instead of the grit of sand it really is, smiles mischievously at him. "I promise not to hurt you, poochy."

Merrill scratches his buzz cut and says, "Okay, victim, turn your back. Bad guy, sneak up behind.

Put your hands around vic's neck and pull her toward you."

Again giggling and fooling around. And major overacting. Mostly from Sol and Hy.

Merrill says, "Victims, he's got you by the throat. You're frightened and you know you have to think fast. What do you do?"

Lola, who must have been one of those prissy kids in school who always shot her hand up first, as she does right now, says, "I know. I know. Don't fight, let your body go limp."

"Very good," the instructor comments. "Your bad guy won't expect that."

Sophie and Bella begin to tiptoe out of the circle, with Sophie's hands still around Bella's neck. They are trying to be inconspicuous.

Ida, who never takes her eyes off them, calls out. "Hey, class isn't over yet."

"Gotta go," Sophie announces. She drops her arms and makes a show of looking at her wrist to read a watch she isn't wearing. "Previous pressing engagement." She pulls Bella quickly along with her.

Ida waits to see which direction they take. No longer paying attention as the victims twist about ready to counterattack, Ida breaks away, too. She apologizes to Pat Nancy. "I'm off."

Pat Nancy says plaintively, "Don't go. I need to attack you."

"Next time," Ida promises.

Evvie calls after her, wanting to know what's going on. "What?"

"Later." And Ida hurries after the two culprits.

She turns at the same corner they took. She can't believe her eyes. They're gone. They knew she was going to follow them and they've taken a different route.

Ida is flummoxed. What the heck are those two ninnies up to?

The chimes ring out. It is a delicate tinkling sound. Sophie watches as every woman in the room stiffens with anticipation and awe. Bella pinches her arm in excitement. A dead husband is calling out to be heard. Their guru is attentive and ready to let the voice of the dearly departed speak to them, from the other side, through him.

So far, in the three times they've been there, he's contacted half a dozen dead husbands for the widows. Each one was such an emotional experience. Sophie is eagerly waiting for their turn to be called. The room is utterly silent as Baba Vishnu tilts his shining blond head to one side as if to listen better.

The chimes stop. Their guru is connected. He reminds them once more, "Don't ask for a description of heaven or hell. They're not allowed to tell."

His voice lowers. "Arlene, I wish to speak to Arlene Simon."

Arlene, a lovely blond woman in her eighties, who looks no older than sixty, stands up from her seat. She waves her arms up and down, thrilled to be called. "It's me, Ronnie, I'm here."

"How's it going, Arles?"

She turns to the group, blushing. "He always called me that." Then, to her dead husband, "I'm good, but I could be better."

"What would make you feel better?" Ronald asks, his voice abrupt, as if his wife had always annoyed him with her "wants."

Now Arlene's voice hardens. "You know."

"I don't know."

The suspense is building. Sophie is fascinated as every woman wiggles to the edge of her seat. They stare, back and forth, from Arlene to their guru, whose face contorts to fit the harsh personality of dead Ronald Simon.

Arlene frowns. "I looked everywhere, Ronnie. Where did you put it? You always hid your winnings under the mattress, but I couldn't find anything. Were you allowed to take it with you?"

A few women giggle. Sophie has to pull Bella's hands away from her arm or Bella will pinch her black and blue.

Ronald answers her with an oily lying voice. "I'm sorry, sweetheart. I lost plenty on those nags at Hialeah. But most of it went on the tables in Vegas. That's what caused my heart attack, when I dropped dead in my two-hundred-dollar-a-night suite in Harrah's. The kids have plenty of money. Get it from them."

Arlene chokes up. "They won't give me a penny, those ungrateful brats."

Silence. "Ronnie?" she asks.

Baba Vishnu shakes his head. He straightens up as if he's been in a trance. "We've lost contact, Mrs. Simon."

Mrs. Jerry comes quickly to Arlene's side, handing her a small slip of paper. As they were forewarned, the phone calls to heaven or hell are considered long distance and cost seven dollars a minute.

The chimes ring again. All eyes look up front except for Mrs. Simon, who stares into space, disappointment written on her face.

Baba Vishnu listens again. "Bella Fox?"

Bella gasps. Sophie leans toward her. "This is it. Now, don't cry. You always cry when anyone mentions your precious Abe."

Baba asks again. "Mrs. Bella Fox? Identify yourself."

Bella waves her hands; her throat is already choked up. She can't speak. Her eyes widen in frustration. Sophie raises her hand, and points at the now dumbstruck Bella. "Here she is."

All eyes turn to this next lucky widow.

"Bella, it's your Abe." Abe speaks through the guru.

Sophie pokes her. "Say something."

Bella starts to whimper. Then sniffles, which turn into cries which accelerate into sobs. Her body heaves, tears pouring down her paralyzed face.

The group can't stand it. Someone yells, "Say something already."

Bella is frozen to her seat. No words can come out of her mouth.

Sophie stands up. "May I speak for my friend?"

"Speak away," says Abe through Baba.

"Why do you always make her cry? Did you used to beat her or something?"

Shocked silence fills the room. Bella manages to gasp. Silence from Abe.

Baba Vishnu speaks. "Contact disconnected." He rises gracefully from his pillow. "Session is over." He bows and leaves the room through his private door.

Mrs. Jerry heads for Bella, waving a bill. Sophie negotiates. "Since she didn't say anything, you shouldn't charge her."

Mrs. Jerry is haughty. "Crying counts." And she shoves the little piece of paper into Bella's shaking hands. Sophie notices that they are the very same order pads used by Jerry for his customers in the deli.

The room empties out. None of them look at the woman who blew her phone call from heaven. Or hell.

Humiliated, Bella sobs again.

Sophie pushes her toward the back exit. "It's all right, *bubbala*. Maybe he'll call again."

11

GETTING READY

I think I have every halfway decent outfit I own littering the bedspread. I bend down deep inside my closet to dig out a pair of fancy shoes I haven't seen in who can remember how many years. I hear Evvie walking through the apartment. She calls out to me.

"Where are you?"

"In my bedroom."

Evvie yells. "I think we have a mystery on our hands with the girls. They're behaving weirdly."

I glance up at her as she rushes in. "I can't see you: What hit this place? A tornado?"

"I'm in the closet trying to find my black satin pumps. But then again, they'll be too much. What about the girls?"

"Never mind. It will keep. You left a message to get over here ASAP, so here I am and what's the emergency?"

I drag myself up and out of the closet and throw my weary body on top of my heap of clothes. "I can't make a decision about what to wear."

Evvie moves a pile off to one side in order to sit down near me. "Okay, here I am. Tell me, what's the occasion and where are you going? I thought you intended to stay home tonight and watch your latest DVRs after an exhausting day at the beach."

"That was my plan, but Jack had another idea. We had a talk about Michelle. He thinks I'm intimidated by her. I think *he* is and won't admit it. Since she'll be leaving soon, instead of just calling to say bye-bye he already made plans to have a farewell dinner with her tonight. I naturally wasn't happy about it, so he decided to take me along."

"Wow, does that sound like a bad idea. Where is he, anyway?"

I sigh. "He went to a car wash to get the Caddy washed and polished." I give her a knowing look. She returns it.

"Since when does anyone around here do more than just soap and hose their cars down?"

I sift through the outfits on my bed, looking for inspiration. "When? When it involves going to dinner with a rich, famous, and gorgeous ex-love. He promised me he'd make it short. We're going to

Nona's because it's close by. Inexpensive, so it won't dent our budget. Casual wear. Simple pasta dishes. They're famous for their quick turnover. Kill an hour and good-bye Mme. duBois forever."

"So why are you looking for black satin pumps? In Nona's you could wear sweats and be considered overdressed."

"I am going to look my finest, because I know she's gonna be judging everything about me."

"Why do you care since she's leaving anyway?" Evvie shrugs. "That was a dumb question. Okay, what do we have that's simple yet classy? Subtle yet sexy?" She lifts item after item and quickly discards them all.

"Probably nothing. I can imagine what she pays for her clothes."

"Why did you agree to this madness? You could have just said no."

I pick up my beige pantsuit; hold it out trying to decide. "And then let him take her to dinner alone? What is it about that woman that gets my teeth grinding?"

"Because she's trying to get her fangs into Jack? Because she's a conniving, controlling over-achiever? Because she acts like a bitch? Because she's a man-eater and has the ego of Marie Antoinette? Little things like that?"

I sigh. "You think?"

We're quiet for a few minutes. I toss the beige

pantsuit. "And what if she isn't all those awful things? What if she's really nice?"

Evvie picks up the beige again and holds a black cotton blouse up in front of it. "Don't you have anything low-cut?" She shakes her head in mock despair.

"Don't be ridiculous. At our age?"

"Do you think she'll behave?"

"No, she'll pull out her whole bag of tricks."

Evvie picks up a lavender dress from among the items on the bed. "Hey, I remember this. You wore it to a New Year's Eve party a few years ago. It's lovely and simple and sweet."

I wring my hands. "But what does it say about me?"

Evvie pokes around the cosmetics on my dresser, looks in my mirror and runs her hands through her curly red hair. "That you live in an inexpensive condo and that dress has long since become outdated and you probably haven't bought anything new in ten years."

I fall back despondently across the bed. "She'll look gorgeous and laugh adoringly at every word Jack says. She'll name-drop all the famous people she knows and tell scintillating anecdotes about them. I'll sit there like a bumpkin."

Evvie pulls me up, grabs my shoulders, and shakes me. "Repeat after me," she says. "No matter what she does or what she says, you will take the high ground and act like the lady you are. Go on, say it. You will take the high ground."

I grit my poor abused teeth. "I will take the high ground."

"Are you ready?" Jack shouts from the entry hall. He hurries into the bedroom and is dumbfounded by the mess on the bed and me still in a robe. He's dressed gorgeously in a black lightweight suit and a gray silk tie that goes wonderfully with his salt-and-pepper hair.

A suit, by the way, that I've never seen before.

Evvie says, "Hello, Jack, and good-bye, Jack." To me she says, "Go for the lavender. It matches your eyes. And don't forget your mantra." She winks at me and leaves.

Jack ratta-taps at his wristwatch. "You've got five minutes to get ready. I'll meet you downstairs." With that he marches out.

I mutter under my breath. "I will take the high ground."

I watch Jack, his hands high on the steering wheel, clutching it. His shoulders are hunched. He's driving faster than usual. He squints in the late afternoon sun. He doesn't like to be late to anything. Nor do I. We both consider it bad manners. But he is overdoing it. Traffic is moving slowly in the clogged area around the hotel. He is impatient and frustrated as he tries to reach the entrance.

"We're only going to be five minutes late, honey. Not a big deal."

He slows slightly. "I'll feel bad if she's just standing there waiting."

Oh, really? Oh, Jack, what is her hold over you?

It takes two more tries and he pulls into the entrance parking area. Because of the book fair, the revolving doors go round and round, emptying out mobs of people at the end of the day's activities. Groups on their way to dinner places. Or parties. Still chattering about what they did and what they accomplished. These are people who've been enjoying themselves and intend to keep the "high" going. A busy doorman uses his whistle constantly to round up the cabs. We both peer out, searching among the crowd for Michelle. There aren't too many with her vivid red hair color. But there's no sign of her.

The activity finally dissipates. Cars, limos, taxis are on their way out. The doorman relaxes, turns to gab with his fellow employees. Still no Michelle. Why would a "star" ever be on time? The name of the game is to make an entrance. I know Jack is not too thrilled, but I won't say a word about my having had to rush to be on time.

She flies out the door twenty minutes later. Looking both frazzled and gorgeous. She's talking on her cell and she waves when she sees us. She is dressed to kill. An appropriate description, I think. She is wearing a stunning lime green silk cocktail dress, off one shoulder and low-cut. She obviously found time to get to the beauty salon. Every man within the entrance area stares at her admiringly. Well, she'll sure make a splash at lowly Nona's Spaghetti House.

Jack leaps out of the car to greet her. She aims her usual air kiss next to both his cheeks. My window is open so I can hear them. She signals Jack, with her finger touching his hand, to wait as she finishes her call. I assume long distance since she's speaking French. Which takes another five minutes. At last we hear, "*Bonsoir, mon ami. À bientôt.*"

"I am so very sorry," she says to the both of us. "But I simply could not get off the phone. Friends back home wanting to know how Colette is. And they want to talk so much."

Of course I know how that goes. My girls call each other back and forth all day long. Not quite the same as talking to France. And look at my darling. Not the least bit upset with *her* for being so late.

Jack opens the back door. "Not a problem, Michelle. They're pretty flexible at our restaurant." He looks surprised as Michelle doesn't get in.

She looks back toward the door. "It just occurred

to me that I left my laptop upstairs. I never go anywhere without it."

Jack immediately says, "Give me your key and I'll run back and get it." She starts to put her hand in her purse, then looks at me. I'm trying not to show any reaction. Then she turns back to Jack and shrugs. "Oh, never mind, we won't be gone long."

"Are you sure?"

She looks deeply into his eyes. "Yes, I don't want to put you out."

Again Jack indicates she enter the back door.

Michelle addresses me. "*Gladeze,* I am so sorry. I meant to tell Jacques earlier. I cannot sit in rear seats. I have the chronic back pain and need to be able to sit up front with the seats straight up."

Jack is nonplussed but I get the message. I climb out of the front and gracefully indicate that she should take my place.

She beams a star's smile. "Thank you so much for understanding."

Jack shrugs and so do I. I do so love the way she says my name with her lilting French accent, *Gladeze.* Sounds like the product name of a cheerful fast-working kitchen scrubbing soap.

He helps her into my seat. I start to climb into the back, but I change my mind. Two can play that game. I wait for Jack to do me the same honors.

Which he does and winks at me. Translation: I get it, but you're still my gal.

As we reach the end of the street, Jack is about to make a left turn. Michelle puts her arm on his. "No, Jacques, turn to the right." He reacts instantly and changes directions. She half shifts her body so she can address me at the same time. "I was speaking to the concierge and he said I absolutely must try The Excelsior before I go home. He insists it is the best restaurant in the entire city. And the darling man even made the reservations for us." With her idea of a beguiling smile, she asks, "Is Miami Beach very far from here?"

Jack is uncomfortable. "Well, it is a ways."

Hah! Only an hour's drive in rush hour traffic. Not only the farthest but also the most expensive restaurant. No wonder she's all gussied up.

"Please, Jacques, please. It has been such a tense few days, we deserve a relaxing dinner, don't we?"

They deserve? What am I, chopped liver?

Jack looks back at me and I answer him sweetly, "You're the driver." Meaning the ball is in your court. Do you stick to our plans, or...?

Well. So much for that. Off we go inching our way south on the congested I-95.

Jack reminds Michelle to fasten her seat belt.

And if Evvie were here she'd be imitating Bette Davis in *All About Eve: Fasten your seat belts; it's gonna be a bumpy ride.*

* * *

The Snake watches as the man's car pulls away from the curb. He stands at the far end of the hotel, leaning on a wall, pretending to read a newspaper. He is enjoying his new glasses. So good not to have to squint anymore. Another woman is in the car with them. Good. Good. He rubs his hands together. They are dressed up and they will go out to dinner and now is the time to find the manuscript. When the redheaded woman loses that, she will have no more defenses and she will be doomed. He hurries into the hotel.

12

MÉNAGE À TROIS (OR DINNER FOR THREE)

The Excelsior is an expensive place. Dark gleaming mahogany walls with subtle accents of beige—or would they call it "ecru"? Gilt-trimmed mirrors reflect the diners and the Renaissance-style dark paintings hanging above them. If some wealthy bride and groom happened to arrive, these diners would be perfectly dressed for the occasion. I hear champagne corks popping hither and yon. And those tablecloths—whiter than white. Cloroxed and starched into crackling crispness. Exquisite huge bouquets overwhelm every available surface. Voices are hushed. Chandeliers shimmer, winking down at us with the perfect amount of flattering light. I notice all of this as the maître d' leads us to our table, a cash register cha-chinging in my head, calculating how much it will cost us to help keep this place rich and snobbish.

When we reach our table, Jack immediately comes to my chair, to pull it back for me to be seated. At that same moment, we both see Michelle standing, tapping her fingers along the back of *her* chair. I see the indecision on Jack's face and I practically throw myself into my satin brocaded armchair. Jack rushes to Michelle just as the maître d' reaches her. A clumsy moment as neither moves away. Finally Jack lets the maître d' take over and seats himself between us. The maître d', infatuated with this exotic creature, lifts Michelle's napkin, snaps it open, and places it delicately on her lap. She thanks him with a dazzling, practiced smile.

As quickly as I can, I toss my napkin onto my lap to prevent this from turning into a scene out of a Charlie Chaplin comedy as both Jack and the maître d' are about to charge toward me. Whew, that was close. I could imagine them fighting over who gets to play "snap-the-napkin" with me.

A waiter introduces himself as our "wait person, Charles," as he places the wine list in front of Jack and announces the "specials," overwhelming us with fancy names and exotic ingredients for twelve different dishes—most of which are covered in heavy sauces and undoubtedly fattening. By the time he gets to "Pompano Papillote with freshly squeezed lime and an *outrageous* spiced mango sauce, with the slightest drizzle of *aglio e olio*," my eyes have glazed over. Michelle seems to absorb every word of every delicacy.

Charles bows and positions himself slightly away to give us time, all the while ogling Michelle's décolleté. Low-cut sounds so much sexier in French.

Jack examines the wine choices. I see him furrow his brow and I bet the prices are staggering. So much for our having an inexpensive dinner tonight.

Michelle reaches out toward the wine list. "May I?" she asks. "While living with the winemakers whom I tear apart in my next exposé, I learned a great deal."

Jack hands her the four-sided laminated card. "Be my guest."

I almost shout "Don't!" I shudder. Doesn't he realize she'll pick the most expensive bottle?

And indeed she does. The highest-priced French champagne they have. Jack winces when she points it out to our waiter, who simpers immediately to her side.

And so it goes. When it's time to choose an entrée, Michelle waves to her "Jacques" and requests he choose for her. He always knew what she liked. Oh, boy, talk about double entendres. Another choice French expression. Under my breath I hum to keep from speaking.

I choose quickly. The very cheapest thing on the

menu, a small appetizer. I explain I'm not too hungry. Jack gets my message. At least my part of the bill won't bankrupt us.

Michelle waggles a naughty finger at me. "Now, now, *Gladeze,* that is not a good way to diet. It's not the amount of food you eat, but the ingredients."

So now I'm fat. I take a deep breath. It's time to mentally chant Evvie's mantra. I will take the high ground. I will not throw my tiny ounce of champagne in her face. I took only enough to wet my lips, leaving the rest for her, and she does guzzle most of it. I only pray she doesn't order another bottle (I might have to kick Jack under the table to stop her). Nor do I retort with a snappy quip about the size of *her* hips. No, not I. Nor do I respond when she "congratulates" me on my clothes, for being thrifty and for shopping *prêt-à-porter.*

"That refers to department stores," she translates.

"I know," I tell her. "I saw the movie."

She sighs. "If only I had a shape that could wear clothes off the rack, but, alas, they never fit right."

Not one word from me, but oh, how I'm tempted.

She yaks on. "I'm forced to have all my outfits made especially for me."

"How sad for you," I say, hardly hiding my sarcasm.

"But, however, I have lucky genes. I can eat all I desire and never gain weight." This she proves by ordering a fat-streaked steak and garlic mashed potatoes.

She looks to Jack. "I haven't gained any weight at all since you saw me last, have I?"

"Look the same to me." His response is bland.

For some reason, Jack seems oblivious to her antics. And he isn't saying much. She chatters away about her life in Paris, her darling *petite maison* with its six bedrooms and five baths in the charming part of the seventh arrondissement with its lovely view of the Eiffel Tower.

Wanna bet that's the wealthiest neighborhood of Paris? No takers?

She prattles on and on. The people she knows. An endless list. She dredges up how much Jacques adored going to the Sorbonne with her. He just loved Montmartre and the Centre Georges Pompidou. The modern art museum. "But I think our favorite was the drive down to Chateau de Versailles." She nods to Jack; he parrots a nod back.

I tune her out. Jack listens as if mesmerized. I eat quickly, hoping to rush things along. It's already been two lengthy hours and I want out! But not

Michelle, she lingers over every bite of every course.

Finally, she daintily pats her mouth with her napkin and beckons her very own Charles and asks for the dessert menu. She explains to me, "Ever since I wrote my latest book, *Bonbon, Non Non!* I've become an expert on *chocolat.*"

I stand up. I've had it. "I don't want any dessert, Michelle. No need to order for me." I head for the ladies room, muttering, "The high ground, the high ground."

Jack is startled as Michelle suddenly grasps his hand. She seems mortified. "Oh, Jacques, what have I done? Your *Gladeze* is upset. I have insulted your fiancée."

"Michelle, Gladdy is a mature woman. I'm sure she isn't insulted." Oops, that wasn't the right thing to say. Now he's insulted Gladdy for being old and Michelle for being a child. *I feel like I'm on a high wire,* he thinks. *I'm going to lose either way.*

She sighs. "Too long have I lived alone. Too long have I made my own decisions. You had picked out a sweet small restaurant, *non?* But I make you go along with my plans. So selfish. I pick the restaurant. I pick the wine. The dessert. Me, me, me. That's who I think about. But I was trying to please you and selfishly did not think of her. What should

I do? Apologize? How can I undo my bad manners?"

Jack smiles at her. "It's all right. I promise Gladdy will be fine." He hopes. "She's a wonderful woman if you had time to get to know her." Why didn't he make it clear to Michelle how much he loved Gladdy? Suddenly he couldn't get words out of his mouth through dinner? That's gonna cost him.

"Will you give her my apologies? I feel such an inconsiderate fool."

Jack is touched. This is the Michelle he once knew.

The Snake looks up and down the hall. So far, so good. No one is on her floor. His waiting is finally paying off. The maid parks her cleaning cart in front of the redhead's suite.

He waits a little longer, hoping the woman will clean one of the bedrooms first. He plans to hide there until she finishes her cleaning and leaves.

But he decides it's too risky to wait out in the open much longer. When he enters the suite, he passes the vacuum cleaner sitting in the middle of the living room rug. He hears sounds coming from the master bedroom. The Snake tiptoes around the corner and looks in. The maid is standing in front of the closet mirrors. What is she doing? Aha, she is trying on Mme. duBois's clothing, specifically a scarlet cocktail dress and a diamond necklace. He scowls. To him the maid is a homely middle-aged hag. A too-fat stomach bulges out of the outfit, so it stays unzipped. Her black, frizzy hair is unkempt and the snood she must wear on her head doesn't help, either.

What to do? She hasn't seen him yet. He can just grab the laptop and sneak back out. Amazing that the woman forgot it. She always has it with her. He cannot miss this opportunity. But his plan is to make it part of a robbery, so it will seem like the laptop was just one of the stolen goods. A common occurrence in hotels. He could come back and try later—kill his mark at the same time. But he hesitates. What if she brings her guests back to the suite? This might be his only opportunity.

He watches the maid enjoying seeing herself dressed in such expensive clothes; doesn't she realize what a pig she looks in them? Now she tries on a black silk gown. He shudders at the lumpy body in her cheap underwear. Doesn't she have other rooms to clean?

Enough! He has not yet had his dinner. He will linger no longer. He pulls on a pair of leather gloves and walks boldly into the bedroom.

"What is going on?" His voice reeks of cruelty.

The maid gasps. She gropes for words. "I didn't mean anything, honest." Half hiding behind the *closet door, she rips the gown off and quickly hangs it and the other outfits back in the closet, apologizing all the while. "Please, I'll lose my job. I need this job..."*

She throws the necklace back on the dresser and dresses hastily in her uniform. She stands, paralyzed, waiting to find out what he will do. She inches slowly toward the door, but he moves right with her. From the change of the look on her face he realizes she has understood the situation. Her hands go on her hips, indignant now.

"Who are you? This is not your room. You are not a guest here. You don't work here. You're old!" She starts to laugh. "You're crazy."

"Shut up, you cow," he shouts at her. Nobody disrespects The Snake! He sees her freeze at the sight of a knife appearing in his gloved hand.

The maid falls to her knees, begging. "Please, don't hurt me. I won't tell anyone, I swear. I've seen nothing. Nobody. Do what you came for. Let me go."

"And you think I believe you won't run to the manager immediately?"

Her hands are shaking and she can't stop them. "I wouldn't tell him, because he would fire me for going through guests' private things. You couldn't tell them about me. That way, we are both safe. I promise I've never seen you." She climbs back up, clumsily, never taking her eyes off him. Panting, not daring to move.

"Say au revoir." He moves menacingly toward her, angling the knife.

The Snake waits for the expression that always comes to his victims when they know death is near. Terror first, then their eyes roll back in dazed acceptance.

But merde, not this one. She runs for the door, screaming.

For a ninety-year-old, The Snake has fast reflexes. She never makes it. He catches her by her uniform apron string. But she still doesn't give in. She fights for her life. He smacks her. She grabs onto his pocket so as not to fall. He doesn't notice that his glasses case has fallen out in the struggle.

As he walks over her dead body toward the door, he wonders if the café down the street has the calf's liver special again. He must remember to tell them to leave the bacon off to the side.

13

WAITER, *L'ADDITION*

Something's changed. I watch the dessert eaters. Michelle's head is down. Am I imagining it that since I've returned to the table, she hasn't looked at me once? I would expect her to lick up every crumb of her chocolate almond mousse, since she was so set on choosing it. But no, she is moving the spoon around the dish, pretending to eat. Suddenly she's lost her appetite? Jack barely takes small bites out of his raspberry sorbet, looking from me to Michelle with a rather odd expression on his face. I can't quite read it. I reach over and take a teaspoon-sized bite from his portion. He smiles at me, it seems, gratefully.

Michelle pats her lips daintily with her napkin and then stands up. "I'll be right back," she says, tossing Jack a little wave in the air as she ambles away.

I look at Jack. So poker-faced I still can't read him.

After too much silence, I have to say something. Be careful, *Gladeze,* I tell myself. "Well, this was an illuminating experience."

He glances up to see if I'm being sarcastic. But I'm sure my face is bland, my tone as well.

Jack replies equally mildly, "You might call it that."

"Oh, oh, here it comes. Brace yourself." Our very own Charles is bringing a dainty silver dish with the check. "Wanna bet what it comes to?"

Jack manages a weak smile as he reaches for his wallet. His humor's coming back. "Maybe I'll just hand him my Visa and not even look at it. Less painful that way."

"I'm betting we could have had eighteen dinners at Nona's with what this cost."

Charles bows. "I hope everything was to your satisfaction."

"Beyond my wildest expectations," I say, bracing myself.

As Jack reaches for the dish, Charles places it in front of Michelle's place. We both look at him in surprise. Charles explains, "Your very charming dinner companion has already paid. This is her credit card and her receipt." He bows again and says, "Have a pleasant evening."

I look at the plate with astonishment. "Well, I'll be..."

"That was very nice of her."

"Maybe it's another kind of manipulation."

"Maybe she realized she could afford it better than we can."

"Wanna peek?"

I start to reach over. Too late. Michelle is bearing down on us. She doesn't bother to sit. She picks up her card and the receipt. "Are we ready to leave?"

We both get up. After all, Madame has set all the rules. She's ready to go, therefore we go. Jack manages the usual cliché. "But you shouldn't have."

"Nonsense. *Mon plaisir...*" She puts her arm through Jack's, then waits for me to catch up to his other arm.

That woman is full of surprises.

As a parking lot attendant brings us our car, Jack's cell phone rings. He answers as the doormen help his two women in. Naturally Michelle sits up front.

Suddenly I'm aware of Jack's voice getting louder. He moves away from us and paces the driveway back and forth, listening to something that must be disturbing. Moments later, he quickly tips the attendant and slides into his seat. He takes off like a shot.

"What's wrong?" I ask.

He looks to Michelle. "That was my son Morrie calling. He's at your hotel suite. Somebody broke in and robbed the place."

Michelle is horrified. "No, it isn't possible. No!"

"And worse," he tells her. "A woman was found murdered there."

When we arrive at the hotel, this time Michelle doesn't play the "who will Jack help out of the car first" game. She's out and running for the revolving doors. Jack does me the honor of giving me his arm. But he isn't walking me to the hotel entrance. He's guiding me to the driver's side of the car, where he left the motor running.

"Go on home, dear," he says to me. "Morrie or one of his men can drop me off."

I glance at him for a moment, then I reach over, remove the keys, and hand them to the hotel parking attendant, who is standing right there. Heading for the doors, I toss back at him, "Not this time, honey. You're not going to a crime scene involving Madame while I wait hours until you get home and report in. I'm staying this time."

Jack is startled. He realizes I am not going to change my mind. He catches up to me and we hurry inside. "Okay, Ms. Private Eye, you're officially on the case."

When we get to Michelle's floor the crime scene has been secured. The yellow tape is up. Hotel guests walk by, curious of course, but they are told to move on. We arrive as a body bag is being carried out by Morrie's men. Frankly I'm glad I didn't get to see the dead woman.

An elegantly dressed man, fifty-ish, watches and takes notes. From the tightness of his lips and his rigid posture, this is a man who is clearly worried.

I glance around. So this is where Michelle gets to spend her nights. Elegant. Expensive. In superb taste. It sure beats our tiny little inexpensive condo. This is a woman who travels first class wherever she goes—does she enjoy all this beauty? Or does she take her entitlement for granted?

But right now I get to watch Michelle storm her way inside the ransacked suite, ignoring the police. She reaches the faux Queen Anne desk and starts smacking the wood, looking under and around it. She groans.

Jack asks Morrie, "Who's the victim?"

"A hotel maid. The unsub knifed her."

My eye is immediately caught by the bloodstains on the carpet.

The elegantly dressed male speaks. Now I realize he is the hotel manager. He wears a name tag that says so. In fact, he could have come from central casting—the perfect hotel stereotype. Ever so officious and I'll bet ever so concerned about a lawsuit.

"In all the fifteen years I've been working here, this has never happened," he says. "We have security men everywhere. How could he have slipped by them?"

Morrie answers, "The maid's cart is still in the hall. He either got her to open the door for him, or he snuck in when she wasn't looking."

Jack adds, "Perhaps he took a key from Colette."

Morrie shakes his head. "No. We ascertained that she had her own room key with her when she was attacked. It was with her when she was brought to the hospital." He turns to Michelle to ask about her key.

I add, "He got lucky that the maid was here while we were out, but not so lucky for the maid, poor lady."

But Michelle isn't interested in what we are talking about. She races from room to room in the spacious suite, screeching at the same time. "Where is it? Where's my laptop?" She turns to Morrie. "I don't see it. Do you have it?"

Morrie is not happy to give her the news. "If you had a laptop in here, I'm afraid it's missing. Perhaps you would look around and tell us what else is gone. It might help."

She is out of control. "Help what! I don't give a damn about anything else!" She tears at her hair in frustration. "How could I be so careless? I never leave that computer. Never!"

One of the policemen tries to give her a cup of water. She smacks it out of his hand. "Leave me alone."

She paces the room again: a caged tigress. "You want to know what else is missing?"

I watch the woman lose total control. She runs her hands feverishly through her jewel box lying open on a chest of drawers. "Two diamond bracelets and a pendant." She tosses the box onto the floor, upending it, scattering the rest of her jewelry. She flings herself down on a chair in anguish. "And what do I care anyway."

Jack walks slowly up to her. "Michelle, please try to stay calm. What can I do to help?"

I fully expect her to smack him or something else in her rage and frustration, but Mr. Magic seems to be the only one able to comfort her. She drops her head down, starts sobbing.

Jack says, "I'm so sorry I didn't go back up for the laptop."

She looks up at him, tearfully. "My fault, not yours. Oh, how could I do that? I never, never go anywhere without that case. Just this one time..."

She looks up at him, poignantly. "I can't bear it."

"I know. I know," Jack says soothingly.

Yeah, I know, too.

"Brandy." She points to the mini bar. The hotel

manager hurries over and removes one of the bottles and pours her the drink. He passes it to Jack, who reaches down and hands it to her. She sips at it, and then shudders.

I watch all this, fascinated. The amount of rage inside her and her obedient reactions to Jack; she is something to watch. The men have no idea how to handle her volatility, even while they're attracted to her beauty. I may be the only female on the premises, but I know she wouldn't take kindly to Jack's fiancée trying to comfort her so I stay out of her line of sight.

I try to imagine what must have happened while we were at dinner. If the thief knew the maid was inside, why did he go in? Probably because he knew Michelle was out, but he didn't know for how long. Perhaps he didn't think he had enough time to wait. It seems obvious that the missing jewelry is just a diversion. He wanted that computer. And no one was going to get in his way.

Morrie walks over to Michelle and shows her an eyeglass case in a plastic evidence bag. "Is this yours?" She shakes her head.

I recognize the unique logo of Eye Openers. "Morrie, that's from a shop in the Sawgrass Mills Mall."

Morrie comments, "We found it under the larger bed. Might have belonged to a former guest, and not swept up after they left."

The manager speaks up again, trying not to be confrontational. "We are a five-star hotel. I assure you, our staff is trained to thoroughly clean the rooms before, during, and after each guest's stay with us."

Morrie places the eyeglass case in a box with other filled bags. "I'll have to check this out." To the manager, he says, "Please move Ms. duBois to another suite. This is now a crime scene."

He nods. "Right away." He starts out of the room.

Michelle adds, "And hurry." She is staring in horror at where the maid's body had lain.

Morrie and his team have gone. We are the last to leave. We waited until Michelle was relocated to another room, where she's now languishing on the couch. A policeman has been assigned to guard her. She's finished three of the little brandy bottles and it's quieted her down. I can tell Jack is reluctant to leave.

"I'm so sorry," he says to her. "This has been a bad-luck trip for you."

"I can't wait until I can take Colette home." She's hardly able to keep her eyes open. She no longer plays the grand dame. It's as if all the stuffing has been pulled out of her. I feel sorry for the woman, in spite of all my conflicted feelings about her.

I would like to say something kind to her, but even in her pain, she ignores me. She speaks only to Jack.

She yawns. "I need to sleep now."

Jack agrees quickly. "Yes. You should. You are safely guarded. The thief is long gone." There's a soft plaid throw blanket on the arm of the couch. Jack tenderly covers her with it.

Oh, Jack, look at you. And that expression of so much concern. But then again, I was thinking of doing the same thing. If I did it, she'd probably snap at me. But it's unnerving to watch my love do something that intimate to another woman.

As we head out, Michelle's eyes are closed. She doesn't hear us leave.

We pass the policeman standing guard outside the door. He nods to us. It's past midnight by now and the hotel is very quiet.

"Do you believe what you said?" I ask Jack, who takes my arm as we head for the elevator. "That she's safe and he's long gone?"

"Not really. But I didn't want to frighten her even more."

"Are you thinking what I am? About the coincidence of her suite being robbed?"

He nods. "Probably fifty or more rooms and hers gets picked? Not too likely an accidental choice."

We get off the elevator, being replaced by a noisy group of revelers still wearing their convention name tags. Looks like there will be some painful hangovers in the morning.

I share my thoughts with Jack. "My guess, it's the laptop he wanted. The jewelry was supposed to fool the police. The thief left all the other expensive pieces. Following the logic that she has many enemies, then perhaps the attack on Colette wasn't an accident—it was Michelle he was after. Not just for whatever is on that laptop."

The lobby is equally quiet. Here and there I see a lone reader who isn't ready or able to sleep yet. The night clerk ignores us as we exit the building.

It's gotten cooler and I wrap my arms around myself while Jack retrieves his car. I am not a happy camper. I thought tonight was good-bye to Michelle for good. But I'm not rid of her yet.

Once I'm seated in my usual front seat, Jack turns the heater on for me. I can still smell the residue of Michelle's perfume. It almost feels strange for me to sit in "her seat." I wonder if that thought strikes him as well.

We're quiet for a few minutes, both minds busily at work.

Traffic is fairly light now and we drive quickly

back toward home. Jack speaks first. "I was thinking along the same lines. Someone who doesn't want that book published and knows enough of Michelle's habits to go for her as well as the computer. And the manager's comments about the safety record in his hotel makes me sure this is a professional job. I'll talk to Morrie in the morning and tell him what we know. Or think we know."

So much for our dinner tonight being a farewell. Jack is very quiet now. And I wish I knew how he feels about this evening. Suddenly, our once easy relationship appears to have shifted. Are we no longer going to share our every thought as we did before?

However, the private eye in me is getting excited. Something about the eyeglass case waves a red flag at me. I wonder...

"Gladdy." I glance over at Jack when he speaks, but he keeps his eyes on the road. "I'm sorry about tonight. I thought this would be the last I'd see of her."

"I thought so, too."

"But I can't just walk away now."

"Can't you just let Morrie handle it?"

"It's not that simple. Whoever's after her is getting impatient. He took a chance breaking into the room with the maid there. He missed her in the book room and now in her suite. He must know that she will leave the country very soon. I have a strong feeling he's about to make his next move. I need to be in closer contact with Morrie and Michelle."

"I suppose you do." I try not to sound like I'm whining.

He finally throws a fleeting glimpse at me. "I don't want to, but I should. That was another terrible shock she got tonight. I have to help in some way. I'm sorry."

The Snake peers out from the stairwell, glancing toward the redhead's new suite. He's not surprised to see a police guard sitting on a chair, sipping coffee from his thermos. The Snake smiles. Part one is fini—he has the laptop. Gaston had better be prepared to pay him well after he finishes off this pesky flea who buzzes around his ear. The Snake grows tired of this so-called Sunshine State. No comparison to his beloved Riviera. And besides, just before he left, a new yacht had pulled up alongside of his, with a luscious female appearing topside. He smiles at the memory. A nice rich widow, he hopes.

14

AT THE MALL

The next morning Evvie and I step out of the Phase Two elevator. I already have my car keys in hand. Abruptly Evvie punches my arm and turns me to look at what she's seeing. "What's with them?"

Ida, Bella, and Sophie are standing in the parking lot in front of my old Chevy, yelling at one another. Rather, Ida and Sophie are doing the shouting as Bella kind of backs away from the conflict. A few neighbors see them but walk right on by. We increase our pace and reach them. Ida and Sophie wave their multicolored canes as if they are about to strike one another.

"Hey, hold it. What's with the war?" Evvie tries to stand between them. They push her away.

Bella says timorously, "Make them stop."

Ida says defiantly, "I hate liars. You know how much I hate liars!"

Sophie humphs. "Miss Perfect. And you never told a lie in your life? Besides, we weren't lying."

Ida addresses us. "I run into them yesterday morning. Being friendly, I ask where they're going."

Under her breath Sophie says, "And what was it your business anyway?"

Ida ignores her. "So one of them says they're going out for a stroll, the other says at exactly the same moment, they're going to the post office. Both look guilty as hell."

Sophie is insulted. "I don't need to listen to this." She turns her back on Ida and sticks her fingers in her ears.

Ida fiddles with her hair at the back of her head. In her anger, her thick bun is coming undone. "So when I follow them a little bit just to see, they don't stroll or buy stamps, they go into Jerry's Deli."

Bella and Sophie exchange panicky looks. What's going on here? Why are they so upset? Maybe I should interfere, but Evvie seems to be on top of it.

Sophie turns back to Ida. Waving her cane she screams, "You what? You followed us? I think I'm going to hit you." She lashes straight out with her cane, chanting the Cane Fu instructions. "Swing hard. Hard as you can—"

Evvie grabs Sophie's cane away from her, drops it to the ground, and jumps on it.

I hold up my hands, trying to calm them. "This is not a big deal. So the girls must have changed their minds and gone for breakfast."

"Yeah!" Bella says eagerly. "No big deal."

"Yes, big deal," Ida says ferociously. "My morning class was canceled, so I decided to join them for breakfast and when I got to Jerry's there was no sign of them."

"We're fast eaters?" Bella whimpers, looking at Sophie in terror.

"You lied." Ida crosses her arms and glares at Sophie. "You could not possibly eat that fast. I demand to know where you went!"

Sophie puts her hands on her hips. "You demand? Who are you to demand?"

Evvie warns, "Don't say anything you'll be sorry for later."

"Keep out of it, Evvie," Sophie says as she points her finger right into Ida's gut. "Maybe we wrapped our take-out egg salad sandwiches and went to the park. Maybe we walked in, decided we weren't hungry, and walked out again. Maybe we saw a cockroach on the wall. There's a thousand different possible explanations."

Ida grimaces. "None of those are true. How about the other 997 lies?"

Sophie's had it. "You want the truth? Okay, here's the truth. We saw you coming and we didn't want to eat breakfast with you."

That does it. Evvie is right. Those are words that can't be taken back. Ida is in shock. Bella tries to hold back her tears. Evvie shakes her head in disbelief and Sophie pulls her cane out from under Evvie's feet and thumps away.

Oy. The last fight any of us had was back around ten years ago when a lone handsome senior bachelor came to pick out a bride. It was hell, sheer hell. This is not good.

All three girls walk off quickly in different directions.

Evvie calls after them, "Come on back here. We're going to the mall—with or without you. Right now."

Evvie gets into the front passenger seat. I follow suit and take my place as the usual designated driver.

One by one, still scowling, the other girls take their seats. What a sight. All three of them scrunched together, arms tightly crossed and refusing to look at one another.

There's one way they'll forget their animosity. I filled them in briefly when I phoned them early this morning about why I wanted to go to the mall.

Now I'm giving them more details about dinner with Mme. Michelle. Followed by returning to the hotel after it was robbed and the poor maid was killed. They listen openmouthed with the avid attention they give their favorite soap operas.

The rest of the ride is me being battered by dozens of questions. What did she wear? What did she say? What did you eat? How did Jack handle it? And their shock to learn that Jack went back to see her today again. To comfort her?

Sophie sums it up. "What a piece of work she is. I'm glad she lost her computer. So there!"

Frankly, by now I'm sorry I invited the girls along to go to the mall to look in on Eye Openers, the eyeglasses store. I should have left them home. They start bickering again as soon as they get out of my car and are facing one another. Fortunately this time they run out of steam quickly.

Finally Sophie says, "I still don't know why we're doing this. Isn't it Morrie's job?"

"Morrie has enough on his plate trying to track down the killer. Tracing eyeglasses will be low on his priority list, and I have a strong hunch this is important. We can give him a hand."

"Are we there yet?" Bella whines like a three-year-old who's been taken on a long trip and wants out.

Sophie says, "You know how she hates walking through this mall. It's the size of Chicago."

"You shoulda entered at the north entrance. We're going the long way," Ida adds to the chorus of kvetchers.

The three adversaries click their canes along the tiles as emphasis for their arguments.

Since today is a weekday, the mall is not too crowded, so we're able to move at a good pace. Evvie had been enjoying the window shopping, but now she's annoyed. "Stop exaggerating. And complaining. And why did you have to schlep those silly Cane Fu canes along? Watch out, they'll make you so crooked, you'll really need them." She doesn't bother to hide her sarcasm.

Sophie humphs. "And someday you'll be glad we did. Maybe we'll stop a purse snatcher or something." She looks around searching for suspicious faces.

"Yeah, sure," Evvie adds. "That'll be the day. If you're not happy, go home."

"But I want to go detecting. That's our job," Bella whines again.

Ida snarls. "You detect? That's a laugh."

Sophie puts her arm around Bella. "Look who's talking. What do you contribute?"

I've had it. "Enough already. When are you going to stop this silly argument? Finger pointing.

She lied. No, she lied. Who cares? We have to live with each other."

Ida humphs. "You call this living?"

Evvie looks at me. "Let's leave them here right now."

Bella startles. "Noooo...we'd get lost and we don't have a car."

Ida stamps her foot. "That's a cheap shot. You know we'd never find our way out of here."

Bella sits on a bench to tie her sneaker. Sophie immediately joins her, seemingly exhausted even though we've been here only fifteen minutes. Ida moves away, arms crossed, her cane leaning against the wall. It's her favorite stubborn position.

I chide the group. "You know I'm trying to help Jack solve his problem. Until it's solved I'm stuck with Mme. duBois in my life. You promised to help. Whining is not helping. Arguing is not helping. I need us to work together."

Evvie points her finger at the three of them. "You heard how that French piece of stale pastry treated Gladdy at dinner. Like she was some bit of chewing gum under her shoe. How she humiliated Jack by paying the check behind his back."

Ida grins. "Lucky for you she did. You'd be eating peanut butter and jelly sandwiches for the next few months to pay for it."

"All right already. So stop fighting and be of some help." Evvie stares them down.

The three enemies look properly ashamed.

Evvie points. "And see—there's the store now."

"Sorry," says Bella, head down, blushing.

"Yeah, me too." Sophie pulls her ample shoulders back and straightens up, ready for work.

Evvie asks, "Ida? With us or against?"

"With. With! What are you all waiting for?" With that, she troops ahead of us, cane slapping, right into Eye Openers.

Even though Sawgrass Mills is an outlet mall, this store has delusions of grandeur. High-tech design. Very well lit. Glass mirrors everywhere. Frames for designer eyeglasses on display in towering Lucite cases.

At the moment, we are the only shoppers. In the back, I can see through a glass partition that the optometrist is testing another customer.

Seeing five possible buyers, the two female clerks both amble over.

The tall skinny blonde in mauve speaks first. "May we help you? I'm the manager, Ashley."

The petite brunette in black linen smiles an encouraging smile and chimes in. "I'm Tina."

Bella bursts out, in singsong, "I'm Bella, they're Evvie and Gladdy and Sophie..." Glaring, she adds, "and Ida."

Ida nudges her. "Who asked you?"

"We're just looking," Sophie says, pulling Bella

with her to pretend to scan the wares, but close enough to listen in.

Ida can't help another retort. "Don't break anything or you'll pay for it." Evvie elbows her in the ribs to shut up.

I address the two young hip-looking women. "We're from the Gladdy Gold Private Detective Agency."

The saleswomen look dubious, hiding smiles of derision. I quickly whip out two of our business cards and hand them out.

Evvie immediately kicks in. "We are senior detectives solving senior problems."

The saleswomen are amused. I get the feeling they're bored with no customers around, otherwise they'd ignore us.

Ashley says to me, "What do you want to know?"

"We're looking for someone who very recently bought a pair of glasses here. Perhaps even yesterday. Unfortunately we don't know his name or what he looks like or the brand he bought.

"I recognize this eyeglass case." I point to the type of case that Morrie found in the hotel suite.

Ashley smiles proudly. "This is one of our very newest designs. People have commented on them."

Tina's eyebrows go up. "Yesterday was a busy day."

Ashley is keen to help. "You know it's a male.

And he had our newest designer case. Anything else?"

I say, "He may have very recently come to this country."

Evvie says, "I'm assuming he paid with cash."

Condescendingly, Tina says, "Doesn't ring a bell. Not too many people pay with cash these days. Sorry."

They are about to walk away when Evvie pleads, "Listen, this guy tried to rob someone." My sister is smart. She isn't mentioning murder—that might scare them. "Last few days, did anyone seem suspicious to you?"

Ida pipes up, "You two seem like very sharp gals. I bet you can look at a customer and know whether they'll buy or not."

Tina takes the bait. "*We* think so. And there are always the looky-loos."

Ashley adds, "We can spot them right away."

Evvie asks, "So who didn't fit in?"

The two women look at one another and begin laughing.

Now Bella and Sophie move in closer. It's starting to get interesting.

Ashley says, "There was this old guy. Really old. And dressed pretty shabby, all in gray."

Old, really old? That's odd. Is it possible? Jack's thinking a professional hit man. Couldn't be a senior.

Tina continues, "But when he got closer, we could tell his clothes weren't cheap. It's just that he looked like he slept in them."

Ashley giggles. "He was going to pay in euros, but then he changed his mind for some reason."

Bingo.

I'm excited now, as are the girls. "I think he might be who we're looking for. Tell us everything you can about him. Did you think he was French?"

Now the saleswomen are into the game. They take turns.

Ashley says, "I think so. He spoke in English, but badly."

Tina says, "It's hard to describe him. He looked so...bland. He was short, skinny, and...bland." She looks to Ashley. Ashley shrugs in agreement.

She obviously can't find a better word, but maybe that says something about how he can sneak around without being noticed.

Ashley says, "He didn't care what the glasses cost, but he needed them fast."

She adds, glancing toward the back room, "We told him he first had to have his eyes examined. Weird that he didn't know that. An old man who never wore glasses before? You should have seen how scared he was of the exam."

Tina says, "And then when we informed him he'd have to wait an hour, I thought he'd have a conniption."

Ashley says, "He said he'd pay triple if he could get them right away. He was starting to get scary so we told him we would do the best we could. Maybe forty-five minutes. We could see him waiting out in the mall, pacing back and forth, looking at his watch."

Evvie asks, "So if he didn't give you his euros, how did he pay?"

Ashley, knowing what we'll ask next, heads for the payment desk. She flips through a file. "He used a credit card." And in another second, she whips out his receipt.

We all crowd around her. Ida grins. "We've got him!"

I wonder. Can it be this easy?

15

MISSED CALLS

Evvie and I are back at Lanai Gardens in the laundry room. I have my cell phone with me, waiting for Jack to call. He's with Morrie; they're checking out the old guy's credit card.

Since she's keeping me company, she's doing a load, too. And she has her cell, waiting to hear from Joe. She's always on edge when he goes to the hospital without her. He insists that she have days without him. " 'Go have fun,' he keeps telling me. As if I could. He's on new medications. I don't know how I feel about him taking them," Evvie says. "He's so frail now that if these don't work they'll weaken him even more." She looks at me with tears forming. "It might even shorten his time."

I put my arms around her and hug her. She can't even say the words that mean the end of his life.

Evvie shakes off her depressed mood. "I just try not to think about it."

The dryer dings and it's time to get my clean wash out, so she can put hers in.

She shakes her head sadly, still thinking of Joe. "It took this long to get us to be friends again. Even lovers. Why do we always have to learn life's lessons the hard way?"

This doesn't call for an answer. We know the answer. There is none. We concentrate on our chores.

Evvie smiles. "We haven't had any time to discuss stuff alone. I'd rather talk about the narrow escape you had at your so-called farewell dinner. If it had been me I would have skewered her with a salad fork and that would be that."

I laugh. "I wish you had been there, but I took your advice and remained a lady."

"You really thought I meant it? I wanted you to show her up as the phony she is. Nah, you did it the right way."

It's my cell that rings first.

"Jack?" I listen. "It's only the noise of the washer and dryer. Can you hear me?" Evvie leans over, trying to hear. I tell him, "Let me repeat what you're saying. Ev's with me."

I move closer to the door so I can hear better.

Now I frown. "That's what I was afraid of." I repeat for Evvie. "The killer used a stolen credit card. One of the convention people. Some man from Boca. Dead end." I listen. And repeat again. "Yes, at least Morrie now has some sort of a description. The hotel manager has been informed and their security people are on high alert. They are searching everywhere for him, including going through all the security tapes." I listen again. "What?" Evvie is waiting for me to repeat for her, but I suddenly can't hear Jack.

I inform Evvie that his cell phone is breaking up.

"What, Jack? Where? Hello? Hello?" I give up. "All right, dear. I'll see you when I see you." I hang up, not knowing if he even heard what I just said.

"What happened?" She folds clean laundry on the small plastic table put here for that purpose.

"Well, as we suspected, the credit card was stolen. Then he was trying to tell me something about good news, and that's when I lost him."

The laundry room door opens. Tessie is there holding a basket full to the brim on her hip, with one hand to balance it. She's got an ice cream bar in her other hand. "How much longer you girls gonna be in here?"

Evvie answers. "Maybe forty more minutes."

"Okay," she says, leaving her basket inside. "By the way, Ev, I just saw Joe drive in, in case you were looking for him."

"Thanks, Tess." Tessie, who doesn't have the word diet in her vocabulary, leaves, licking away at her treat.

Evvie steps out on the landing and sees Joe heading for the elevator across the way.

"I better go." She picks up her basket of folded laundry. "I'll come back later for the rest."

She and I look at each other. Are we both worried about the same thing? Losing the man we love?

When Jack walks into Colette's hospital room with Morrie, he is pleased to see that she looks so much better. The color has come back into her young cheeks. Michelle sits on the edge of her bed, smiling.

Michelle says, "Good news. Perhaps my Colette will be able to go home in a few more days. And as soon as that is possible we'll leave directly for the airport and home."

"I can hardly wait," Colette agrees, as she looks lovingly up at Michelle.

Jack watches Morrie draw closer, notebook open, ready to interrogate. Though she tries to hide it, Michelle stiffens.

"Are you all right about answering some more questions?" Morrie asks.

Jack stays in the background, watching both

women and how they react. Michelle tries to look relaxed, but she isn't. Colette seems fragile and unsure.

"Yes, of course," Colette answers.

Michelle fluffs Colette's pillows so she can sit up more comfortably.

Morrie sits, pulling a chair closer to the bed. "You remember what happened that night? All of it?"

Colette says, "I think so, but I'm not sure. I came into the closed book room, using the passkey I had. When I tried to turn on the lights, they wouldn't work. I assumed there was some electrical problem. At first I thought not to go in, but the lights from the hall helped me find my way."

Her body shakes as she speaks, perhaps reliving the fears she felt that night. She stops, reaches for her glass and sips some water. Michelle helps her hold on to the glass.

Morrie says, "I know it's hard for you. Would you prefer doing this later?"

"No. Please, now. Let me tell it and help me understand. You know how it is when something feels wrong? It occurred to me I might not be alone in the room. I called out, but no one answered. I assumed it was my imagination, but even so, I decided to drop the books on the shelf and leave as quickly as possible."

Jack watches Michelle as Colette relates her story. She looks grim.

Colette continues. "When I was up the ladder, I knew something was amiss. The ladder was shaking and then it seemed like the bookcase was as well. And then I saw a...shadow...and I am still not sure if I imagined it. I thought it was some kind of apparition." She pauses for more water. Michelle leans closer to her, her head next to Colette's to comfort her.

Jack muses. Michelle is tough, manipulative, and impatient with most people, but not with Colette. She's gentle and clearly loves her niece.

Morrie speaks softly. "Can you describe what you think you saw?"

"Everything began shaking even harder and I knew I would fall. All my energy went into trying to right the ladder and the bookcase. But in my mind I thought I saw a gray head of a very old man behind the bookcase, pushing it."

Jack and Morrie exchange glances. That matches what Gladdy learned in the mall.

Michelle closes her eyes and barely shakes her head. Colette looks at Morrie, inquiringly. "But that's not possible, is it? I thought it was a ghost. Isn't that silly?"

"Did you see a face?"

She thinks hard. "Yes, but only for a moment,

and then just the top of a head and withered old hands pushing. Isn't that strange?"

Michelle hugs Colette, but Jack senses she is hiding what she is feeling. She says, "*Chérie,* you must put all of this out of your mind. Whatever you imagined happened is over and you are going to be well and home very soon. That's all that matters."

"But why did I fall?" She looks to Morrie, but Michelle quickly answers.

"You know how wobbly that ladder was. Somehow you must have grabbed the bookshelves, which shook the ladder, and you lost your grip on the ladder and pulled both down on yourself."

Jack watches Michelle gloss over the truth so as not to worry the girl. Morrie nods to him. He's getting the same message.

Colette is confused. "Is anything else going on that I should know about?"

Again Michelle doesn't let us say anything. "Nothing you have to worry your pretty little head about. I've already completed my contract with the convention, so we're ready to leave when you are." She gets off the bed and straightens the blanket. "You should rest now."

Colette unwillingly agrees. "I am tired."

That's that. They all say their good-byes and leave Colette.

Down the corridor, out of Colette's hearing, Morrie stops Michelle, who is walking at a fast pace. Michelle knows what he will say, so she beats him to it. "There is no point in telling her about the robbery and the killing of the maid and the loss of my laptop. I want her to get well quickly without any emotional setbacks."

Morrie says, "I understand and I agree. But we now know for sure that there is someone out there gunning for you. And as odd as it seems, apparently he is old. But still dangerous. He meant to kill you, not Colette, that night; you know that."

Jack jumps in. "I agree. He is a very determined character and he won't stop until he finishes the job."

Michelle's hands are on her hips. Jack senses that she is equally determined to have her way. "That's why I want to get out of this country as fast as I can."

Morrie insists, "We have to talk more so that we can figure out who hired him."

"All right, we'll talk. But not now. I have a terrible headache." She turns away from him.

Morrie is even more forceful. "You're in great danger. He seems to know your every move and no one has been able to spot him. We have to protect you until we find him."

"I can take care of myself."

Jack says, "Be reasonable; listen to my son."

Michelle's voice is loud now. "It won't matter if

I'm with someone. Even if I'm in a crowd, he might get me."

Jack says, "You have a better chance with someone trained in protection at your side. And if you stay in your suite most of the time."

"No! You want me to spend twenty-four hours a day with some total stranger? I won't have it." She starts to walk away. "That boy you left to guard me? So young. He would be useless."

Hospital personnel pass them in either direction, but Michelle pays no attention as they stare at this shouting woman.

Morrie is getting impatient with her. "If you don't have confidence in my officers, then I suggest you hire someone to protect you until you leave."

Jack tries a different approach. "If something happens to you, then what will become of Colette?"

That stops her. To Jack's surprise, she moves up close to him. She takes his hands in hers. "You do it, Jacques. You will stay with me and keep me safe. Won't you?"

He could kick himself. She's blindsided him. If Gladdy were here, she would have seen it coming and avoided it. Too late. Michelle was way ahead of him.

Her voice is syrup. "You said it yourself. It's only for a few days. Your *Gladeze* will understand, *n'est-ce pas?*"

Jack shudders to think what his *"Gladeze"* will say to that. *Say no, now,* he tells himself, *before you get into hotter water.*

Tears form in her eyes. "It's only you I trust."

"All right." He turns to his son, whose eyes have just widened. "I'll be there tonight. Can you have someone with her until then?"

Morrie doesn't answer for a few moments. Finally he nods. "I'll have one of my men there waiting for you at the hotel." He looks at Michelle pointedly. "Someone older."

With sarcasm, he adds, "Until Jack arrives. Someone really old."

"Thank you," she says to Morrie tearfully. To Jack, she says, "I will wait for you at the elevator. You will drive me back to the hotel?"

She quickly walks away from them, leaving the two men staring after her.

Morrie shakes his head. "Do you realize what a Pandora's box you just opened?"

Jack sighs. "Yes. But Gladdy will understand. She won't like it, but she'll understand."

Morrie grins. "Did she even know you were coming here?"

"I tried to tell her, but my cell phone conked out." He looks at the expression of disbelief on his son's face.

"Dad, you were always my hero. I thought you were sophisticated and worldly. Imagine my shock to find out you're naïve about women. This former French flame of yours is coming on to you. If I were Gladdy, I'd want to shoot you."

"I wouldn't blame her. I could even oil my old service revolver to help her do it."

Morrie can't hide his grin. "I'd love to be a fly on the wall when you tell her."

16

JACK BREAKS THE NEWS

I'm sitting out in my Florida room having a glass of wine and reading. Actually I haven't turned a page for quite some time. Instead I look out of my screened-in patio, watching the early evening traffic go by. And the sun settling down for the night. Where is Jack? When he called, he was with Morrie, having just spoken to the hotel manager. Not a word since his cell phone went out. I tell myself to stop looking at the clock. Funny, I'm not in the habit of doing this waiting thing. In our easygoing relationship, I have my plans and he has his, and we do many activities together. We usually keep in touch during the day, but not necessarily so. Nor do we interrogate each other about details of what we've been doing apart.

Face it; ever since Mme. Michelle has come upon the scene, I'm constantly waiting for the proverbial other shoe to drop. I never saw myself as a jealous person, but the more I think about her, the more irritated I get. What is it about that woman being near Jack that sets my teeth on edge? As if I didn't know. She blatantly wants my guy, that's what.

I look at the clock again. Only fifteen minutes have passed. And it's Jack's night to cook dinner. I mean, there's no reason why I can't cook something, but it's been fun switching our cooking detail.

Hearing the door open, I'm relieved and I hurry to greet him. But I stop short at the sight of Jack fairly covered with a huge bouquet of roses and two huge paper bags with the logo from Vittorio's Villa d'Este, a fairly expensive restaurant.

When I reach him, he gives me a quick kiss through his three bundles, both of us wary of getting scratched by the sharp paper bags, the thorns on the flowers. Then he hurries to the kitchen to set his packages down.

"How are you, sweetie?" he says. "I hope I didn't keep you waiting. Are you starved? Are your taste buds ready for chicken Parmesan? Some gnocchi? A Caesar salad?" He opens each cupboard. "Where do you keep the vases?"

"I'll do it." I follow him in and fetch a vase from an upper shelf and take the flower arrangement of pink and red roses and place them in the vase. They're beautiful. And probably quite expensive, too.

Jack removes each of Vittorio's cartons with the well-known decorative estate logo. He places the contents in various pots to heat up.

"Something smells wonderful. How come you didn't want to cook?"

He smiles. "Just lazy, I guess."

I can't believe my reaction. Suddenly I'm an accountant, figuring out what he spent on these items. A lot. And the flowers? Why do they remind me of so many novels and movies when the husband brings home an especially large, ostentatious bouquet because he is guilty of something? And, I think irrationally, that the word "bouquet" also comes from the French.

Jack is oh so busy heating the food and setting the table and lighting candles—and, I might add, he hasn't really looked at me since he got home.

He's on edge. He has something to tell me and he's working up to it. Very slowly. And I know I'm not going to like it.

"Isn't this great?" he says. "Fewer dirty bowls to wash. That's a plus. I mean you can do the same anytime you aren't in a cooking mood."

I can't help myself. If he isn't going to talk about where he was today, then I'm going to ask. "Where were you off to when your cell conked out?"

Do I imagine he stiffens, for only a second? He places the silverware on the napkins, paying attention to everything being perfectly aligned around the table.

"Morrie and I were on our way to the hospital. Colette's memory has come back and he went to chat with her and find out what she remembers."

Uh-oh. *And why did you have to go with him?* "Was Michelle there?"

Pause. "Yes, she was." Then quickly, "Colette remembered seeing an old man, but because she doesn't know what we now know, she thought she imagined it."

I don't say a word and he is forced to fill the silence.

"Michelle made sure that Morrie didn't tell Colette what's been happening, so as not to upset her." Jack pours two glasses of wine. A nice Pinot Grigio—nicer than usual, I might add.

The food is ready. Jack serves the dishes. He places the vase with its gorgeous bouquet in the center of the dining table, taking up a lot of space. It reminds me of Michelle, overwhelming every room she inhabits.

"And?" I wait. "And? There must be an 'and' in here somewhere."

Neither one of us is eating. We're picking and moving food around our plates. We'll have leftovers tomorrow. Funny. I have a sudden memory of my childhood. My parents got along fairly well, but when they quarreled it was always at the kitchen table. Ruining everyone's appetite. I've heard this from so many people over the years. Why is it always when we're just about to eat? But is there ever a good time or place for anger?

Jack sighs. "Now that we know Michelle was the intended victim, Morrie wanted her to have a professional stay with her until she gets on the plane for home."

I jump out of my seat, almost overturning my dinner plate. "*You* volunteered!"

Jack bows his head. "I tried to say no."

I am speechless.

He continues while I stare into space. "I suppose you're furious. And I don't blame you."

I sit down again on the edge of my chair. "Why? Why didn't you say no? What is this spell she's cast over you?"

Jack doesn't say anything for a few moments. He finishes his wine too quickly and pours another glass. "I don't know. Maybe she reminded me of my mother, who always used to cry to get my father to give her what she wanted. He always gave in."

Isn't that interesting? He, too, thought of childhood memories. That's a subject we've never discussed. "All right, break it to me gently. What's the deal?"

He takes a deep breath. But he needn't bother telling me. I know exactly what he's going to say.

He finally says, "Want to hear something funny? Morrie thought you'd want to kill me and I agreed, but I told him you'd also understand."

And darn it. I do. As long as he keeps remembering his mother.

I watch Jack pack the suitcase that's sitting on our bed. I sit on the other side of the bed, arms crossed. His sense of humor is coming back. "Are you checking to see that I don't include my sexy pajamas?"

I sort of growl at him. "You don't own any sexy pajamas."

We both smile.

He stops packing for a moment and walks over to me. "If you tell me to do it, I will go to the phone right now and call her and say I'm not coming over."

Yes, yes, do it, my pitter-pat heart is saying. "No, it's all right. I trust you."

"Let me make myself very clear. I am going over there because I know this mad old man intends to kill her and I am determined to stop him." He reaches into the bedside drawer, removes his gun, and places it on top of the table.

Then Jack sits down next to me and holds me

tightly. "She is nothing to me anymore. I love you. I will always love you. Just remember that."

"I know." With that, we kiss. And fall backward on the bed, knocking the suitcase off onto the floor.

"When do you have to leave?" I ask between kisses.

"Whenever I'm ready. I'm waiting for it to get dark enough so I can sneak out of here without the yenta patrol seeing me."

I smile. "Then we have plenty of time."

And we stop talking.

It's eleven o'clock and we peek out the window to make sure no one is outside.

"All clear. Be careful, dear, please."

"Don't worry. I will. And I'll call you every chance I get."

I give Jack a final hug and he sneaks along the shadows on the landing toward the stairs.

Jack is torn. As he drives to the beachside hotel, his mind is racing. He knows how much he's hurting Gladdy by coming here. But the truth is, he believes Michelle is terrified and all her bravado is to hide her fear. He feels he owes her. Maybe it's the old guilt about walking out on her. He never forgave himself for behaving in such an ungentlemanly manner. But that was then and now is now. He has to concentrate on how this strange old man might try to kill Michelle. And who could he be? Gladdy's theory is that the man must have been hired by the people who want Michelle's next book stopped— the men who own the winery she's about to expose. Jack intends to get their names from Michelle and send them to Morrie.

Please, he thinks, don't let Michelle open her door wearing a slinky negligee. He is unable to suppress a grin. *Negligee,* a French word, of course.

The police guard is waiting for him outside of Michelle's suite and reports that all's quiet. Jack thanks him and the cop leaves. He takes a deep breath and knocks.

Michelle checks through the peephole, making sure it's him. She opens the door and greets him wearing a T-shirt and jeans. No makeup. Barefoot. Jack is relieved, then thinks, she's too clever to have been that obvious. *Watch your step,* he warns himself.

"Want something to eat or drink?" she asks him. She seems very relaxed and cool. She's drinking from a brandy snifter. Jack settles for a bottle of water.

"Shall I show you your room? It was to be Colette's room, now yours."

"I'm not here as a guest, Michelle." Jack places his small suitcase on the rug near a paisley armchair. "Guards don't sleep on the job, except for a small catnap or so."

"But that will be so uncomfortable, with a perfectly good bed a few feet away."

He shrugs. "I'm not here to relax."

She settles into the matching couch, feet tucked under her. The coffee table is loaded with snacks.

Jack asks, "You should tell me your schedule. I don't want to keep you up too late."

She shrugs. "My hours are flexible. I eat when I'm hungry and sleep when I get tired. Travel upsets one's natural routine."

Jack sits down gingerly on the armchair. "Are you up for some questions? I feel we're getting close to a solution. We have to know who hired that old man. Let's talk about the winery you worked at."

She raises her arms, stretching. "Not tonight. We'll talk when I'm fresh in the morning. Over breakfast. They do a wonderful buffet."

"We won't be going down for breakfast."

She smiles. "I know that. They bring me anything from the buffet that I might want."

"Very nice," he says.

"Need some entertainment? I've got a stack of DVDs and we can watch a movie." She picks up a box from the assortment scattered around. "A few good French ones. I even have the popcorn to go with it."

Jack muses. He assumes she's found something they went to see together. He manages a yawn. "It's pretty late. You should turn in soon. Tomorrow we have a lot to talk about."

She smiles a cat's smile. "We certainly do." She starts for her bedroom.

Jack sends her a little wave. "Good night, then."

When she closes her bedroom door, he breathes a sigh of relief. He feels as if he escaped from something dangerous. He brings his small travel case into the guest bathroom and realizes this bathroom doesn't have a shower. Obviously the master bedroom is probably much larger and fully equipped. So he'll have to shower in her room. Oh, boy.

He looks around. He didn't pay attention when he came up to the first room for a drink, or even after the break-in. He imagines the rooms are similar. What luxury. Silk and satin everything. Wall-to-wall mirrors. Darn it, a very sexy room. Gladdy would love it. He goes back into the living room.

A moment later Michelle opens her door. "Don't you think I ought to leave my door open? In case our dangerous little old guy does show up."

Jack is stymied by his carelessness. Of course she has to leave her bedroom door open. His feelings are getting in the way of his training. "Yes, definitely." He hopes she doesn't notice how red his face is.

"Pleasant dreams," she calls back to him as she walks away.

He goes immediately to the suite door, then the terrace windows, making sure they are securely locked.

She's right about the door, and he feels foolish that she had to point it out to him. He grabs a throw blanket from the couch and sits down on the armchair, trying to make himself comfortable.

A few minutes later, he hears soft music coming from her bedroom. He recognizes famous French love songs. The lyrics playing now are "*Chérie, je t'aime beaucoup.* Darling, I love you a lot. I'm thinking of you. Are you thinking of me?"

It's going to be a long night.

17

THE MORNING AFTER

I'm eating my lone breakfast and feeling a bit sorry for myself when there's a knock on the door. It's Ida and Evvie. They are dressed in their sweats for our morning exercise. I'm surprised to see them.

"What are you doing here so early? We don't meet for another half hour."

Ida helps herself to a piece of rye toast. "We couldn't wait."

Evvie pours herself a cup of coffee. "Inquiring minds need to know. Where did Jack go last night?"

I knew it. There's no escaping the yenta patrol. He should have waited until three A.M. and then *maybe* he'd have gotten away with it. "Okay, who saw him leave last night?"

Ida says, "Tessie was making a late run to Publix before the market closed. She had a craving for cherry pie. If we didn't know she was an obsessive overeater, we'd think she was pregnant."

This brings howls of laughter from the two of them, being that Tessie is fifty-six.

Evvie adds, "She thought it was a burglar at first, and she had her cane ready to attack, when, luckily, she saw the suitcase and looked closer and then realized it was Jack."

Swell. One of these days these crazy broads are going to hurt themselves with that Cane Fu nonsense.

Ida searches the fridge for cream cheese. "She then told Lola who told me and I told Evvie and here we are."

I am turning red. I knew it. Nobody can mind their own business around here. Next thing I'll hear is that someone knows I didn't sleep very well last night because my light was on so late. I tried to read, but it was hopeless. I was creating scenarios in my head featuring Jack's first night alone with the French Dragon Lady.

Evvie looks at me closely. "Tessie said he looked 'furtive.' I didn't think she even knew that word." Then it hits her. "He didn't...He couldn't...He wouldn't have gone over to *her*?"

I sigh.

Ida is aghast. She almost chokes on her toast. "With a suitcase! Gladdy! What is going on?"

I stall for time. "How come Sophie and Bella aren't here to help with the interrogation?"

Ida hovers over me, tenting me with her arms so I can't escape. "They went to that secret whatever across the way. I saw them go into Jerry's Deli again and I bet it isn't for bagels and lox."

Evvie nudges Ida. "Don't let her change the subject. Glad...fess up."

I sip at my coffee, but that buys me only seconds of time. The two of them are waiting me out.

"All right. The update is that the police are now sure that Colette's fall wasn't an accident and she wasn't meant to be the victim. As I suspected, Michelle is the target."

Evvie sits down at this news. "The police want her protected. And Jack is her guard?"

A small whimper escapes from me. "Twenty-four hours a day until she leaves the country."

Ida stops eating the toast. "He stays overnight? You're doomed. Oy. Good-bye, Jack."

"Nonsense. I trust him."

"But do you trust her?" Evvie looks me straight in the eye.

I get up and walk to the dishwasher and put my coffee cup in. "Not for one single second."

Evvie helps with the rest of the small cleanup.

"What's her angle? What does she want from him? She knows darn well Jack loves you."

"I think I've finally figured it out. It was the inscription in her book about forgiveness. Jack told me he was the one who broke up their relationship."

Evvie jumps in. "Wow, this is wild. She comes to this country and accidentally runs into Jack and then gets this great idea. Nobody ever turns her down. This is a woman who must win, or else. She has no intention of forgiving him."

Ida says, "Wait, you're going too fast for me. Isn't she in danger?"

I say, "Yes, and now she has it both ways. She lures Jack into guarding her life and gets even with him at the same time."

Ida is dumbfounded. "What is she? Some kind of nutcase?"

Evvie says, "She means to punish him by breaking the two of you up. All Jack has to do is make one little mistake, if you know what I mean."

Ida shakes her head in wonder. "Boy, does she have guts. If someone were out to kill me, that would be the only thing on *my* mind."

I wipe the kitchen table of its crumbs. "Talk about cold-blooded. Think of it. She lives with people she intends to destroy and doesn't bat an eyelash. Looks them in the eyes and goes right ahead and traps them. And makes a fortune writing best-sellers about them."

Evvie goes to the stove and pours another cup of coffee. "And the world treats her as a heroine because the people she turns in swindled the public."

I sigh. "I guess fame and fortune and even fear aren't enough to keep her busy. She makes time for chasing after probably the only guy who ever ditched her. He did it because he felt he was doing the right thing. He was too old for her. What a joke."

Evvie tries to make me feel better. "Jack will be able to resist her."

Ida says, "Oh yeah? Think of that warm, gorgeous young body with that silky unwrinkled skin. That sexy long red hair. Climbing into his bed. The right time, the right place, the right circumstances, any man would give in to temptation, even if they know they're doing wrong." Ida paces the room. I can see that her mind is speeding at a hundred miles a minute. "And it won't take much. Even if she gets Jack to give her one little kiss, he's done for. Jack has too much integrity. He'll never forgive himself for betraying you. He'll bow out of the marriage."

I sort of laugh. "Thanks a lot for that. Just what I needed to hear."

But when I look at Ida there's something in her eyes, a kind of pain. Is she speaking for herself or someone she knows? There's still a lot we don't know about our friend.

We all grow silent, deep in our own thoughts. Maybe thinking of long, long ago when we had those young, supple bodies?

The phone rings. I jump. Is it Jack, I hope? But my smile turns into a grimace—it's Trixie, the wedding planner, wanting to take me out and show me wedding gowns.

I tell her I'm not sure I want to hire her, or anybody. She assures me this is just a dry run to show me how she works, no strings attached.

Yeah. Right. I shudder as I repeat this info to the girls.

Evvie says, "Why not? We need to keep up a happy face around here. Tell her you're going." She looks toward Ida, who nods her head. "We'll all go."

Wouldn't you know it; Trixie ("call me Trix") drives a Pepto-Bismol-pink Caddy convertible. She even provides scarves for those who don't want their coifs blown away. I can't believe I agreed to do this. Evvie and Ida busily tie their head scarves on, grinning, imagining this as a fun adventure. Maybe for them. Not me. I sneak my cell phone into my purse in hopes that Jack will call.

As we're about to pull out, sure enough Hy and

198 • Rita Lakin

Sol are out in front of the building schmoozing. Darn it. They whistle at the sight of the obnoxious-colored car.

"Where are you broads off to?" tactful Hy wants to know.

Evvie calls out, "We're shopping for wedding gowns."

"Don't answer them," I say with disgust. As if they would be put off by that.

Hy cackles. "And where's Jack, as if we couldn't guess."

Ida takes a run at an answer. "He took his suitcase out to a store to get matched luggage for the honeymoon."

Trixie leaves the parking area with a squeal of tires. The guys' cries of derision follow us down the road. "Yeah, sure. Shopping at midnight."

"Idiots!" Ida calls back at them.

"My dears," Trixie implores Ida and Evvie, sitting in the backseat, "talk sense to the bride-to-be. There are places to go. People to see. And time keeps ticking away and yet nothing is on the dotted line. I have the car companies waiting to hear your choice of a wedding vehicle. The flower arrangers need as much time as possible to gather their—"

Evvie quickly interrupts her. " 'Gather ye rosebuds while ye may.' "

Trixie looks confused.

Evvie smiles as Trixie eyes her through the front mirror.

" 'Old time is still a-flying,' " I add.

" 'And this same flower that smiles today...' " Evvie laughs. We are playing old familiar memory games.

Even Ida looks baffled.

I finish with, " 'Tomorrow will be dying.' " I raise an imaginary cup in toast. "To the virgins."

Ida gets annoyed. She hates being left out of things. "What virgins? What are you two raving on about?"

Evvie raises a cup also. "To the virgins. Poetry, Ida. Robert Herrick. Poetry."

Trixie, I see, cannot be derailed. She turns to me and says, "And what about the music? Do you realize how far in advance you need to book a good wedding band?"

Evvie leans over my shoulder and winks at me. " 'Music hath charms to sooth the savage breast.' "

This is always a test to see who remembers the stuff we learned at school. Lose and you pay the winner a point. You'd think my having been a librarian might give me an edge. But Evvie is a voracious reader with a memory like a steel trap. I jump in. " 'To soften rocks, or mend a knotted oak.' "

Ida crosses her arms. She always does that when annoyed. "You two are really rude."

Evvie gives her a little hug. "Yes, aren't we?"

Suddenly Trixie swerves wildly. We all hang on for dear life. A car has just pulled away from the curb. "Parking spot," she trills. She backs in. She pulls out. She misses the curb. She goes over the curb. She starts over and over again. The way she weaves in and out is enough to make one carsick. Finally she grinds to a stop and grabs her key out of the ignition and waves it on high. Proud of herself, she grins at us. "I have parking place karma. We're here."

Evvie pokes me to look at what Trixie accomplished. She's parked about two feet away from the curb.

Trixie steps out of the Caddy and points to a huge glass window. The store sign reads, "Ye Olde Wedding Shoppe," and the wedding gown in the window, against a background of red and white polka-dotted wallpaper, could have been made for Scarlett O'Hara.

Evvie whoops with laughter. I groan.

I try on a gown that turns me into a flapper from the 1920s. Lots of satin and lace, cut on the bias. The veil hangs just low enough to hide my eyes. And a snappy red garter perches above one knee. All I'm missing is a Camel cigarette in a long sleek ebony holder.

Evvie playfully selects outfits to model, too. She

has a laughing fit looking at herself in the full-length mirror in an overstuffed rigid Victorian number, bustle and all.

Ida wants no part of our shenanigans. She sits opposite us and reads an old dog-eared issue of *People* magazine. She pretends not to watch us go from gown to gown, stepping up on the small platform to show ourselves off. But she does take a peek every so often and, of course, scowls.

Trixie has left us to our own devices as she busily yaps with the buxom, overly face-powdered fiftyish owner of the shop. Thank goodness, the one saleswoman is busy with a teenager with a suspiciously large belly and an unsmiling mother.

Evvie comments, "I bet old Trix brings all her customers here and then, dare I think it, she gets a kickback on what they buy."

Ida, nodding at the other potential customer, adds to that. "The young ones come in all dewy-eyed about planning the best wedding in the world and don't even look at the price tags."

I glance at mine. A mere three thousand dollars. I feel guilty wasting Trixie's time, but she's clueless. I've never seen a woman smile so much over nothing. At least she sort of keeps my mind off waiting for my cell phone to ring.

"Hey, try this one," Evvie says pushing another gown at me.

I shrug. When I come out of the dressing room,

I'm in what I can only call a Bavarian beer hall waitress outfit. With lots of pink ribbons flying out of the skirts and a short round veil. As I twirl on the platform, Evvie pops out of the adjoining dressing room, wearing the identical garment. We break up laughing. This time even Ida smiles.

We do a silly little dance together on the platform. Evvie sings, " 'Love and marriage...Go together like a horse and carriage...' "

This time we've caught the attention of Trixie and the manager, who now come toward us, still chatting away.

Evvie pokes me. "I've got a great idea. Why don't we make it a double wedding?"

Ida drops her magazine at that, eyes wide.

Even I'm startled at the suggestion.

Evvie says, eyes glistening, "It would make Joe happy."

Only I know why she's teary-eyed—though I suspect Ida has guessed how ill Joe is, but says nothing.

Trixie and the owner come gushingly to our sides, having heard Evvie's comment. Trixie is ecstatic as she looks us up and down. "Perfect. Wonderful, and with matching twin gowns." They must be drooling at the thought of two credit cards with those great big numbers, three thousand and three thousand plus tax. She beams at us. "You both look adorable."

Ida is trying not to choke.

Evvie starts for her dressing room. And I head toward mine. My sister says haughtily, "We'll have to think about it."

The owner looks crestfallen. But not our Trix. I'm sure we'll spend the entire trip home with her driving us crazy, trying to talk us into buying those dreadful outfits.

Ida says good-bye to Evvie and me as we each head to our own apartments. We are both still chuckling at the wedding gown store caper.

Ida decides to stop at her mailbox on the way into her building. Suddenly, she spots Bella and Sophie turning right from the back of the building and heading toward her. Their arms are filled with brown paper bags from Jerry's Deli. She recognizes the logo immediately—two huge smiley-faced bagels with a bright red heart between them.

Still annoyed with their antics, she ducks behind the mailboxes out of their line of sight. Now what are they up to? she wonders. All those packages; are they planning a brunch party? Hardly. They never entertain. Sophie is too cheap and Bella is too terrified. Ida, on the other hand, being an expert cook, could give a party if she wanted to. Which she never does.

The two girls are giggling and bumping into

each other playfully. When they get to the corner of the building, they look around, seemingly to make sure no one they know is outside. Again, Ida is irked by how odd they are acting.

They cross the courtyard together. Aha, they're both going to Bella's apartment. Ida longs to go up-stairs, kick her shoes off, have a nice cup of tea, and watch Judge Judy. But this is irresistible. She has to know what those two are up to. She decides to wait a few minutes, then find out once and for all what they are hiding.

While she waits she peruses her mail. Why does she bother? All she gets are bills and flyers for things she doesn't want. Years ago, when she first moved here, each time she opened the box her heart would flutter. Maybe one of her grandchil-dren would write. But she finally gave up hoping to ever hear from them, and eventually her friends stopped asking questions about her family that she would never answer.

She looks at her watch. Five minutes should be enough. Ida takes the staircase to the second floor. Since Bella lives right next to Evvie, she doesn't want Evvie to happen to see her from her kitchen window, so she approaches from the farther side.

She grins. This ought to be fun.

She knocks. No answer. That doesn't surprise her. She rings the bell. Nothing. She knows she is being watched through the peephole.

She puts her eye to the little metal circle. "I know you're in there, so open up."

More waiting, but she knows they'll cave. She is stronger willed than the two of them put together.

The door finally opens. Bella stands there nervously. Sophie is right behind her, blocking Ida's view.

"Yes?" Bella asks timorously.

Sophie is less tactful. "What do you want?"

Ida smiles sweetly. "I just happened to see you walk by with all those heavy bags from Jerry's. I thought maybe you might have an extra bagel to share." With that, Ida pushes her way inside.

The girls nervously turn to follow Ida as she looks into the kitchen. "Hmm. No bags in the kitchen?"

She turns toward the dining-living room area. Bella's apartment always amuses Ida. Everything is painted or wallpapered in wishy-washy colors. Watery beiges, light whites, insipid grays. Just like the clothes she always wears. Sometimes she imagines Bella will fade into her wallpaper, never to be seen again.

Aha. Suddenly, Ida gets the picture. It wasn't food in the bags, but stuff—now emptied out all over the off-white couch. Posters. Chimes. Crystals.

"What's that awful smell?" She wrinkles her nose.

Sophie's hands are on her hips. Petite Bella practically hides behind her generous girth. "Incense and it's none of your darn business."

Ida walks around the room. She picks up a hammer and looks at a poster with wild colors of a sky with many stars in it. That's a surprise. "Redecorating, are you?"

Bella can't help herself. She is near tears. Ida is amused. The poor darling's home is under siege.

"We're creating a meditation area," Bella says waveringly. "And you should really go home."

Ida keeps poking and sniffing among their things. "Since when does Jerry sell stuff like this? I don't recall seeing rocks on the menu."

She makes room for herself and sits down on the couch among the many brochures lying in a pile. She reads each one aloud: "*Crystal Healing. Cleansing and Balancing. Focus Meditation. Tai Chi for Beginners. Journey Through Your Chakras.* Hmm, I didn't know the sacral chakra is for creativity and sexual expression. Just what we need to know at our age. Well, well. Fess up. Where did you get all this stuff?"

Bella can't stand any more. She blurts, "We belong to a club."

Sophie puts her hand over Bella's mouth. "She doesn't need to know."

Ida shows not the least interest in leaving. She scans the pamphlets, humming a little tune to herself. "And where is that club and what's it got to do with Jerry's Deli?"

Bella pulls Sophie's hand away. "I don't care if she knows. I just want her to stop tormenting us."

In an unusual show of aggressiveness, Bella plants herself directly in front of Ida. "We meet in the back room of Jerry's. We have a guru who teaches us about better health. We learn how to get rid of stress. And right now that's what you are. Stress."

Ida is not perturbed. "You're in my space."

Startled, Bella lurches backwards, away from her.

Ida leans farther back into the couch. "A guru? Really? Just hearing about all this, I already feel relaxed. So what's the name of your club?"

Like lightning, Sophie pulls Bella away, and faces her, nose to nose. "Not another word."

The two of them turn and look daggers at Ida. She smiles. "I can wait. I have no pressing engagements." Ida's eye is caught by a receipt atop one of the purchases. "Twenty-one dollars for a long-distance call? Huh?"

Bella closes her eyes, defeated. She finally turns to Sophie. "You know she's gonna blab to Gladdy and Evvie. Then *they'll* be all over us. I can't stand the pressure, so let's just get it over with."

Sophie shrugs. "It's your funeral."

Bella startles and waves her fingers at the air. "*Ptui, ptui.*"

Ida stares at her as if she's crazy. "Stop that."

Bella keeps waving. "But I have to chase the bad spirits away." To Sophie, she says, "Don't say things like that. It's like having someone walk over your grave."

Sophie shrugs as she heads for the kitchen. "You and your superstitions. I'm raiding the fridge. All those Jerry bags give me an appetite. Go confess your heart out. You'll be sorry."

Bella moves close to Ida, right back in "her space." She puckers her lips and fairly spits the words out. "It's called the Dead Husbands Club and we get to talk to our...our dead husbands. And that was a bill for three minutes. Not that I was able to say a word. So there!"

With that Ida jumps off the couch, almost knocking Bella over. Her composure is finally undone. "You what!"

Bella smiles calmly now. Confession is good for the soul.

Michelle sleeps late, Jack discovers—gratefully. It's already nearing ten A.M. That gives him fewer hours of walking around a minefield with her. He stretches. Every muscle in his body aches from trying to relax in the armchair. He did drop off a few times, but any little sound woke him up again. A car alarm going off. Garbage trucks backing up. Conversation in the hallway.

He can't wait for his turn to shower. On the other hand, he thinks about not bathing at all, just to avoid going into her bedroom—a double minefield. Then he laughs at himself. Does he expect her to climb in once he's naked and lathered? Like he's such a great catch? But he wouldn't put it past her. And how would he feel? How would he react? Would he have to fight her off? Any man's fantasy woman? He feels himself sweating. What an idiot he was to allow her to manipulate him into this. Gladdy was right about her ability to twist him around to do her bidding. He realizes he doesn't know this woman at all.

Craving coffee, he digs around the well-equipped kitchen area and finds an open package. And in minutes he's made his own full pot. There are even croissants in the fridge. Naturally. He warms one up in the microwave. As he butters the flaky delicacy, he recalls, with a pang, his recent dinner with Gladdy. Their evening of dinner at a French restaurant and a French movie, when he officially reinstated their engagement. Somehow it seems a long time ago.

The Miami newspaper is waiting outside the door to the suite and now he can enjoy Gladdy's and his favorite pastime of the day. The morning coffee and the morning paper.

After a while he hears shower sounds coming from her bedroom. He finds himself staring at her half-opened door. He sighs, bracing himself. For when she'll come out.

But when she does she surprises Jack again. Instead of wearing some slinky robe, she's already dressed for the day. Even casual in a white linen pantsuit and no makeup, she's still gorgeous. And doesn't she know it.

"*Bonjour,*" she says.

"And good morning to you," Jack greets her.

She lifts her arms, stretching, causing her jacket to open and reveal another of her low-cut silk shirts. "I slept so well, knowing you were here to watch over me."

She heads for the coffeepot and fills her cup. "How domestic of you to make coffee. You could have ordered room service."

"No problem."

She sits down next to him at the elegant dining room table and sips. "Good," she says. She peers at one of the sections of the newspaper on the table. "Weather is supposed to be perfect. Balmy. What shall we do today?"

Jack is startled. "Do? We're supposed to stay right here and stay safe."

She pouts, gets up and walks to the balcony door. "I can't stand being cooped up."

"You don't have much choice. And please don't go out there."

"You see too many of your violent American movies. Do you think he's out there with a rifle trained on this particular window?"

"Michelle, we don't know where he is or what he's planning. I don't want to take any chances. You're my responsibility."

"But I have to visit Colette."

"You can talk to her on the phone. Hopefully the police will find him soon, now that we have a description. And hopefully, even if he changes his appearance, they'll spot him anyway if he's anywhere in this hotel or close by."

She turns and grimaces. "There must be some way we can sneak out so he won't see us. He can't be everywhere. We can have a bellman bring your car around. After you get in, I sneak in and lie down on the backseat until we are far from the hotel."

"Michelle. Not a good idea."

She walks back to where Jack is seated. "*Mon cher,* I'll go mad closed up like this. *S'il vous plaît!*"

Jack isn't about to share *his* feelings about being cooped up. What if he's stuck here for more than a few days? He'll want to put a fist through a wall. Believe it—he wants out of here more than she does. Because he's indoors he imagines all the outdoor places he'd rather be. When he was a cop, he was always outside, always on the move. Even during those years married to Faye and raising the kids. He'd be taking them camping. Skiing. Fishing on some lake. Gardening. He already feels the four walls closing in.

She reaches out to touch him. "I beg you."

Jack quickly stands up. "I think I'll shower now. Why don't you order some breakfast?"

She straightens up, rebuffed. "Very well. What do you want?"

He picks up his overnight bag. "Surprise me."

He walks into her bedroom, avoiding looking at the unmade bed and her personal items lying around. He tries not to look at the wall-to-wall mirrors.

When he gets into her bathroom, he fixates on the lock, tempted to turn it. He hesitates, then doesn't. Laughing at himself. Does he really believe she'll slip in next to him? He's not surprised to see mirrors again everywhere. A huge sunken tub. The large, beautifully appointed room smells of bath soaps and perfume. It's overwhelmingly feminine. And intoxicating.

He turns on the shower and as he undresses, he keeps his eyes on the door.

Jack smiles ruefully and thinks, *Gladdy, save me*.

18

GETTING THROUGH THE DAY

By the time the lunch hour rolls around, I feel like I've spent the whole morning staring at the phone, willing it to ring. But I know I'm being unrealistic. How can he talk when she's around? Besides, he wouldn't call me when he's "on duty."

I open the fridge to find something for lunch. Some cottage cheese and tomato? Boring. Leftover Caesar salad? Wilted, uninteresting. Which reminds me, yet again, of last night's flowers and fabulous dinner, then spoiled by Jack packing a suitcase and leaving. I play this scene over and over in my mind. I think of myself standing here at the open fridge eating whatever I find. Is that what I'll be going back to if I lose Jack?

I pace. I can't read. I can't nap. I can't stand my negative thoughts.

Knock. Knock. Knock.

I answer the door. To my surprise the girls troop in. Carrying boxes.

Evvie says, "We got hungry; thought you'd be, too."

Ida says, "Chinese take-out."

Sophie says, "Egg rolls. Mu shu chicken and wonton soup."

I smile to myself. Since when did Chinese become the national comfort food? Notice how, in so many movies, when you see someone lonely and unhappy, there are always the little white cartons and chopsticks on the table?

Bella adds, "And we stopped at the video store and got the latest George Clooney so we can drool over our fried rice."

The way Ida and Sophie and Bella avoid looking at one another and keep their distance tells me they haven't quite made up yet. There's still plenty of tension between them.

We line up at the kitchen counter and dole out portions. I bring out a pitcher of iced tea. The girls lay place mats on the coffee table in the Florida room. Evvie slips the movie into the VCR slot. She warns us that the guy in the video store said DVDs have almost completely replaced tapes, and very soon they'll be gone forever and we'll be out of luck. And there's even talk about something "blue" that might replace them, too.

We bring in our plates and drinks and go for our usual seats. My slat-backed rocker is always mine. We settle in for food and entertainment.

When Clooney appears, a happy groan goes round the room.

"Oh, to be forty years younger," Evvie says, sighing.

"Oh, to be forty pounds lighter," Sophie adds.

Bella jumps in. "He should be forty years older and I could live in Hollywood right next door to him. I could knock on his door to borrow a cup of sugar."

Ida feels compelled to dash their dreams. She has not one romantic bone in her body. "So, why isn't he married? There must be something wrong with him."

Evvie counters, "Hey, if you looked like him and made the money he makes, believe me, you'd stay single and have all the fun you want."

Sophie snipes at Ida. "You always have to spoil everything, don't you?"

Bella gives Sophie a little shove to try to keep her quiet.

Ida flares. "You starting up with me again?"

Bella shoves Sophie harder. "Don't."

I sigh. Here we go again. "Girls, what is it going to take for you to be friends again?"

Ida stands up, waving her chopsticks at them. "A confession to everyone for being liars, that's what."

Evvie hits the mute button on our movie and turns to them. "Let's have it, already. This is getting tiresome."

Sophie and Bella cower into one another. Poor things, they look terrified.

Ida says, "Allow me. If you let them tell it, we'll be here all day while we drag it out of them. It seems that our gullible friends have done it again."

Sophie sits up stiffly, glaring at her. Bella hides her face in her hands.

"They've joined a club. Apparently there's a secret back room at Jerry's Deli where not only do you get a guru and incense, but you get one hell of a scam."

Sophie jumps up and shoves her. "It is *not* a scam."

Bella whispers, "We get vitamins, too."

"Didn't you learn anything after Mme. Ramona duped you?" Ida shoves Sophie in return. Harder.

Evvie rushes to them and pulls them apart. "Enough. Sit down."

Bella moans. "I'm getting a heartburn already." She gropes for Tums in her purse.

Ida spouts out the venom she feels. "Not a scam? It's called the Dead Husbands Club and they make phone calls, I assume, either to heaven or hell. It cost Bella twenty-one dollars to be able to speak to her Abe!"

"I didn't say a word." Bella pushes two Tums in her mouth, tears beginning to run down her face.

There is a moment of silence. Evvie and I exchange glances. How funny! Actually paying money to talk to heaven? Or hell? But we mustn't laugh. Evvie finally breaks the silence. "Oh, boy." She shakes her head in wonderment. "Did you actually hear Abe's voice?"

Sophie answers as Bella searches once again hurriedly through her purse. "They speak through our guru, so of course it isn't the actual voice. And don't make fun of him."

Bella answers, her nose in her purse. "He's a saint."

Ida blurts back. "What do you know from saints?"

Sophie shoots Ida a poisonous look. "Feel better? You like making her cry."

Ida shrugs. "It's the principle of the thing. You lied because you knew the rest of us would disapprove. They're breaking the law. They should be in jail."

Evvie tries to mediate. "But are they hurting anyone? Doesn't sound like much of a scam. You're talking a few bucks. Not a big deal."

Ida scowls. "Okay, if you are so sure you aren't

being suckers, then let me go with you to the next meeting."

I look from face to face. I should say something. But I feel like the last person who should criticize Bella and Sophie for wanting to reconnect with the husbands they love, so I stay silent.

Sophie hmphs. "Come. Don't come. It's a free country. Do what you want."

Bella timidly adds, "But don't forget to bring extra cash for phone calls."

Ida scoffs at that. "Hah! That'll be the day."

Evvie tries to appease all three of them. "Maybe I'll come, too. As a visitor. But don't tell Joe. He'll resent being thought of as dead."

She makes the joke to ease the tension, but I see the worry in her eyes.

"Wait, I have something." Bella finally finds what she's looking for. She brings out two small wrapped packages and hands one to me and the other to Evvie. Her nose goes up in the air as she passes Ida. Nothing for her.

Evvie and I open the packages. Inside, I find a thin red leather cord, holding metal chimes with small crystals dangling below.

Bella explains. "They're special chimes. You hang them up somewhere and when the chimes ring, someone you loved and lost will return. Let me show you how to do it."

She takes my chimes and goes to the window.

Tiny Bella reaches as high as she can. She has trouble hanging the cord from the top of my curtain rod.

Evvie jumps up to help her. "Thanks for my gift, Bella," Evvie says, hugging her.

I smile at my two very sad friends. "It's lovely. Look at how the colors of the crystals move in the sunshine." I go to Bella, too, and kiss her on the cheek. "Thank you."

The tears are really falling now. Bella turns to Ida, chest out, head high. "If something I do makes me happy, why do you have to ruin it? I don't care if I lose my five dollars. Every time I go, I feel good, and isn't that what matters?"

Ida looks uncomfortable. I think she feels cornered. And puzzled. If she's sure she's right, why aren't we agreeing with her?

She forces a smile. She can't believe all of us are against her. "Let's go back and watch the movie. Okay?" She hands Bella a tissue as she heads back to her seat. Bella takes it and sniffs her tears away.

Sophie swivels so her back is to Ida and looks at Evvie. "On with the show."

Evvie quickly turns up the sound again and everyone settles down as George Clooney smiles his irresistible grin and seems to be looking directly at each one of us.

I try to join them, but I can't stand not knowing

what's going on with Jack and Michelle. What are they doing? What are they talking about?

After a few minutes, I get up and start out of the room with my picked-at plate of food.

Evvie calls, "While you're up, Glad, wanna bring me some more mu shu?"

"Actually, I need to get out. I really appreciate your coming by, but I must get some air. Enjoy your food and Mr. Gorgeous."

They look at me, disappointed but concerned.

"Want us to come with you, wherever you're going?" Evvie starts to get up.

I gently wave to her to stay down. "I don't have a clue as to where I'm going. I'll be back soon."

As I leave the room, I hear Bella say to Evvie, "Why didn't you put it on pause? Now we missed a whole lot."

I hear Evvie answer her with weariness, a question asked and answered a hundred times. "We can rewind, Bella. R.E.W.I.N.D."

As I grab my purse and keys, I suddenly know where I'm going. If I can't see the father, then I'll visit the son.

Eventually Jack had to agree with Michelle. After a few hours of playing cards and watching dull TV sitcoms, both of them needed a break. Some fresh air. Especially since Michelle still refused to talk about the man who was trying to kill her.

He enlisted the aid of the hotel manager, who helped them escape through a service entrance that led to a private staff parking area, where one of the valets had brought Jack's car. To his surprise, the hotel manager handed them a picnic basket filled with a gourmet lunch and expensive wine— apparently, Michelle had called room service while Jack was getting ready.

Now, as Jack watches Michelle leaning her head and shoulders back against a tree, satisfied after the delicious lunch, what he's thinking about isn't her but his recent picnic on the beach with Gladdy. He wishes he was spending this beautiful afternoon with the woman he loves, instead of sitting here growing impatient with Michelle's attitude and her refusal to help them wrap up this investigation. He knows they weren't followed from the hotel, but he can't stop his eyes from moving in perpetual motion as he examines everyone near them, looking for the murderer.

"I never want to go back." Michelle sighs happily.

"Enough fun for today. It's about time we got down to business."

She is all sweetness. "Do we have to?"

"Yes. You've been avoiding this discussion long enough."

"I'd rather talk about us." She starts to crawl closer to him.

"Stop." He motions her to stay where she is.

"But it's such a lovely day. It feels good not to think about problems."

Jack takes a notepad and pen out of his jacket pocket. "I want the names of the people you met when you worked at the winery. The owners."

She laughs. "You can't be serious. Those pathetic losers? You think *they're* trying to kill me?"

"It makes sense. Who else would want your computer? Why were you so angry when it was gone?"

She says angrily, "Believe me, I'm still angry. Because of my rivals. The press. There's always someone who's looking for a scoop. Or a way to steal ideas from me. You have no idea how many vultures there are out there. A writer has no privacy anymore."

"But not enough to want to kill you. The winery people already know it's about them."

She cannot hide her amusement. "Jacques, *chéri*. I lived with those people for months. They are four unintelligent people incapable of any complex action. And the whole idea of them hiring an elderly assassin? To track me down in Florida? Ridiculous."

"That old man 'hired gun' tried to kill you and

came very close to killing Colette instead. He murdered the maid at the hotel when he went after your computer. I think that's enough to take very seriously. What's in the next manuscript that's important enough to kill for?"

She sighs. Jack assumes she's annoyed that he isn't going to let go of this idea. "All right. They were 'blue fining,' something they shouldn't have been doing because it's dangerous and banned in many countries." She stops.

Jack waits. She's going to make him work for it. "What is it and why is it dangerous?"

Being facetious, she grins. "Why don't you wait until the book comes out? Then you can read my twenty pages about the whole process." Michelle tilts her face up to catch the sun's rays. "I hate to waste this glorious day on serious talk."

"Michelle. Enough playing games."

Another bored sigh. "Very well. Wine growers afraid of clouding in their white wines use hydrogen cyanide to remove the copper and iron that cause the problem. Needless to say, the cyanide can decompose in the bottles. Growers are supposed to test the wine to detect residual levels. But they never did. And believe me, they were guilty of many more infractions of the law. Enough already. No more questions."

"Thank you," he says, not hiding his impatience.

"Besides, others have tried to get me and failed.

This guy's already blundered and I'm sure Morrie's people will apprehend him soon."

"His blunders may make him even more reckless."

Michelle slides closer to him. "Why should I worry? I know I'm in good hands."

Jack watches her glance around, smiling at passersby, untroubled. She ignores his pleas to be concerned. It's as if she spins a web around herself—sure, because of who and what she is, that she's immune to being hurt. The woman reminds him of a moth, more like a butterfly, who fearlessly flies closer to the flame. He must keep her focused. But is it for her sake or his?

"The names, Michelle." He removes the cap of his pen.

She shrugs. If he must insist on this boring subject, very well, she'll play it his way. "Pierre LaRoche, his brother, Oswald, and the fat wife of Oswald, Hortense. And their partner, Gaston Dubonet." She intends a joke. "Sorry, I don't know the name of your elderly assassin with gray hair. Their winery is Le Vin de Bordeaux Sud."

He studies her for a moment; she is shaking out her red hair, pretending to be unaware of how sexy her movements are. Hah. As if she didn't know that everyone looks her way admiringly. Maybe envying this sour old daddy next to her. Surely no one would think he was her lover. "Why did you insist I guard you day and night?"

Her eyes lower, her lips form a seductive smile. "You can't guess?"

"No, not really."

She's now close enough to touch him. "Perhaps it's because you left me so abruptly in Paris, we never had a proper ending. All these years, you never thought of me once?"

Jack doesn't intend to get into any old intimate details. He moves away from her and gathers the remains of their lunch, packs what's left of it into the basket. "I think we should go."

She pouts prettily. "A few minutes more. Please. Look, on the bandstand. There's a group of musicians about to play."

Jack sighs. "All right. I can call my son from here. One song. After that, we leave." He lifts his cell phone out of his inside jacket pocket and dials.

Morrie answers, but is busy on another line, so Jack quickly reels off the names Michelle gave him. Morrie makes a quick note of them and promises to call right back.

Michelle removes the wine bottle and her glass from the basket. "Just a few sips more."

The band plays its first selection. A French song. "April in Paris." She claps her hands in delight.

Jack puts the phone down. She refills his glass

and passes it to him. He hesitates a moment, then takes it.

I don't even bother to call Morrie. In my agitated state, I rush over to his office hoping he'll be there. And he is. He's surprised to see me. He gestures for me to wait as he completes a call. When he finally hangs up, he smiles.

Never mind the niceties. I jump right in. "Why didn't you talk your father out of becoming Michelle's guard?"

His eyes widen. "Not even a hello, how are you?"

"Hello. How are you? There. Happy?"

Morrie walks me to the chair opposite his desk and sits me down. "Dad and I share a stubbornness gene. When we make up our minds, nobody can change it."

"It was his idea?"

"No, hers. She manipulated him into it. She's very persuasive, as you probably know." He stands over me. "Want a drink?"

"No, thanks."

"Funny you should drop in. I was about to call him. With news."

I mutter under my breath, "Wish I had phone privileges." Then I realize he just said something important. "News? What news?"

Morrie sits down behind his desk and puts his feet up. "I've had a most amusing phone conversation with a *commissariat de police* in Paris. An Inspector Bonnard. I explained who I was, gave him my phone number. Reported the situation about Michelle and her niece and all that's happened. Dad had just given me the names of the people who own the winery. I turned them over to the inspector. I informed him that we feel these people sent over a professional assassin to murder Mme. duBois while she's here in America. My French was deplorable, but I muddled through.

"He seemed very busy and was constantly being interrupted. It was hard keeping his attention. But that changed when I said I had information about the assassin and I needed his help. When I mentioned that the man we are looking for is elderly and has bad eyesight, there was a pause. I heard peals of laughter in the background as he rattled off a fast barrage of French to the others in the room. Then, after a few choice words which I won't repeat, and didn't understand but got the gist of, he hung up on me."

I manage a smile. "I can understand why. An elderly hit man does seem implausible."

Morrie picks up the phone. "Maybe Dad will have an idea." He dials and Jack answers.

My frustration is unbearable. The two of them

can chat anytime, back and forth, and I don't dare call.

Morrie turns on the speaker phone so I can listen. I want to wave to him not to, but I don't. There may be a reason why Jack hasn't called me. But I'm curious to hear what's going on.

Morrie says, "I spoke to Paris a few minutes ago."

Jack's voice comes up with background noises I can't quite make out. Music?

Jack says, "Were the French police of any use?"

Morrie answers. "They were all right until I mentioned the elderly assassin."

I hear a woman's voice. A woman with a French accent. Guess who?

She is speaking to Jack. "*Alors.* I told you the police would never believe you."

I scribble a note to Morrie. Morrie nods.

He asks Jack, "What's that noise in the background?"

There is silence for a moment. "Michelle was restless and needed to get out. We're at a park and a band is playing."

Michelle pipes up. "We had a lovely picnic. I wish Jack would dance with me."

My head reels. Morrie avoids looking at me.

Silence. Then Jack asks, "Why is the speaker phone on? Someone else is in the room?"

I quickly stride to the door tossing out my exit

words. "Not anymore." I walk out. In the hallway I take a deep breath. This is too much. She's really trying to do it. She will find a way to destroy our relationship.

I make my way down the hall. Morrie comes out of his office and hurries after me.

"What?" I ask.

"Dad says he'll call you later and explain."

"Explain what? Everything is quite clear."

Morrie is stumped. He doesn't know how to comfort me. And I feel foolish for exposing how upset I am. I dig deep into my purse for my car keys so I don't have to face him and see his pity.

I ask, still looking down, "Did he have an idea?"

Morrie says, "No, he'll try to think of one."

We both stand there. I want to leave. He wants to get back to his office and we're both frozen. Finally, I say, off the top of my head, "Call the French police back. Tell them to look up the family background of the four owners. There's got to be some connection there to why the killer is so old. I have a hunch something will turn up."

I walk out of the building without looking back.

As I turn the key to open my car, I think, *You better not dance with her, Jack Langford!*

19

WATCH YOUR STEP

Evvie and Joe are making an effort to pull me out of the wretched mood I'm in. It's not working. Joe tries with the dinner he prepares. He made a special pasta for me with eggplant and mushrooms. The two of them even set the table with what I recognize as Evvie's best dishes, used only for special occasions. Evvie delights Joe with reporting our antics at the bridal shop. I'm in their apartment because I know Jack will phone me at home. He may even have done so by now but I don't want to talk to him. Obviously Mme. Michelle is calling the shots. You don't take a possible murder target out of a safe room in a hotel to go dancing in a nonsecure park. That's unprofessional. And dangerous, and Jack knows it. Incredible how she is able to control him.

"Didn't we look cute in the matching gowns?"

I suddenly realize Evvie is trying to get me to join in the conversation. "Yes, adorable," I answer.

Evvie says softly, "Joe has good news. His new medication seems to be working. The doctor says he's in remission."

I perk up. "That's good news indeed."

Joe grins. "I may be around longer than ol' Ev would have wanted. You know. Like the movie, *The Man Who Came to Dinner*. I think she expected me to take the last leap into the great unknown a lot sooner."

Evvie gets up from her dining room chair and bends to hug him. "You know that isn't so, you silly fool."

To the surprise of both of us, she holds onto Joe's chair and lowers herself down to her knees. No easy feat with her arthritis.

"Hey, doll, what are you doing?" Joe looks worried. "Are you hurting or something?"

She grins. "No, dummy, I'm about to propose to you." She looks up at me. "Maybe I was kidding in the store, but I'm serious now." She takes both of Joe's hands in hers. "Joe Markowitz, would you marry me? Again."

As Joe stares at her, startled and thrilled, I feel she is doing this partly because she really means it and partly to do something dramatic that might stop me from agonizing over Jack.

Joe bends down, kisses her hair. "You're serious? You want this old fossil back in your life for good?" She nods, with a smile so bright as to be luminous. He helps her up, nuzzling her as he does. "You betcha."

They both stand hugging each other. Joe grins at me. "And you can't get out of it, because we have a witness."

They are practically jumping up and down with joy. Evvie says, "A double wedding, Joe, with Gladdy and Jack."

Bless my sister who loves me so much. She is sending a message to me, the way she always does, her thoughts reaching out to my heart. She's telling me Jack will marry me. Of course he will. He loves me no matter what this nonsense is with Michelle. She wants this to comfort me, but instead it's breaking my heart.

She adds, giggling, "But of course, not with wedding gowns. It's a little late to be wearing white."

We're all laughing, but I've got tears in my eyes.

I'm finally allowed to leave, though they keep trying to hold me there. "Shall we play cards? Watch some TV? Phone the kids and tell them the news?" But as much as I don't want to go back to my apartment, I need to be alone.

*　　*　　*

My thoughts are elsewhere as I leave Evvie and Joe's apartment, and in my hurry toward the elevator I don't see the package of vitamins in front of Bella's door. I trip and suddenly I'm falling. And now I'm on the ground and I know I've hurt something. My ankle is throbbing.

I shout for Evvie. "Evvie, help. Help!" She comes running out with Joe. But so does Bella who lives to the left of Evvie. And so do Lola and Hy at the farthest end of the walkway. In moments, Joe and Hy get me up, but I can't stand on my left foot. So careless. Did I unconsciously want to hurt myself?

So back to Evvie's. On her couch. Everyone scurries about to help. Evvie has ice cubes in a kitchen towel on my ankle. Lola brings a pillow to elevate my leg, at the same time asking if Evvie has any frozen peas in the freezer. She used them once on a hurt knee. They're easier to wrap around than ice. No peas so I settle for the ice. The two men chat about the walkway not having enough light and insisting that it should be taken up with the condo committee. Evvie reminds them she is on that committee. My sister wants to call a doctor but I talk her out of it. It's probably only sprained. Everyone is involved with my condition and I could punch myself for not being more careful.

Bella has disappeared, but now she returns. She walks over to me and hands me her candy pink decorated cane. "Now you can join Cane Fu class for real," she says helpfully.

Finally Tylenol lowers the pain enough that I'm able to limp back to my apartment with Joe and Evvie holding on to me.

Evvie insists, over and over, that I call Jack. "Tell him you're hurt. He'll rush right home and that will be that."

"No. Absolutely not." I repeat this every time she mentions it. "I'll tell him in my own time." I am weary. "Thank you both, but please go home. Please."

Reluctantly they leave me, Evvie not happy about my being alone. And yes, there is a message from Jack telling me to call, no matter what time. How ironic. Suddenly it's all right to call him. But I don't want to because I know I'll weaken and end up confessing about my fall.

Jack paces the living room in Michelle's hotel suite. From the master bedroom he can hear Michelle talking to her niece, Colette. She is almost ready to leave the hospital, thank goodness. Let this be over and done with. He's bungled things with her and with Gladdy. How could he have been so stupid as to take Michelle outside? He feels he is no longer able to think clearly.

He needs to talk to Gladdy. To explain what's going on. He assumes she is not answering the phone on purpose because she's angry at him. And rightly so. When Morrie put the phone on speaker, Jack should have guessed that Gladdy was in the room. But why was she there? Probably to get news of him through his son, because he hadn't gotten in touch with her. He cannot believe how poorly he's behaving. Michelle is clouding his judgment. Maybe after this Gladdy won't even want him back.

"Gladdy, please pick up the phone. Please."

Jack looks up. Something's different. Suddenly he realizes what it is. Michelle is standing behind him. He turns. She's changed her clothes, and this time she's in a gorgeous black silk negligee. She comes closer and he can smell her heady perfume.

"*Chéri,* we must speak. Something most important."

"Yes." He clears his throat. "We need to clear the air once and for all. Michelle, I can't—"

Michelle holds out her arms to him. Her voice is tender. "I cannot help myself. *Je t'aime.* I love you. I never stopped loving you."

20

CONFESSIONS

Jack pulls back as if he's been burned by fire. Michelle starts to move closer, the silk of her gown swishing like a soft wind in her wake.

He throws his hands up as if that will halt her motion and the words coming out of her mouth. He tries not to look at her body, every curve of which is accentuated. Her pale creamy skin is made even more exquisite by the ebony black of her gown. "Don't. Please," he says.

She stops, breathing hard. "I can't go on pretending. I can no longer help myself, *chéri...*"

Jack moves behind the couch, would that it could protect him. "You mustn't say such things. It's impossible."

"I have to say what's on my mind. I cannot keep

my passion inside me for another second. I never meant for this to happen. You left me and I knew you would never return. But I still loved you and I thought you loved me. Even though you made it clear that you meant for us to be over."

"Michelle, please. No more." He thinks of Gladdy, trying to imagine what she might be doing now. What she's imagining. Why he isn't home yet.

She can't stop herself. "When I knew I was coming to this book fair, I told myself I would not look you up, nor had I any intention to call. But when we met by accident, I took it to mean that fate wanted us to be together again."

Jack thinks he must look a fool cowering behind this frilly couch. His mind is reeling.

Say something. Don't just stand there, he tells himself. "Michelle, we were caught up in a fantasy. The confused American and you, amused by his awkwardness, coming to his rescue. An old guy easy to seduce. Mad passion on my side. Entertainment on yours. It was a game to play. Nothing more."

She gazes lovingly across the room at him. "It might have been that at first. But not after we made love."

Jack shakes his head. "Michelle, admit it. I was just an amusing fling to you. I even thought at times you felt sorry for me. You couldn't possibly have fallen for this old man."

She smiles. "But I did, and I know you loved me, too."

Jack groans. He needs a drink to get through this soap opera discussion of their affair. He helps himself to the Scotch bottle on the bar near him and pours himself a double. He pulls his jacket off and tosses it onto the back of the chair.

"I thought so at the time, but how could I not be infatuated? Who wouldn't be enchanted by your beauty and your youth? I was flattered, and grateful for your attention. I thought you were intentionally gifting me with what was probably going to be my last love affair."

"You didn't believe I loved you?"

"I imagined you thought you loved me. But it was timing. Another month or year, in a different mood, another man in your life, you wouldn't have even looked at me. When I happened to appear, you were ready for someone like me."

"*Mais non,*" she protests.

"Yes. You spoke so often of your beloved father. I felt that's what I was to you—a father figure." Jack thinks that his feet are hurting, that he wants to sit down like the old man he is. But he dares not move.

As if she reads his mind, she smiles. "Shall we sit down?" She seats herself gracefully on the couch, tucking her legs under her.

Gripping his drink as if it were a lifeline, Jack

thankfully drops down into the armchair farthest from her.

"Being here with you again, being this close, moment by moment, made me realize this was no fantasy for me. It's real," she says.

"You tricked me into being alone with you."

"Yes, because I wanted you to accept the fact that you still loved me, too."

"Michelle. You can have any man in the world you please. You could do so much better than a beat-up old codger like me."

"*Non. Non. Non.* Men want me for many reasons. My body. My success. My money. An entrée into my world in which they want to belong. I never met a man who truly loved me. Nor did I love any of them. But with you I was comfortable. I felt safe. You were the only honest man I ever met."

Jack sets the drink down on a table. He thinks suddenly of his daughter, Lisa, and recognizes the similarity of feelings. He sighs in relief, like a puzzle has finally been solved in his head. He feels like a father to Michelle. He wants to wrap his arms around her and give her the comfort and safety she needs. Yes. But if he tried, she would misconstrue it.

She leans forward, fervently. "Do you know what happened to me after you left? I was angry and grew bitter and cynical. I changed. There would be no other man after you. I turned myself off. I became obsessed with work. No more good guys. What did I decide to love? I loved the idea of finding worthless, dishonest men and punishing them. And there were so many. The more I succeeded, the more arrogant and distant I became."

"I'm sorry you felt you needed to do that," he says quietly.

They are silent for a few moments. He stands and takes a deep breath. He has no other choice. He must break the thread between them forever. He did it wrong the first time. There was no closure. He'll have to hurt her again, like a doctor cauterizing a wound, but hopefully she can go forward when it's over.

"I do love you, Michelle, but not in the way you want. You have to get on with your life and leave the fantasy behind. I wish someday you'll forgive me."

She jumps up, gasping. "Don't say that. Don't."

"I'm so sorry, Michelle, but I can't stay here anymore. It's wrong for you, and for me as well." Jack gets up and reaches for his cell phone. "I need to call Morrie and find someone to replace me."

He strides to the door, desperate now for some breathing space. "I'll call from the hallway."

As he reaches the door, Michelle runs to him and grabs his arm. "Kiss me, Jacques. Please." She raises her lips to his. "Please."

For a moment, neither one moves. Then Jack gently pries her away.

He opens the door. "I'll be just outside, for a few minutes."

He watches as her eyes tear up. "If there was no Gladdy, would your answer be different?"

He shakes his head and walks out, closing the door behind him.

The Snake watches the woman's suite as usual. Leaning casually against the wall, near the elevator, gives him a quick exit if he needs it. He holds an open newspaper, his prop. Suddenly, he is hit with a sharp pain in one of his teeth. Now what? A toothache?

But never mind that. Abruptly, he is alert. The flic is coming out, punching a number on his cell phone as he does. The Snake quickly presses the elevator button, but the cop looks down the hallway and sees him. It's too late to turn away. They lock glances with each other and The Snake sees recognition in the enemy's eyes—a perfect match to the description of the man they are all looking for. He can almost read his mind—should he come after him? But what if he's wrong? It leaves the woman vulnerable. But the cop thinks he is right. He reaches for his gun—but he's left his gun inside the room.

The Snake is in luck. A trio of older women,

laughing, round the corner and arrive at the eleva-
tor. He grins and immediately puts his arm around
the waist of the woman nearest him. If she screams
or slaps him, he will be a canard mort, *a dead duck.*
And he will be forced to press the blade of his knife
at the woman's fleshy neck to take her hostage.
Then it will get very messy. Fortunately, his luck
holds. She is surprised and delighted at his atten-
tion, and her friends smile also. He whispers in her
ear, softly, using his French accent charmingly, re-
assuringly, as the four of them cheerfully enter the
elevator. He tells the woman he mistook her for his
wife. The door closes on the women's laughter. At
which point he discovers she is wearing a gardenia
corsage. He sneezes. Three times. Damn his aller-
gies.

Jack stands in the hallway, unsure. For a moment
he was certain that little guy fit the description of
the assassin but it was a false alarm. The man had
simply been waiting for his wife. Once again, Jack
is upset with himself. How could he have walked
out without his gun? Another mistake. What if the
man near the elevator had been the wily killer? But,
then again, if Jack had gone after him, he'd have
put the ladies in the elevator at risk. Argh. He slaps
his thigh in frustration. He is too involved to think
clearly. He must bring someone else in here quickly,

before his ineptness gets Michelle or someone else killed.

Jack reaches his son on the phone and explains what's been going on. He listens impatiently as Morrie recites his version of I-told-you-so.

"Never mind the lecture. Get some men over here, fast. In fact, I'm not sure, but I might have just seen the guy—or at least someone who fits the general description." Just to be on the safe side, when he hangs up, he alerts hotel security.

He unlocks the suite and goes back inside, but Michelle is no longer in the living room. Neither is the bottle of Merlot that had been on the kitchen counter. Her bedroom door is closed. He pauses, then walks over and calls out to her. "Michelle, are you all right?"

For a few minutes there is no answer. He knocks this time.

"Go home, Jacques. Go home to *Gladeze,* where you belong."

"Come out, Michelle. Please."

"Enough has been said. Leave me alone."

He hears the sounds from her portable CD player. French love songs again. He sits down on the couch with his head in his hands, feeling like a rat. And wonders how long it will take for Morrie to find replacements.

He hopes that Gladdy won't lock him out of her bedroom as well.

21

BELLA'S GIFT

The pain in my ankle is making me restless, so I decide to try sleeping in the rocker in the lanai room, fluffing pillows behind my back for comfort and resting my hurting leg on the ottoman in front of me. But I'm kidding myself. The ice on my ankle helped a bit. So did the Tylenol for the pain. But what can I take for a broken heart?

I close my eyes. I can still hear the bandstand music playing in the park and Michelle asking Jack to dance with her. Did he? Did he hold her in his arms the way he's held me? Is it time to tell myself the truth? That he wants her and not me. Not that I can blame him. Nonsense! I do blame him.

If he's that shallow, I tell myself, then he isn't for

me anyway. He's just like any other gullible male after all.

Why did he have to come into my life? Life was settled. Easy and comfortable. I have my sister and my friends. I live in a place where we all care about one another. What more should I want? To be jealous at this age is a bad joke.

I cover myself with the colorful afghan that my daughter made for me. Right now I wish my Emily was here to comfort me. I try to relax. My radio plays softly. I have it tuned to the same station all the time—playing all the hits of my teenage years. Swing era, the announcers call it. Well, we're not swinging anymore. Out of style and out of time. Funny how I can still remember all the words of those hits of the forties and even earlier. I sing along. " 'He's my man, I love him so...' "

Ha! I really need to hear that right now. The tissues come out as the sniffles begin. Next they're playing the Andrews sisters singing "I'm in love with you, you, you. I could be so true..." Stop already with the love songs! I smile, though, remembering my beloved best friend Francie singing, crooning actually, these same songs, totally off-key. Like everything she did, she did it with gusto and joy. Yes, like the Andrews sisters, she used to accentuate the positive and eliminate the negative. Is it possible it's nearly two years since she was murdered?

I sigh. "Oh, Francie, why aren't you here when I need you?"

I hear an unfamiliar sound and my eyes pop open. I look everywhere. There, the curtain rod. It's coming from the hanging chimes that Bella gave me. They're ringing? But how? There's no breeze in here. But they're ding-donging loud and clear. Ha. Ha. Very funny. Next thing, I'll see someone dead.

"Dead, but hopefully not forgotten."

I jump up so fast, I bang my head on the side table lamp and knock it over. Francie is standing there, arms akimbo, the way she so often did. She's wearing shorts and her favorite sweatshirt, the one her grandkids gave her. "Death by Chocolate" it says.

"What are you doing here?" I back away from this apparition, stupidly acting as if she's really in front of me.

"That's a nice way to greet your oldest and dearest best friend." She plops herself down on the ottoman I just abandoned.

I can't believe my eyes. "I'm imagining this, right?"

"No, it's me. You called me and I came."

"I called you? How did I do that?" I just keep staring at her. She looks exactly the same. Tall, willowy, salt-and-pepper hair mixed with ginger, in her usual pageboy style. Big smile. Wide hazel eyes, still twinkling with humor.

"Bella explained it to you. When you desperately need someone, you only have to say so and poof—here I am."

I feel foolish and tearful. "You had no right to die and leave me, darn it!"

She shrugs. "Like I wanted to croak? I ate that poisoned piece of chocolate birthday cake and that was the end of me."

"You could have worn a different sweatshirt." I regard the prophetic words ruefully.

"Forget the fashion statement. By the way, you and the girls did a hell of a good job figuring out who did me in."

"Thanks." What else should I say? I feel a little crazy right now chatting with a ghost.

"So you want to know why I'm here? You're having a crisis of love and you need my help. You're thinking of dumping that gorgeous hunk you latched onto. You think the French tootsie got him back? Have I got it right?"

"How do you know all this ... if you're dead?"

Francie waves a hand at me, dismissing the question. "I could explain the chaos theory, but now's not the time. Stand tall!"

I immediately obey her, though I pay for it with a jolt of pain to my ankle.

"Shoulders back! Where's your guts, old girl? I remember you as the gal who knew her own mind.

She was wise and witty. Who is this pathetic wimp who took over her mind and body?"

Now I'm getting sore. "This is what I get? You come back just to lecture me?" I want to reach out and shake her. But if my hand goes through her like it happens in the movies, I'm going to faint right this minute. I go along with the craziness. "So, tell me, where are you living these days? I mean where's your dead zone? What's it like? I can make history and get rich telling the world I know all about the afterlife."

"Stop blathering. I don't have all day for this. Tell me you still trust Jack."

"You don't even know him. You never met him."

"I know everything. Men like him are rare. You'll be very sorry if you lose him. He's loving and honest and loyal. And damned good-looking. Don't worry. The girls will come around"—and here she grins mischievously—"eventually. I know he's true to you and he loves you madly. Don't blow it by stupid jealousy. Don't nag, and no interrogation. Believe every word he says. Love him as much as he loves you."

I huff. "Thank you, Dear Abby. And by the way, have you met her up there or wherever it is you hang out?" I move a little bit closer. Dare I reach for her? "And while you're here, tell me how much time I have left. When do I get to check out and join you?"

I fairly jump when the chimes ring again. "We have more dead people coming?"

My visiting ghost walks over and removes the glittering crystals from the curtain rod and places them on the side table. "My time's up. You won't need these anymore. Only one visit to a customer. So, quick, my darling Glad, tell me you won't screw it up."

"All right, already. I promise."

"I love you," Francie tells me.

"I love you, too." I bend down to pick up the fallen lamp. When I turn around, Francie is gone and I drop the lamp again.

Someone is shaking me. Is Francie back? I open my eyes slowly, afraid of what I might see.

"I would have left you sleeping, but I thought you'd be more comfortable in our bed. With me."

It's Jack, leaning over me. I practically leap out of the rocker and into his arms. "You're home!"

"For good, if you'll have me."

"I'll have you. I'll have you!" We kiss and I hope this isn't a dream, too. When we finally release lips we heave large happy sighs. I continue to hold onto him.

He looks around the room, concerned. "What's happened around here? Are you all right? You broke your lamp."

I look down. My lamp is on the floor, in pieces. The shade is hopelessly bent. I quickly glance up at the curtain rod. The chimes are gone. No, they can't be . . . Yes, they're on the table where Francie placed them. It was a dream. Of course it was. It had to be. There is no other possible explanation.

There's a little hesitation in his voice. "I suppose you want to know what happened tonight."

My mouth is just about to say You bet I do! Instead, I count to three. "No, not really. If you want to tell me, it can wait until tomorrow." I take his hand in mine and start to lead him back to our bedroom.

It's then he notices that I'm limping, and at the same time he sees Bella's cane. "What's this? What happened?"

"Just a little thing. I tripped and twisted my ankle. No biggie."

He is upset. "And I wasn't here to help you."

I tug his arm tighter. "You're here now, and besides, my ankle feels a lot better. Honest. No guilt, please."

He still frowns.

"I'm waiting for a smile. I'm not moving until I get it."

He smiles at me then, tenderly. Francie would be proud.

We straighten up the bedroom. Jack helps me re-make the bed. When he goes to get clean pillow-cases, I murmur, "Thanks, Francie."

"You're welcome," I hear in a faraway whisper.

22

GLORIOUS MORNING AFTER

Still in my bathrobe, I sip my morning coffee and can't stop smiling. My guy has come back to me. All's well with my world again.

I hear a pounding on my door. Evvie rushes in without waiting for me to answer.

She bends down to hug me. "I just saw Jack getting into his car. He was whistling and looked so happy. He's back. For good?"

"For good."

"No more Michelle?"

"Well, at least he's no longer 'guarding' her."

Evvie helps herself to coffee. "So where is he going?"

I pass her the plate of whole wheat toast and the cream cheese. "He's off to see Morrie to describe the old man he saw last night. Jack's sure he's the bad guy. The police artist will do a sketch."

"Did he tell you how he managed to escape Michelle?"

"He said it's a long story and he'd tell me later in some romantic setting, just the two of us. Sounds like he wants me in a good mood."

Evvie chomps on her toast. "I can't believe you were able to wait and that you didn't drag it out of him last night."

"Francie advised me on how to behave."

Evvie rightly looks puzzled. "Who's Francie?"

"Our dear Francie. She came to me in a dream. At least I think it was a dream. And that's another long story. Maybe I should save it for when all the girls can hear it. Especially Bella."

"I can hardly wait." Evvie pulls her chair closer to me. That isn't very far in my tiny kitchen. She's very excited. "Listen, I have an idea. Let's get married as soon as possible."

I blink my eyelashes and make my voice gooey. "Why, darling, I didn't know you cared."

She gives me a playful shove. "Our double wedding, as fast as we can get it together."

I'm in such a playful mood. That's what pure joy does to you. "Why? What's the rush? Are you pregnant? Ha-ha."

She laughs. Then smirks. "You must have had one heck of a welcome home party last night."

I blush. "Never you mind."

Evvie turns suddenly serious. "Because I want it for Joe. Sure he's in remission now, but for how long? Being married again with the chance to do it right this time would mean the world to him."

I reach over and hug her. "That's reason enough. Why don't we all elope? The four of us could go to city hall and then go on a honeymoon somewhere."

She shakes her head. "I want Joe to have our families there. And all of our friends. It might be the last time he'll see them. And on a happy occasion instead of..." The tears start to fall. I reach over and brush them away.

I jump up. Ouch. I remember my ankle a little late. "Okay, call Trixie. Once and for all we have to tell her we are doing this on our own. We can't keep stringing her on."

"Hah!" says Evvie. "Are you gonna be the one to break the news to her?"

"I was kind of thinking of letting you have the honor."

"Thanks for nothing."

"We'll do it together—but remember we have to be strong. Meanwhile I'll get dressed."

Jack leans over the police artist's shoulder. "The nose should be a little longer and sharper."

Lee Shiller, a slim, relaxed young man, works at a table over to the side of Morrie's desk. He makes the change with a few short strokes of his pencil. "Like this?"

Jack nods. "Better." Jack is surprised he still has the knack. He used the same method in the old days, when in his mind he photographed mental pictures of the suspect.

Morrie is at his desk, shuffling through papers. "Now where did I put that French inspector's phone number?"

Jack glances at him. "What time is it in Paris now?"

"Six hours difference. It's four P.M. Ah, here it is." He walks over to Jack and Shiller. "So that's what he looks like?"

"Pretty close." Jack tells the artist, "Make the gray hair shaggier, like he doesn't do much combing—or cutting, for that matter. The cheeks slightly more hollow. And set the eyes a little closer."

After Lee does so, Jack takes the rendering and gives it to Morrie to examine. "I think that does it, Lee, and thank you."

The artist gets up. "You're welcome." He picks up his gear and leaves the room.

Morrie shakes his head at the sketch in his hand. "This old guy looks like a strong wind could knock him over. He must be about ninety. You sure it's him?"

"Maybe that's why he's never been caught. Nobody ever pays attention to him. There was something about his eyes. In the way he looked at me. Maybe it's my imagination, but I saw just the slightest flicker of arrogance in his expression. Like he was daring me to recognize him. And when he put his arm around the woman, there was the smallest moment of hesitation on her face, as if she was deciding whether to go along with the guy or not. I'll bet he seemed harmless to her. Then she smiled."

"Well, I'm making copies for the hotel security. And I'll fax this to Paris. Let's give them another call now. Maybe with you on the line as well, he won't think I'm a nutcase."

"Might as well."

Morrie grins at his father as he picks up the phone. "So Gladdy took you back."

"No comment."

"Did you tell her about Michelle's passionate pleas?"

"Not yet. I'm working up to it. Hopefully, I can leave out that part." Jack worries about sounding foolish to Gladdy. That a young woman would throw herself at him. He's kidding himself. She'll want to know why he left Michelle in such a hurry.

Morrie can't resist. "Maybe Michelle could become interested in a younger man. Like myself.

She'll think I'm debonair. There's a good French word."

Jack shoots him a dirty look.

"Just think, if I get lucky, you can have her as a daughter-in-law."

The father pretends to raise his hand to his son. "You're not too old to spank."

Morrie smirks. "Yeah, right. You never laid a paw on me as a kid—too late now."

"Never too late to pull off the old leather belt and whack you."

"You don't wear a belt."

Jack shrugs. "You've got a point."

The two men laugh and reach out to hug each other.

"All I can say, Pop, is you're quite a Romeo. Who'd have imagined? Well, I guess if you can be a hottie at your age, maybe we can believe in the possibility of a very old killer."

"Never mind that. Go make the phone call."

Morrie, still grinning, hits the speaker button and dials the long international number. After a few rings, the phone is answered.

The man is abrupt. *"Bonnard ici."*

Morrie tries out his French haltingly. *"Bonsoir,* Inspector. *Je suis* Detective Morgan Langford. Fort Lauderdale *dans* Florida."

The inspector rattles off some French to whoever is in the room with him: "It's the crazy American again; the one who called to tell us Madame duBois is being stalked by an ancient assassin. Now he's trying out his bad French again."

Morrie hears laughter in the background. *"Peutêtre..."* He gives up on the French.

The arrogant inspector chuckles, then in a heavy accent he answers, not even hiding his sarcasm. "Don't bother. I will speak only in English. We are all forced to take it up in school for just such an occasion as this—when some crazy American calls."

Morrie refuses to get aroused by his attitude. "I'm here with another detective." Jack introduces himself. "Jack Langford. Formerly from New York City. Retired."

Bonnard seems to be in a room full of men. Men who are easily amused. "Have you caught your ancient assassin yet?"

Jack answers. "Not yet. But we now have a description. In fact, we'd like to fax it to you."

Bonnard says, "By all means. We will examine it quickly before your suspect dies of old age." He recites the fax number and Morrie jots it down.

Morrie takes over. *"Merci.* Thank you. I will send it off immediately. I don't suppose you checked on the winegrowers whose names I furnished?"

Jack thinks the inspector seems to be playing with something on his desk, maybe keys from the sound of the clinking. "As a matter of fact we did.

They are simple winegrowers. I personally don't like their Cabernet Sauvignon, too fruity, but, *alors,* to each his own."

"And?" Morrie waits for an answer.

"And nothing. They have no criminal records." Bonnard pauses, curious. "You think these people hired someone to do the dastardly deed—to kill the famous, beautiful writer?"

Jack says, "Yes. Because they want to stop her next book from coming out."

Morrie leans in closer to the phone. "Her next book concerns this winery, and because she intends to expose them in such a way as to ruin them, we feel sure that they are the ones trying to kill her."

Someone in the room calls out to the inspector. He translates what he's just been told. "There have been such rumors. But there have been no attempted attacks as far as we know. Mme. duBois lives in the seventh *arrondissement*. A very rich neighborhood with a substantial police presence."

Jack says, "Here's our thinking. Logically, if someone were to put out a contract, they would naturally hire someone young. Which makes sense. But the odd fact that this man we're searching for is old makes us wonder why. They might worry that a hired killer is an unknown factor? Something might go wrong?"

Morrie jumps in. "Is it that they couldn't afford it, or wanted to keep it quiet? So, perhaps in one of their families, there was such a person? A contract killer who's now old? Retired?"

Jack adds, "Perhaps he's a killer who never got caught."

Bonnard coughs, but they sense he is paying close attention. "A most original idea."

Jack smiles. It's a good thing they don't know it was his darling Gladdy who came up with that idea. That would cause another round of derisive laughter. Nor would he inform Bonnard that he and Morrie also thought the idea preposterous originally.

Jack speaks again. "So the next question is—any criminals in their family trees?"

There is a sound of something falling. And another barrage of French. This time the voices speak quickly and excitedly. *Vous ne croyez jamais. Il a trouvé Le Serpent. Après trente-cinq ans! Interpole, vite. Enfin.*

All Jack can understand is the word Interpol. From a slight distance he hears the inspector excitedly calling out to him and Morrie. "It is nothing. Only my chair fell over. I will be right back. Hold on."

Morrie uses the time to fax the drawing to Paris.

Bonnard is back. "I went to our wall with the most-wanted list. One man has been on this Interpol list for thirty-five years. His name is Anatole Oliviere. Also known as The Snake."

Other voices call out to remind him. "Also he uses phony passport names. Pierre Gimpe. Michel Avedon. Louis Phillipe."

Bonnard adds, "He has killed at least twenty people that we know of. There could have been more. In our never-ending search for him, we interviewed a distant cousin, many, many years ago, Gaston Dubonet. The very same winery owner. But it seemed at the time to mean nothing. Dubonet had never had contact with this very distant uncle. He was shocked to think such a person might be in his family. We let that go by. Eventually the killing stopped. We all breathed a sigh of relief. We thought he was dead. Now we think, thanks to you, retired."

Jack smiles at Morrie—they've struck pay dirt.

Jack agrees, "No longer retired."

Bonnard says, "I am looking at your fax. What the murder book tells us is that at about fifty years of age, he was a very thin man. Short of stature. Shifty, close-set eyes. Wiry. Skimpy black hair."

Morrie adds, "Gray now, but that's a pretty close description."

Bonnard says, "We have only one possible photo of him, but it is blurred and has proven useless." He adds grudgingly, "The Snake is considered the master of them all; none can compare. He'd slither his way in and slither his way out. Quick, efficient, and deadly."

Bonnard's voice grows gloomy. "We never came close to catching him. He always outsmarted us. Maybe age has slowed him, but I would think he is still someone to fear. Now tell me everything that has transpired in this case of yours. Paris will work hand in hand with you to capture this elusive killer."

Jack high-fives Morrie. About time. They've got to get Michelle safely out of the country and back home. If they can't catch The Snake here, then Inspector Bonnard will be waiting for him in Paris. He can't wait to tell Gladdy how her hunch was so right.

23

A SECRET REVEALED

Trixie waits for us inside Jerry's Deli. She's dressed as usual in a loud patterned flowery dress with a matching wide-angle hat. We pass chubby Jerry and his equally chunky son, Larry, busy behind the counter slicing, chopping, and nibbling. Evvie and I say hello. Jerry grunts. A man of very few words—none of them pleasant. His usual dialogue consists of "Wadda ya want" and sometimes "Hurry up. Order. I ain't got all day."

Trixie waves us over to join her in her booth. She is excited to see us, ready to hear our good news. Which won't be so good after we've explained our position.

Before her sits a massive plate of pastrami and scrambled eggs, hash brown potatoes, a bagel with cream cheese. And a side of pancakes, swimming in butter and syrup. Cholesterol heaven.

She greets us happily. "Did you girls eat breakfast? Go ahead, order."

Her look is disdainful as we ask Jerry for shredded wheat. "That's a breakfast?"

Evvie assures her it's enough for us. "And coffee also," she calls to Jerry's receding back.

Trixie settles down to business, but not missing a mouthful. "So, you took my suggestion. A double wedding. Now we're ready to do business together. You two will look adorable in those sweet gowns you tried on. I already made a call and told the owner to put a hold on. So what sizes do you wear?"

Evvie and I look at each other. Our eyes say, You do it. Not me. You.

I'm about to tell Trixie, tactfully, I hope, thanks but we can't spend much money, so we intend to buy our own outfits, in our own favorite store with prices we can afford, which means, we really have to say no to you, when Evvie jumps in. "No white wedding gowns. We're wearing cocktail dresses. Ones we already own. I mean, we only wore them a couple of times. It's wasteful to buy something new that we won't ever wear again."

My shameless sister doesn't blink an eye as she lies.

Trixie's lower lip forms a pout, but she recovers

quickly. She jots down a note in her immense workbook, saying as she does, "Call and cancel the gowns. Okay, cocktail dresses are nice. You already wore white."

Jerry brings our breakfast, places the dishes in front of us with a grunt.

Trixie is coy. "But remember: Something borrowed, something blue. Something old, something *new*."

Evvie says, "We're already supplying the old. Us."

"Now, now girls. You're only as old as you feel."

Oy, I'm thinking. *She's going to recite every cliché she knows*. I kick Evvie under the table for continuing this charade. We have to stop Trixie now. But which one of us cowards will have the guts to break the bad news? The way we're handling this is slow, painful torture.

Trixie busily checks her list of what she wants to do and in what order. "I have about twenty places we can visit for wedding halls. Depends on whether you're going for a big religious do, or not."

"Not." Evvie chugs down her coffee and waves to Jerry, who's wiping tables, indicating a refill. "Actually we decided on using Lanai Gardens' great lawn." She smiles cheerfully. "The price is right: Free."

That, at least, is the truth. Trixie swallows the

news along with a dripping bite full of pancake. I can tell her adding-machine mind is already deducting wedding dress and wedding hall commissions from her fee. Through clenched teeth, she says, "Free is nice."

I shoot Evvie a look. She shoots it back at me. Now? Trixie is a very large woman. What if she gets violent? Neither Jerry nor his son would come to our rescue. Too bad none of the Cane Fu experts are in sight. Even though I have Bella's cane, I wouldn't know what to do with it.

Trixie rolls up her sleeves. She has a most determined look on her face that's crying out—Where's the money?

She heaves a huge sigh. "All right. Let's talk about the guest list and the wedding invites. There's a darling little paper shop—"

Evvie jumps in. "No need for that. We'll call our folks and put up flyers on all the Phases' bulletin boards. Everyone's invited."

Trixie's eyes go glassy. "Okayyyyy," she drags out. Another X in that box. "No invitations. But then how can we tell the caterer how much food we'll need?"

My turn to add to Trixie's suffering. "Look, Trixie, what we're trying to say is…uh…people around here like to contribute their special dishes. To show off their culinary skills, you know? It's kind of a tradition. Sort of a potluck." I am such a coward.

I think Trixie is getting apoplexy. If she has a fit, no one will be able to lift her off the floor if she drops. "Potluck! Potluck! That's suicidal! You know what happens at potlucks? Desserts, that's what! Everyone brings desserts!"

Evvie shrugs. "If it was good enough for Marie Antoinette, it's good enough for us."

"Marie...Antowho? Who the hell is that? Did you talk to another wedding planner behind my back?"

I look pleadingly at Evvie. *Get us out of this already!*

Evvie pats Trixie on her arm, hoping to calm her. Trixie is shoveling the food down like there's no tomorrow. Well, food is cheaper than Valium. "Marie Antoinette was the queen of France. She said, 'Let them eat cake.'"

I watch as Trixie's eyes now seem to roll around in her head. "No caterer." Hardly daring to hope: "Flowers?"

"Well," Evvie starts to say.

Trixie sighs. "Don't bother; the lawn has plenty of flowers."

I try to look benevolent. "Yes."

She nods dejectedly like someone heading for the guillotine. Like Marie Antoinette. "I know," she says. "Free."

She heaps a huge forkful of the pastrami and eggs into her mouth. "So, what date are we talking about?"

Here we go. I say it softly and recoil just in case. "Actually, next weekend, but—"

Trixie leaps up, spitting out her mouthful of food. Most of which lands on her ample bosom. She's stuck in the booth, so her huge body lifts the tabletop up. Everything on it starts to move downhill toward us! Evvie and I slide out of the booth as fast as we can. We're lucky. Only a few bits of food hit us. I didn't know we still had such good reflexes.

Trixie shrieks and everyone in Jerry's turns around. "Next weekend? Next weekend! I ask for a year in advance and you want next weekend! I haven't even started!"

Evvie tries to pacify her. "I'm sorry, we've been trying to tell you—that's why we can't use you. However, we'll pay you for your trouble."

"What! You're crazy! Both of you!"

With that, Trixie stomps toward the door, lurching and tottering from side to side on her pointy-toed three-inch high heels. Evvie calls out, "Thanks for all your wonderful advice!"

The diners go back to dining. The deli is quiet except for an occasional slurp.

I frown at Evvie. "I'm ashamed of us. We were cruel, dragging it out that way."

"Listen. I found out the truth about her. She doesn't have any sick grandchild she's supporting in an iron lung or dialysis or whatever cockamamie story she made up. Her last three clients fired her because she botched up their weddings, and they wanted to kill her."

"Hmm. So when did you expect to share that news with me?"

"I was waiting for the right moment."

"How did you get Lola to confess?"

"Hy told me. Behind Lola's back, naturally. Feel better?"

I grab Trixie's check. It's the least we can do.

Jerry, now at the cash register, looks at us with eyebrows up. "Meshuggeners," he mutters. Maybe we're wackos to him, but he isn't above taking our money.

Evvie humphs as she collects our change. "Who asked your opinion?"

To our surprise Trixie is still outside the deli. I'd have thought she would have taken off in a huff. She's standing with Ida. *What's Ida doing around here?* I wonder.

I can't help myself. "Trixie, I'm sorry we didn't work out for you."

Her nose goes up in the air. "Never mind. I have many other classier clients who are less trouble than you. My personal code of ethics, when I deal with difficult people, is to take the high road!"

I almost choke on that. *You and me, too, Trix.* Somehow that makes me feel better. Trixie is a survivor.

Evvie is curious. "What's going on?"

Trixie comments, "Your friend here was snooping around the building."

Ida says, "So, what's it your business?" She turns to us. "I was just trying to figure out how that guru works his shtick. I know he's a fraud and I'm sure Sophie and Bella are being rooked."

Trixie starts to cackle. A rather weird sound like *heh, heh, heh.* "Your friends are in that dumb Dead Husbands Club?"

All three of us gape at her.

Ida gets excited. "You know something about it?"

Her chin comes up; proud bearer of insider information. "I know everything about Erwin Blatstein. This whole neighborhood knows everything about Erwin."

Ida is not surprised. "Except our loopy friends. Erwin? Is that the guru's real name?"

Trixie cackles again. "Jerry's other son. Haven't your friends noticed the wart on his chin? This one thinks he's too good to be in the deli business. He went to some radical hippie school in Kansas and came back 'enlightened.'"

Ida adds her two cents. "Wait a minute. So if you have so much data about those gullible women who attend, cough it up. What's the secret?"

Trixie delights in revealing all to Ida. "It's the closet where you put your purses and packages. There's also a sister. Phoebe. The waitress? She also has the family wart."

Evvie can't resist a comment. "I doubt if warts are hereditary."

"Whatever. There's a trapdoor to the closet, and while Erwin is guru-ing, Phoebe searches everyone's bags. Then later they Google and learn a lot more."

"Wow!" Evvie says. "Oy. Sophie and Bella will have a fit."

Ida is fairly bursting at her seams. "I knew it! I knew he was a fraud. How does he do the dead husbands' voices?"

Trixie shrugs. "He took up ventriloquism as his major at that half-baked college. He knows how to change his voice."

Evvie comments, "I don't get it. It's like a nickel-and-dime business. Chump change. How much can you make with a few five-dollar bills?"

I add with a touch of amusement, "Don't forget the long-distance phone calls to heaven."

Ida's grin is so wide, she could crack her face. "Hey, we're not talking about that *momza* Bernie Madoff and his stolen billions. Jerry and his sons and daughter and wife are small potatoes. Money is money. Besides, the guru son thinks he's making these widows happy."

Tessie comments, "Jerry thinks he's an idiot."

Ida practically jumps up and down with glee, but Evvie is upset. "Just look at you. You can't wait to tell our friends about this and see how it hurts them?"

"Hey, they started it when they wouldn't admit what they were doing. I hate liars. I told you that. Besides, I'm not going to tell them, I'm going to show them."

Trixie starts off. "Bye, ladies. Don't forget to recommend me to your friends."

Off she goes. Good-bye and good riddance.

Ida imitates the Trixie cackle. Heh, heh, heh. "I know just what to do to trap those goniffs into revealing who and what they are."

As we start back across the street I feel sorry for Sophie and Bella.

24

PLANS

"So, honey, what's your plan?" I ask Jack later that evening. I know he's bursting to get off his chest what I'm longing to hear—that he really and truly is through with Michelle. It must be true, since he's back with me. "Do you want to take me out for dinner? Or I have lamb chops waiting to be broiled. And potatoes waiting to be baked. And cheesecake and coffee for a to-die-for dessert."

Jack seems unsure. "I was going to suggest a long walk first. But not with your hurting ankle. I should have brought you flowers, but I was in a hurry to get home."

"I don't need flowers. Your being here is good enough."

"We could go out for a quiet dinner somewhere. Someplace romantic and expensive."

I can't resist giving him a little dig. "That's something guilty men do. Bribe their women with flowers and expensive restaurants. You don't need to do that."

He reddens. Caught. "Maybe I thought I did. I want to tell you everything, but we need privacy."

"Well, this place isn't bugged as far as I know. We have all the seclusion we want right here. How about we have cocktails in the Florida room and look out at the ducks on the waterway?"

Jack looks pleased. "Sounds perfect. Bloody Marys?"

I'm already heading for the ice.

It's lovely this time of evening. The air coming in the louvers is cool and refreshing. The drinks are strong enough to make us mellow. Just the right amount of vodka and Tabasco. The ducks quack away at one another. Maybe there's some male duck out there confessing to his female counterpart a tale similar to Jack's. Who knows?

Jack is reciting his story in a pretty straightforward manner. No doubt he's toning down some of the lurid parts. And in the telling, the excitement is dampened. But my imagination is filling in what he leaves out. Here was this passionate younger woman throwing herself at him and I'm getting the rational explanation––dryly, professorially, safely explained.

"So," he says, "it pretty much boils down to an impressionable young woman having a crush on a father figure. And me feeling fatherly to her."

I sigh. I know he is leaving out seductive clothes and sexual advances and cries and whispers. I would have enjoyed the juicier parts now that he's safely back.

He finishes up with, "Michelle really is a nice person. She felt bad about you seeing her at her worst."

Frankly, I wouldn't have liked seeing her at her best.

"Thank you, Gladdy dear, for being so patient with me. Had I been you, I would have tossed me out a long time ago."

I won't touch that line with the proverbial ten-foot pole. "Hmm," I say, not saying anything.

Jack fills me in about his and Morrie's discussion with the Parisian police and the realization that the little old man is a former world-class contract killer. I feel good that my instincts led them to this important discovery.

Jack completes his summation. "So, we'll either capture The Snake here or the French police or Interpol will grab him when he tries to get through customs back in Europe. Michelle and Colette should be leaving by next weekend."

That's a lot of news to be getting secondhand. Truthfully I'm not happy about having been left out of this really big case and missing all the excitement. Contributing secondhand is not my idea of being on a case. But never mind, all's well that ends well. However, Jack and I will have to discuss our work relationship from now on. And I shudder to think about how the girls will take his getting involved in our cases.

I cuddle close to my guy on my small love seat—a most applicable name. "By the way, coincidentally, the news here is that the very same next weekend there will be a very big double wedding on the back lawn. Friends and neighbors are cooking up a storm. Every possible chair is being lent out. Bridesmaids and ring bearers are already chosen. Somebody's grandson's garage band will be playing free for the experience. A chuppah is midway toward construction. All plans are in motion."

Jack is pleasantly surprised. "Who's getting married? Anyone we know?"

Indeed you do, big guy. "Gladys Gold and Jack Langford. Evelyn Markowitz and Joseph Markowitz." I can give out information in a dry, professorial way, too. "Just thought you'd like to know in case you want to rent a tux. And drive downtown for a license."

Jack beams. His grin is from ear to ear. "You made this decision without my consent?"

I snuggle closer. "Well, you were otherwise engaged, so to speak."

"You were that sure of me?"

No way am I going to let him know about the awful anxiety-ridden sleepless nights. And I probably should skip the visit of a dead friend to give me advice.

For a moment we are distracted by the duck couple below us. Their meeting seems not to be going well. There is a flutter of wings and angry duck squawks, and some neck nipping, but soon they settle down again. That's a good sign.

I return to my information patter. "Preparations are happening even as we speak. Our relatives were informed and invited by phone..."

Jack stares at me in surprise. "Wow! That's pretty fast."

I am tempted to say that I've had nothing else to do, since he kept me away from working this case. But I hold my tongue. "Of course everyone said yes, but typically complained of not having enough time to buy new clothes. All three families are traveling at the same time and I told them we'd meet them at the airport."

"It all sounds wonderful. What did I do to deserve you?"

I could boast, but I won't. A quick snuggle and I

keep reciting. "I've already put all our thirteen New Yorkers up at a nearby hotel. The four granddaughters are looking forward to sharing their own room. As well as the three grandsons."

"Isn't it wonderful that yours and Evvie and Joe's family and mine have become close friends?"

"We've been blessed." For a moment I think of Ida, who never hears from anyone in her family. It must be so hard for her.

It's as if he read my mind. "And the Bobbsey triplets? Their response?"

"Sophie, Bella, and Ida are so mad at each other, it's more on their minds than we are. But I know they're pleased." I sigh. "The only spoiler is having to walk down the aisle with a cane."

Jack rises and lifts me up in his arms. "You're going to go down that aisle even if I have to carry you."

The doorbell rings. It's eight A.M. and I don't want to get out of bed. I want to stay spooned against my man forever. Besides, I know who it will be—the girls wanting me to get out and exercise as usual. I ignore them. They'll stop eventually.

Wrong. They don't.

From his head muffled under his pillow, Jack mumbles, "Chase them away."

I guess I have to get up.

No big surprise, it's Evvie and Ida. I open the door and move to the kitchen with them tagging along as I start to put up our morning coffee. "Hang on. I'll grab some coffee, get dressed, and grab my cane."

Ida says, "Don't bother. We're not walking."

Evvie adds, "Bella and Sophie refuse to join us. Or rather, won't exercise with Ida."

Ida isn't perturbed. "Just as well. I want to show you something."

Evvie hands me my can of coffee and then opens the fridge for the mocha mix and gets the Splenda packets out of a kitchen drawer. She knows the drill. I start the percolator perking.

From her pocket, Ida pulls out a sheet of paper. "Here's my plan for outing that phony club they belong to. I'm going with them today whether they like it or not."

Evvie and I exchange exasperated glances. She won't give up.

"Here goes. I wrote this fake letter, which will be left open in my purse, now that I know that closet will be searched." She reads. "Dear Sonny boy. This is just a note to remind you of the anniversary of Daddy's death. Please go to the cemetery and bring roses. You remember how he always loved to bring me roses. Throw a kiss to my Murray for me."

She looks up brightly. "That should do it, don't you think?"

I have to ask. "Why can't you let it go? Why is it so important to you?"

Ida pulls at her hair in its bun, a gesture she makes when she's anxious. "I told you. I wish to make Sophie and Bella answer for their foolish behavior."

My coffee has perked long enough. Evvie pours us each a cup. She hands Ida hers and says, "Be careful, Ida. Sometimes what you wish for backfires and bites you in the rear."

Jack calls from the bedroom. "Is that fresh coffee I smell?"

I call back to him. "Yes, oh lord and master. Your cup is on the way."

Evvie smiles and Ida grimaces. Evvie gulps hers down and heads for the door.

"Come on, Ida," Evvie says. "I need you to help with the decorations."

Ida follows after Evvie. "I don't do decorations. I'm not good with all those rolls of crinkly tissue paper."

"Then you can blow up balloons. I'll bet that's your real talent." Evvie winks at me. "Bye, Glad. Enjoy the rest of your morning."

I pour Jack's cup and head back to my darling.

25

IDA'S FOLLY

"Isn't it wonderful about how everyone is so nice around here?" Sophie says to Bella as they wave to a neighbor.

Ida fumes, but then she calms herself thinking that they'll be singing a different tune when she makes fools of them in front of everyone. Today will be part one of her plan. Hopefully it won't take too many weeks before she gets called on by her "dead husband." She doesn't want to be stuck in that so-called club longer than she has to.

When they reach Jerry's, she follows the girls to the curtained back door. Jerry smirks as she passes. Ida is tempted to stick her tongue out at him—just wait till he sees what she'll be doing to his business. It'll wipe that sneer from his face once and for all.

They enter the back room. Ida looks around, taking it all in. She shakes her head. Wow. She has to admire the setup. Very holistic and New Age. Very smart.

Continuing to ignore Ida, the girls pay their five bucks and head for seats.

Ida fills out the little entrance agreement. Clever. The "members" are not supposed to tell people about this place unless they believe they'll join. They want no hostility to destroy the guru's "home of peace." *Too late,* thinks Ida with a grin—*the cat is in the mouse house.* And ready to gobble them up. After signing the agreement, she makes a show of being impressed with the books and vitamins and incense. "I always wanted to know about chakras and stuff," she insincerely tells Jerry's wife, who sits at the small table with the cigar box of money open and waiting.

When the woman explains that she has to leave her purse in the closet, Ida pretends to be impressed. "What a good idea. Keeping the room pure." Then she manages to form a worry line on her forehead. "Are you sure our purses are safe in there? I do have a bit of money with me."

Jerry's wife assures her as she folds her arms. "Nobody gets past me."

Yeah, sure, thinks Ida, picturing the homely daughter waiting to paw through her personal things. As she places her purse lovingly in the closet she silently says bye to her so-called letter. *Do the job, babe, sucker them in.*

She takes off her shoes and lines them up with all the others, then makes her way to a seat. All thirty chairs are taken except for two. Bella and Sophie sit at the end of a row. Sophie holds her hand on one of the last empty chairs next to her. Ida knows it's to keep her away. Not a chance. She walks straight to them. "Is this chair taken?"

"Yes," Sophie says. "No," Bella says at the same time. Ida parks herself right there, forcing Sophie to remove her hand or have it sat on.

The guru makes his entrance. Ida is thoroughly enjoying herself. She thinks he's perfect for the part—like he's in some movie, picked out by central casting. As they do their "ohm," he lowers himself down on his pillow and everyone bows. Ida can hardly keep a straight face, but she bows along with them. Ohm indeed.

Baba speaks. "Today we will practice the meditation of the root chakra."

Jerry's wife walks up to the table behind her son and lights the incense sticks. Ida squirms. She hates the smell of incense. But she has to laugh at Jerry's wife, now wearing some *schmatte* on her head trying to look like a religious Indian woman instead of the silly housewife she really is. Sophie and Bella stare straight ahead, never glancing at her.

Baba Vishnu speaks softly. "Breathe slowly and

deeply. Visualize yourself in a perfect place, a very special place, one that made you happy. See it. Concentrate on it. Recognize the beautiful colors. See who is there to share your joy."

Ida sneaks looks around, fascinated by the rapt expressions on the women's faces. It reminds her of the circus of olden days with the slick guys who sold snake oil. What was it Barnum said—or was it Bailey? "There's a sucker born every minute."

"Feel their love radiating toward you, filling you with happiness." Baba raises his arms.

Ida watches as woman by woman, they smile contentedly. *Yeah,* she thinks, *I'm thinking of a happy place. This deli when the police raid it.* She almost giggles. Then, suddenly she finds herself thinking of her Murray. She never thinks about him. Ever. She feels sad and doesn't know why. She senses tears form in her eyes. What's happening to her?

The chimes ring out behind Baba. Softly. Everyone looks up excitedly. Ida gets it. Obviously this is the moment they're really here for. Baba stares out at them, benevolently. It seems like all the women are holding their collective breaths. To Ida, it looks like the guru's trying to go into a trance, but he's probably counting the house to see how much he'll take in today.

Ida recognizes Linda Rutledge of Phase Three, a

sweet gentle lady of seventy who always wears purple. Her wheelchair is parked in front of Sophie. Linda turns to her and whispers, "It's gonna be my turn this time. I just know it."

Sophie says, "Me, too. I feel my Stanley's vibes."

The guru speaks out in a "dead husband" voice. "Linda, my angel. Where are you? I am here for my wife, Linda Rutledge. It's Seymour."

Linda gasps, practically jumping up and down in her wheelchair in excitement. She automatically pats her hair to neaten it. "Yes! I knew it! I'm here, Seymie, yes, indeedy. How are you, sweetums? Are they treating you okay?"

Ida watches the guru move his lips. She shakes her head. Unbelievable that all these women would fall for Erwin Blatstein's bag of tricks.

"Seymour" sounds bereft. "It's lonely without you, honey bun. When are you coming to join me?"

Linda is startled and then flustered. "I don't know. Oh, I would if I could, you know that. When you passed, I asked the good Lord to take me, too."

"Seymour's" voice grows cool. "It's another guy, isn't it? You've got another guy taking my place."

Ida watches, enthralled as Linda's face reddens. "It's only Mr. Finster, downstairs. But we haven't done anything. He likes my chicken soup."

"Seymour" is furious. "I turn my back on you

for sixteen years and what do you do? You cheat on me!"

"Seymour, no! We're just good friends!" Linda looks pleadingly at Baba. But Baba shakes his head. "Seymour" has hung up.

Linda cries daintily into a tissue as Sophie pats her shoulder in condolence.

The chimes ring gently again. Everyone perks up. Who's next?

A voice rings out cheerily from Baba's lips. " 'I got buttons, I got bows. Where they came from, nobody knows.' "

Sophie jumps up so fast that she knocks her chair over. "It's Stanley. It's my Stanley's advertising slogan for Meyerbeer's Notions. Stanley, is it really you?"

Ida has to admire the guru's ability to capture the personality of a man he's never met. She remembers Stanley. He was a huckster through and through. The guru is pretty quick. He must have been a frustrated actor before he turned into this shyster.

"Stanley" speaks. "You look good, Soph, but you put on a few pounds."

Sophie sighs. "Crying over losing you. You know I tend to eat when I'm sad."

"Stanley" comments as if he were looking her up and down. "You always was a good dresser. You could take a belt and a buckle and a scarf and make a Hester Street outfit look like Fifth Avenue."

"That's 'cause you taught me how. I miss you, poopsie. All the time."

Bella, next to her, is clutching Sophie's arm and sobbing.

"I gotta go, doll face, but a word of advice. Someone near is not your friend. Beware."

And with that, "Stanley" is gone.

Ida is startled as Sophie whips her eyes around and stares into hers. "I know who my darling meant," she says ominously. "So keep your distance."

The guru ends the session and Sophie happily pays for the "long-distance phone call."

Ida grits her teeth. *Just you wait,* she thinks.

26

WEDDING DAY MINUS TWO

While Jack washes his car, he puts in a quick call to Morrie. It's his chance to be able to speak to his son privately. Gladdy is busy with wedding plans. It's not that he couldn't make the call in front of her—he's sure Gladdy wouldn't mind—but this is his excuse to be alone and be more comfortable. As he dials, Lola and Tessie, arms full of shopping bags, walk by. Lola grins at him. Tessie blows him a kiss. This kind of overkill has been going on ever since he came downstairs. Neighbors smile at him. Or high-five him. Everyone is happy. His arm is tired from constant waving in return. The wedding news has spread like wildfire and the sense of excitement is in the air.

Morrie puts him on hold, says he'll be right with him.

Sol and Hy trail behind their wives as they map out the races at Hialeah in today's newspaper. They stop in front of Jack.

Hy leers. "So you're really gonna do it, huh? You didn't know when you were well off?"

Jack is benign. "Looks like it."

Sol shakes his head. "It's always better before the wedding ring tightens like a noose around the neck."

Morrie comes back on the line. "Dad, are you still there?"

Jack indicates his cell phone to the guys. "Gotta take this. Thanks for your reassuring words."

The two men amble off, pleased at their advice giving.

Jack works on the hubcaps, scrubbing hard. "It's like a zoo around here, what with everyone having their own version of what to say about the weddings."

"Breaks up the monotony. Gives them something new to gossip about."

Jack can't resist. "So, your dad is having a second wedding and he's still waiting for your first."

"I'm working on it. I have a hot date tonight with a gal I met on the Internet."

"Have you actually seen her?"

"Not yet. Only judging from a photo. But it's hit

or miss. My last blind date lied about her age, her weight, the color of her hair, and her job."

"And still you keep taking chances?"

"Hope springs eternal. Hey, we all lie a bit. Lying seems to be a national sport these days."

Jack washes the car windows. "Good luck. You'll need it."

There's a pause. Morrie says, "Go ahead, Dad. I know you want to ask."

"You're right. I do. How is she doing? Is she all right with the other men guarding her?"

"What did you say to Michelle when you turned her down? She's so quiet now. Not complaining about the guards I assigned to her, both inside and outside her room. She seems listless, like she's just marking time until she and Colette can leave. Which, by the way, will be on the day you and Gladdy get hitched."

"I'm glad she's all right. How did she take it when you filled her in about The Snake?"

"Again, almost disinterested. She just wants to go home."

"And still no sign of him?"

"It's a puzzle. Nothing's happening. It's too quiet. I thought he'd make his move by now. Maybe he's laying low because you spotted him. The entire security staff at the hotel is on full alert. I've also posted extra men around the building and they're canvassing the whole area. I wonder where he is."

The Snake paces his crummy hotel room, holding a plastic bag full of ice to one side of his cheek. He's totally frustrated by how things are going. This job should have been done by now, but his redheaded target is surrounded by flics. He's certain that cop in the hotel guessed it was him. Now he has to re-work his plan. Not that that would deter The Snake. What's making him crazy is this damned Florida. He's allergic to everything that grows here. Every flower makes him sneeze! To make matters worse, first he had to get glasses and now this—the pain in his tooth is getting worse by the hour. Get-ting old, he decides, is the pain in the derrière.

An hour later, The Snake climbs the rickety steps leading to the office of Dr. Horace H. Holiday. The building needs paint and repair. There's an easy alley getaway. The whole street smells of garbage. Good. The Snake has chosen from the yellow pages well. He couldn't appear in some flashy main street office with too many possible witnesses.

At least it's clean inside, and even better, the den-tist's white coat doesn't carry the bloodstains of former patients. He probably doesn't even have many patients. The Snake sums up the man quickly: Overfed. Anxious. Too eager to please. Obviously has no receptionist. File folders lying around. A quantity of old coffee in cardboard cups.

The Snake adopts a pathetic lost-tourist act, heavily accenting his English, pretending not to know the language well. He can see the gleam in Dr. Holiday's greedy eyes; certain he's deciding how much he will rip him off. Pretending stupidity, The Snake effusively thanks the man for seeing him on such short notice. "You are saving the life of me."

The dentist says with false cheer, "Not at all. Always glad to show foreign visitors our Florida hospitality." The Snake introduces himself as M. Merde, *knowing this fool won't know what the offensive word means. He takes enjoyment from these little games he plays.*

The Snake sits down rigidly in the dentist's chair. He is relieved to see the man scrub his hands, and then put on latex gloves. His instruments are waiting in a sanitizing dish. The Snake breathes a sigh of relief. He'd hate to die, poisoned by this hack.

After placing a relatively clean paper bib around his neck, Dr. Holiday smiles broadly. "Now, Mr. Merd, let's take care of your little problem." Holiday opens his new client's mouth and pokes around with his pick.

The Snake watches with amusement as the

man's smile turns to horror. He actually stutters. "When is the last time you saw your dentist back home?"

He pretends to be ashamed. "I don't know. Maybe 1964? About the last time I went to church." He chuckles. Another good one.

The dentist leaves him for a moment, to hurriedly search his cabinets "I need my camera. I must have a picture of your rotting mouth for the next ADA meeting. It's one for the record books."

The Snake's eyes narrow. "Come back here. No pictures."

Dr. H.H.H. is dismayed. He returns to the chair. "In the interests of science—"

"Just pull the bad tooth."

"But you don't understand. There are at least a hundred hours of work in this mouth of yours. I hardly know where to begin. This abscessed tooth—"

"Get the damned tooth out."

Dr. H.H.H. doesn't realize he is about to make the biggest mistake of his life. He glares at The Snake. "Shame on you! These are the worst teeth I've seen in forty years. You're an embarrassment."

The dentist fails to notice the narrowing eyes of his patient. He continues to poke around The Snake's mouth in fast cadence with his growing lecture. "You old people don't understand how important it is to floss! Sure, getting old is the pits, *but that's no excuse for laziness. I'll bet you haven't checked your prostate recently, either. I'll bet it's as big as the Dolphins' stadium."*

The Snake leaps up toward him and grabs him by the collar and tightly holds on. *"Just pull the damn tooth."*

Surprised and suddenly frightened, the dentist stutters, *"Of-of course. Whatever you say."* He tries to pull away. *"I must prepare your anesthetic. We wouldn't want you to feel any pain."*

"You want to give me laughing gas?" His eyes are slits by now. He tightens his grip on the dentist's neck. The Snake smiles, and it's not a pretty sight, what with those awful teeth. He can tell by the rolling of the man's eyes that the dentist's mind is hysterically trying out ways to save himself from this possible nutcase.

"Nobody treats The Snake with disrespect!" With that he pulls out his knife and presses it to the dentist's neck. A tiny smidgen of blood seeps down onto the formerly clean smock. The man gasps.

"Just do it!"

Even though his hands are shaking, the dentist manages to get the job done. In the moment that The Snake's hand loosens in response to the pain, Holiday makes a run for it. But as ever, The Snake is faster. He leaps out of the chair.

"*Please don't hurt me. Listen, this is free of charge. Please—*"

The Snake grabs him.

The dentist looks into The Snake's face, terrified now. "Why are you doing this? If you don't want anyone to know you were here—you weren't. Honest. I never saw you. I had no patients today."

He babbles. "I didn't even hear you mention your name, Mr. Merd." And sweats as he tries unsuccessfully to escape. "I have a divorced wife. Expensive alimony payments. Four children. One ready to go off to school. Do you know what that costs these days? Of course I wanted him to go to dental college, but you know kids..."

"Then I hope you carry a lot of life insurance." With that, The Snake lets his trusty knife carry out its usual excellent work.

Dr. Horace H. Holiday's last dying thought is that his patient's English had improved considerably.

As The Snake leaves the dentist's office, popping stolen pain pills, he begins to plot his new plan to finish the job. First, he will look for a suitable dinner companion.

27

WEDDING DAY MINUS ONE

Early in the morning, when the New York–to–Fort Lauderdale red-eye arrives, Jack, Evvie, and Joe stand at my side. Morrie wanted to come and greet his sister, but he couldn't get away. We stand excitedly outside the baggage claim area, waiting for our three family groups to arrive. Joe even has his camera ready.

Here they come. Joe and Evvie's daughter Martha and her husband, Elliot, rush toward us. Right behind them is Jack's daughter Lisa and her hubby, Dan, and their two boys. The new baby stayed home with Dan's folks. And right on their heels, there's my daughter Emily with her Alan and my four wonderful grandkids.

After the big group hug and many happy shots

taken with Joe's camera, much laughing and much posing, the entire gang suddenly moves backward away from us. What's this?

They line up as best they can despite the interruptions of passengers' goings and comings at the terminal. Arms around one another, they wait for a signal. My Emily gives it with a wave of her hand and a cry. "Now!"

A chorus of familial voices shout out in unison, "What took you so long?"

Back at Lanai Gardens, Ida stands legs apart, hands on hips, in front of the girls. She is annoyed. "You have to come with me."

Sophie mimics her position. "Well, we're not going. We have a hundred things to do today. We need to get our hair done. And do our cooking for the wedding. Right, Bella?"

Bella nods her head vehemently. "Right. And besides, the Cane Fu wedding rehearsal is starting in twenty minutes. And you have to be there, too."

Ida pulls a sour face. She thinks the idea of copying West Point, using canes to make an archway under which the brides and grooms will walk, is silly. "Well, I haven't made up my mind if I'm going to do it or not."

Bella is insulted. "It's for our dearest friends. How can you refuse? It's an honor."

Ida eyes them slowly. "All right, I'll carry my cane. But first you have to go with me right now. The meeting's about to start."

Sophie won't budge. "We've already been there this week. It's enough. Besides, both of us heard from our dead husbands. We don't need to attend today."

Ida is adamant. "But I haven't heard from mine, and I have a strong hunch that today's my lucky day. And wouldn't my friends, meaning you two, want to share my joy?"

Sophie, remembering Stanley's warning, stamps her foot. "You're no friend. Not anymore."

Ida, betting on the fact she knows them so well, tries another tactic. She needs them there to see the Blatsteins' fall from grace.

She sighs, as if giving in. "Very well. I'll go alone. I'll tell you later if you missed anything."

She starts for the back path to Jerry's Deli. In moments, she can hear the patter of their feet following her. The thought of missing anything will do it every time.

To any bystander, the scene is chaos. But knowing that Evvie is in charge of the rehearsal, I have full confidence all will work out. I watch her in action. Like a traffic cop, my sister stands in the eye of the hurricane and dispenses whatever directions are needed. Pardon my mixed metaphor.

Our friend and neighbor Pat "Nancy" Drew rushes up to her, wringing her hands. "We only have fifty chairs. Will that be enough?"

Evvie: "Not to worry. If people have to stand, they will."

Pat scurries off.

Joe approaches, worriedly looking around. "Where are your dingbat girlfriends? They're needed for the Cane Fu rehearsal."

Evvie: "Don't worry. Enlist stand-ins from our many grandchildren. They'll love it. And warn them not to hit anyone over the heads with the canes."

Joe isn't finished. "Hy is being a pain in the neck about which pole he gets to carry for the chuppah. He says he feels unbalanced."

Evvie laughs: "That's because he is unbalanced. Let him pick his pole. Ignore him otherwise."

Linda wheels her chair over. Proudly she introduces the four scruffy-looking teenagers with her, carrying instruments. "Here they are, as promised. My grandson, Run, and his friends, Hop, Skip, and Jump." She smiles wanly. "Their 'professional' names. For their band—Toothpaste."

I don't dare crack a smile.

Evvie, lips pursed: "Pleased to meet you. Find Joe and he'll show them where they should set up."

When they leave, Evvie releases a groan.

I walk closer to her. "Heaven help us."

We both try to hide our giggles.

Evvie says, "Toothpaste? I think maybe someone should put a cap over them."

"Need some relief?"

With her eyes glancing every which way, she says, "Nah. I'm having a ball."

"Very clever of you to give our families little jobs to do. It's quite a sight seeing Dan, Alan, and Elliot redesigning the brush cove we'll be standing in. With their wives decorating with balloons and kibitzing, of course. "

"I missed my calling in life. I should have been a CEO of some major corporation. Like the CIA. Hah!"

"Strange, isn't it? No sign of Bella, Ida, and Sophie? I would have thought they'd be the first ones here."

"I can't imagine why they weren't. Could they be together, considering the war they're fighting?"

Ida tries not to squirm in her chair. She knows she'll be called. She's fresh meat for the Blatsteins. Sophie and Bella, still grumpy, keep looking at their watches. Ida only half listens to the guru's lecture on the central chakra—the heart of the journey.

He drones on, "The symbol for this chakra is twelve lotus petals around a six-pointed star. It is concerned with forgiveness and compassion—unconditional love and true acceptance in both body and spirit."

Yeah, yeah, Ida thinks. *Sounds like all that sixties huggy-kissy stuff. What a joke.*

The guru is interrupted by the chimes. Everyone pays attention immediately. Ida sits straight up in her seat.

The "dead husband" speaks. "I call upon Ida Franz. It's Murray calling."

Yes! Ida jumps to her feet. Sophie and Bella stare, amazed. Her plan is working. She knew it would.

"Murray, darling. So glad to hear from you. I knew you would call. I felt it in my heart." She smiles, getting a kick out of this. She milks it. "My heart chakra told me."

"Murray" continues. "Thank you for telling our son to put flowers on my grave. It was so sweet you still remember."

A crooked smile appears on her face. Ida plays it to the hilt. She takes her time looking around, making sure every eye in the room is on her. "What son? We have no son. And Murray, what is this about a grave? You were cremated." She lets her bewilderment turn into anger. "I have your ashes on the shelf in my bedroom closet, in an old Chock Full O' Nuts coffee can, right next to my summer hats. What's going on around here?"

Sophie and Bella stare at her in shock, their mouths wide open. All the women gape at Ida, horrified by this turn of events.

Ida picks up momentum. She turns on the guru and Jerry's wife. "What kind of racket are you running? I knew you were phonies! I left a make-believe letter in my purse, knowing that you people search them for information!" Her face is getting redder by the moment, but in her frenzy she can't stop. She runs to the back closet and flings it open.

Her voice is shrill and high-pitched. "Where are you, Phoebe? Busing dishes? Get out here, Lenny, stop nibbling at the pastrami already. Come out, come out wherever you are."

She breathes heavily. It gives Ida great pleasure to watch Mrs. Jerry push herself against the wall, afraid that she might hurt her. Poor Arlene Simon, closing her eyes, so she won't have to watch. Ida smiles meanly at the effect she's having.

But then "Murray" calls out again.

"My poor, poor Ida. You didn't fool anybody with your thoughtless letter. They know the real truth. That you put your own daughter in prison and your grandchildren will have nothing more to do with you. That's why they moved to California, to get as far from you as possible."

Ida stops cold. How is it possible...?

Ida slowly turns toward the guru, who is still

mouthing "Murray's" words. She feels as if she'll faint. She grabs onto a chair to hold her up.

The guru locks his eyes onto hers. "Murray" continues in a nasty tone of voice. "I have news for you, my dear wife. Our convict daughter is about to get paroled. And she will be coming after you."

With that, Ida's arms drop from the chair. The last thing she sees is the room spinning wildly around her and then, blackness.

When Ida comes to, the first faces she's aware of are those of Bella and Sophie. They kneel beside her looking worried and frightened. They are both crying. In fact, everyone in the room is tearfully surrounding her. Mrs. Jerry comes over and hands Sophie a damp cloth. Sophie lightly wipes Ida's sweating forehead. All the faces show concern.

Ida tries to talk but can't. She is astonished to feel the sympathy of this whole group of people, sending waves of love out to her.

Baba also looks at her with deep compassion. "May I help you up, Mrs. Franz?"

Ida can barely nod. He gently lifts her to her feet. She stands, wobbly. At that moment Sophie and Bella and every woman in the room reach out wanting to help hold her. She feels their strength and is deeply grateful.

With that Ida bursts into tears.

Bella and Sophie hold onto her arms as they head for home. The sun is going down—she had no idea they'd been at the meeting so long. For a few moments none of them speak. Finally Ida breaks the silence. "You mustn't tell Gladdy or Evvie. It will ruin their wedding."

Sophie smiles. "Not a word out of *my* mouth. Pinkie honor." She rolls her pinkie finger into Bella's.

Bella nods happily as her pinkie accepts Sophie's. "Not a peep out of me, either."

They walk a little farther.

Ida stops. She needs to tell them everything. They sit on a bench under a palm tree. They listen, their faces solemn.

It's hard for her to begin, but she must. "I've lied. About everything I ever told you about my life. I was too ashamed of the things that happened—the things I did. The mistakes I made." She dabs at her tears with a tissue.

"Everybody makes mistakes," Bella offers.

"Shh," Sophie says kindly. "Let Ida finish."

"My daughter and son-in-law were selling drugs and I couldn't stand the life they led, endangering my sweet grandchildren. They were on food stamps. They felt the world owed it to them. Why didn't I recognize my daughter's illness? I tried to help." She shakes her head as she's reminded of the bad memories. "I gave them money to support them until they found work. The money went fast and foolishly. I gave them more with their promises they would reform. When I finally had enough, I shut off the cash cow."

Bella can't help it. "Oy, then what happened?"

"They stole my jewelry. They forged my name on checks and when I found out, they laughed at me. They lied and didn't give a damn how much they hurt me. I couldn't think straight. I called the police and turned them in. My daughter's husband got off, but she went to jail. My grandchildren believed their mother's lies, swearing that I gave their parents all that money and jewelry.

"They blamed me, and hated me so much for what I did to their mother and ruining their lives. They didn't want to ever see me again. My darling babies ended up living with their other grandmother, who had no interest in them. Their lives must have been awful. I felt so guilty." She stops to take a breath. "My daughter threatened my life. She said she'd finish me off when she got out."

Bella gasps.

Sophie is in awe. "And the guru found out about everything."

Bella says, "Because that mean Murray told him."

Sophie shoots her an exasperated look. "No, Bella, those Blatsteins probably Googled Ida's family on a computer. There are no dead husbands calling."

Bella doesn't get it. "But, but, all the husbands came to talk to us. Abe called me, even though I couldn't say a word. I know it was him."

Sophie shakes her head impatiently. "Don't be silly. Ida is right. They were reading stuff from out of our purses and doing research on all of us. The guru just acted it out."

Bella practically stutters. "But you talked to your Stanley."

"No. I knew it was our guru. Doing a great imitation, I must say."

"You mean, you didn't believe them either?" Bella is astonished and confronts Sophie. "So why did you join the club?"

"We can't go to movies or play bingo all the time. It's entertainment."

Bella is furious. "Then that guru is stealing our money under false pretenses. They all ought to be in jail!" She stops abruptly, looking guiltily at Ida. "Oops."

"You know what?" Ida says. "Forget about calling the cops. I only saw happy faces at your guru's place. If there's someone else who's concerned, let them play bell ringer. We have a wedding to go to."

Ida stands, and the girls start walking again. When they reach the great lawn, people are coming toward them. Sophie and Bella instantly lock pinkies again, and Ida relaxes.

As the three of them continue to walk on, now swinging their arms in unison, Sophie breaks into song. "Friendship, friendship, just the perfect blendship..."

Ida and Bella join in.

The rehearsal is breaking up. Everyone is heading back to their apartments. The Cane Fu group drop their canes from their parade position. Merrill arranges to meet with them again later for a last run-through with the three who missed rehearsal. I take a long look around.

Everything seems in order. The charming assortment of the many-styled dining room chairs are finally all lined up in rows, waiting only for the last minutes when the wedding committee will tie balloons to the aisle seats on each row. The waiting chuppah is beautiful, constructed by my loving neighbors. It always brings a tear to my eye, remembering that the four poles that hold the canopy up signify the four corners of the earth, and the blue cloth canopy above is symbolic of the heavens and the wedding ceremony itself.

We had to have a drawing to choose who would hold up the bridal canopy, there were so many volunteers. Evvie had to find some way to avoid chaos. I'm amused that Hy Binder is one of the pole bearers. Lola beams with pride.

I watch Evvie as she organizes all three families as to dinner arrangements. She's sent out for pizzas, which brings applause from the grandkids. Picnic tables and benches are already set up in the rec room. She announces, "There are coolers filled with drinks waiting for you. For the adults I ordered healthy salads." Much relief at that announcement.

Out of the corner of my eye, I see the three missing girls heading toward us.

I applaud my sister. "Maybe you should go into the wedding planner business, too. You do the best wedding-on-the-cheap I've ever seen. So far, we haven't spent a dime, except for new dresses."

"Thanks. Maybe I will, and give Trixie lessons."

"You could even go into partnership with her."

Evvie laughs. "OMDB, as we used to say in school. Over my dead body!"

I spot Jack talking on his cell and hurrying toward me. He looks excited. We wait for him to reach us.

I hug him when he arrives. "What's up?"

He shakes his head. "You are not going to believe this. It was Morrie. No wonder my best man didn't show up for the rehearsal. They found The Snake."

I am relieved. "That's fabulous news. Where did they capture him?"

Jack says, "They didn't. He was found dead in an alley about an hour ago. Badly beaten. Knifed to death."

I have mixed feelings. What a terrible way to die. But that's what he did to others. How ironic.

Evvie says, "That French Inspector Bonnard will be disappointed."

Jack is philosophical about it. "But at least he can close the files on their most notorious criminal. Morrie and his men are heading over to The Snake's motel room right now. They found the key in his pocket. Morrie wanted to know if we would be interested in meeting him over there."

Am I interested? You bet I am. I put my arm through his and use the cane with the other. "What are we waiting for? Let's go."

Joe, who has come to get Evvie, hears the tail end of this exchange and is astounded. "You have a wedding tomorrow and you're running off to visit a crime scene?"

"Wouldn't miss it for anything. Business before pleasure."

Jack says, "Save us some pizza."

On our way to the car, Ida, Bella, and Sophie are directly in our path. They are laughing and singing. What a nutty threesome they are. First they're fighting and now they're a chorus? I wonder how that came about.

Sophie merrily calls out, "Rehearsal over?"

"Yes, and where were you?" I pretend annoyance.

Bella says, "Just hanging around." She grins.

Weird. Whatever they're hiding, they're obviously going to keep me out of it. "Well, never mind; go join the others for dinner in the rec room."

Bella is confused. "But you two are going in the wrong direction."

I explain. "We'll be back soon. We have to see a dead body first."

We don't wait to see the expressions on their faces. We know how they'll look.

28

WEDDING DAY MINUS ONE
CONTINUED

The motel is rundown and ugly. We've seen this cliché in dozens of noir films. Leaky faucets. Rusted pipes. Musty smell. The TV bolted to a table. Even the toilet paper rolls are nailed in so they can't be stolen. But it's easy to see the killer's thinking. No one would find him here. And it's actually walking distance from the fancy hotel where the book convention was held and where Michelle is staying.

Morrie greets us at the door and hands us gloves. "Sorry I couldn't make it for the rehearsal, Dad."

"No problem. Just don't forget the ring tomorrow."

"I know. I know. You reminded me a dozen times already."

I smile at their obvious love for one another. Funny how I met Morrie before I met his dad— even before I turned into a private eye. My very first case. I look around as they chat. The Snake sure traveled light. One other gray suit in the closet. One extra shirt. One extra pair of shoes. Then again, he was expecting to get the killing done as soon as he got here.

I turn to Morrie. "You said he was badly beaten, almost unrecognizable. No wallet? How did you know it was him?"

"Sometimes it's just a fortunate thing. I saw the pair of eyeglasses lying smashed beside him. On the frame I recognized the logo of the store in the mall. And besides, he matched the description. He was small and very thin, with strands of gray hair. His suit had a European styling. When I got to the motel room and recognized that his cologne matched the bottle on the sink, I knew we'd guessed right."

Jack looks at the paperwork on the scarred wooden table. I join him.

Morrie has the assassin's suitcase open, feeling around for anything hidden. "See? It's all there on the table. The airline tickets to France. His passports next to them. Remember Bonnard's list of aliases? He has three of them right here. The airline ticket is in the name of Louis Phillipe."

I pat down his single bed because I see something bulging. I pull down the coverlet. "Look at this."

Morrie and Jack hurry over. There's a knife half under the pillow. It's been cleaned, but bloodstains can still be detected.

Morrie pulls out an evidence bag. "Well, well. No doubt this will match up with the hotel maid's DNA."

"How strange," I say, "that he didn't have it with him."

Morrie shrugs. "He probably went out for a quick dinner and expected to be right back. Lucky for us. Unlucky for him. He had to make a mistake sometime."

Morrie's men finish bagging all the items in the room. Then they leave.

The three of us take a last look around before we take off.

"Well," says Morrie, in the dingy hallway, "it couldn't have happened at a better time. Now we can all take a deep breath and enjoy the wedding. I'll give Michelle a call and relieve her anxieties. She'll be on the plane tomorrow and we can successfully close the case of The Writer and The Assassin."

I catch the troubled expression on Jack's face.

"Why don't you call her, darling? I'm sure she'd rather hear it from you."

Morrie and Jack look closely at me. I can tell Morrie is surprised at my suggestion, but he quickly agrees. "Good idea. I've got to hurry to the station and call Bonnard. I'm sure his next step will be to bring the winery people in for interrogation. So make the call, Dad, why don't you?"

With that, Morrie hurries to the stairs. "See you tomorrow. Say hi to the folks for me."

In the hallway, Jack takes my arm. "Let's get out of this dump. It makes my skin crawl."

"No argument from me."

Outside again, we both enjoy the cool, clean night air. Though the neighborhood is grim, at least there are many lit stores. Besides, I'm with my very own cop, so I feel safe. "Go ahead and call," I say. "I'll walk ahead while you do."

Jack holds me back and says gratefully, "No more secrets." He takes out his notebook and looks up the number of the hotel and punches it in on his cell. It takes a short while for her to answer.

"Michelle, it's Jack."

He listens. "Yes, I know it's a surprise hearing from me."

He's repeating what she says for my benefit, that dear guy.

"I have amazing news. The man who tried to kill you was murdered last night. It's all over and you can leave with a clear mind."

Jack has this habit of walking in circles when he speaks on a phone. I sort of travel along with him.

"I can understand why you don't want the details. It isn't necessary to burden you with such grim information."

Now he turns and circles counterclockwise. It's an endearing habit.

"Gladdy is fine." He pauses, takes a deep breath and forges on. "As a matter of fact we're getting married tomorrow."

He waits, listening, this time not repeating her words. "Yes, at Lanai Gardens. I believe I mentioned it to you. Where we live. A garden wedding."

He listens again. "Thank you for your kind words. I'll tell her. And I wish you a bon voyage." More listening, his head nodding, then he hangs up.

He faces me. "Well, that's that."

I try to read his expression, but I can't. It's all right. Let him close this episode privately, in his own mind.

Later, Jack and I hold hands as we gaze at the two items hanging on our closet door. His black tuxedo and my peach silk gown. It's nearly midnight.

I ask, "Are you sure the peach looks good on me?"

"Gorgeous."

"Maybe Evvie looks better in that color?"

"You both look sensational." He grins. "Cute idea, wearing the same gowns."

He walks over to his tux and flicks away an imaginary piece of lint. "What about my matching peach cummerbund? A little too much?"

Another of Evvie's ideas since she took over as the wedding planner.

He returns to my side. I sigh. He sighs.

I say, "Looks like this is it. Five more minutes to our wedding day."

"Sure seems like it."

"Last chance to back out."

"Ditto for you."

He kisses me on the cheek. "It's about time you made an honest man of me."

Jack turns me around to face him. He places my hands in his.

"I, Jack Langford, do solemnly swear to be the best husband I can possibly be." He nods. My turn.

"I, Gladdy Gold, swear to be the best wife I can be. I hope God will be good to us and let us have many healthy years together."

Jack says, "And that He will keep our children and grandchildren healthy and happy to continue to live useful lives."

"I promise to love and honor, but I'm not much on obeying."

"I, Jack Langford, hope I can be the kind of man you'll respect. I will do everything to make every hour of every day special." He grins. "I also promise no more redheads."

"I promise never to be jealous again."

He laughs. "I pledge a lot of laughter in our home."

"I like that. Do you think we'll feel different being married?"

"Better than ever. I give my word that nothing will ever separate us again."

"Amen to that."

He puts his arms around me and I place my arms around him. We stand like that for a very long moment. I can feel his heart beating against mine. Right now we have just gotten married in heart and soul.

Tomorrow is merely icing on the wedding cake.

We drink a toast with our bedside water bottles.

Jack is aware of the expression on my face. "What? You seem pensive. Don't tell me you've changed your mind and are getting cold feet."

"It's just that something bothers me about The Snake's motel room. But I can't put my finger on it. Where's the laptop? Shouldn't it have been in the room? Something seems too pat."

He laughs. "He may have hidden it elsewhere.

But what does it matter now? At a moment like this when I am wooing you from the bottom of my heart, you think of the dead Snake?" He hugs me. "The cop shop is officially closed. Forget about business. Now, woman, come into my arms where you belong."

How can I resist? I'm already obeying. And loving it.

29

HERE COMES THE BRIDE
AND THE OTHER BRIDE

It's an hour to our wedding vows. The weather is perfect. It's going to be a glorious evening. Everything and everyone is in place. The children and grandchildren are kvelling. As a group, they can't stop grinning. They're thrilled. The beloved father of one side and beloved mother of another are finally tying the knot. Our friends and neighbors are having a wonderful time. Every woman there is delighted to find a small bouquet on her chair. Even the ducks in the pond seem to be quacking out their good wishes to us.

Sophie and Bella, in matching chartreuse gowns, are wandering around telling anyone who'll listen, taking credit for the two love matches. Ida follows along, a little serious today.

I watch Evvie, looking wonderful wearing my twin peach silk, still directing traffic; my "über" wedding planner. It was funny having seen her earlier give orders to Linda Rutledge's grandson's garage band—oy; Toothpaste. Evvie insisted Mendelssohn's traditional wedding march was not to be played with a rap beat. The guys were disappointed. They'd already composed a rap to be sung along with the march. I shuddered to imagine.

Evvie points out to me where she and I will wait, in the farthest corner behind a mass of shrubbery, unseen by the gathered guests. Our cue, of course, will be the Wedding March, no matter how Toothpaste butchers it.

She then directs the Cane Fu gang, who are positioned in front of the grove where we will stand. They're lined up in two rows. Merrill Grant will lead them to the chuppah, at the music cue of a rat-a-tat-tat on the drums. Merrill snaps his fingers and the group stand ready to aim their canes on high, crossing swords, so to speak.

They are all a-flutter with so much responsibility. Jack's daughter, Lisa, and Ida lead the two lines. Bella is right behind, partnered with Sophie. Our two daughters, Emily and Martha, are next. My Emily turns around to brandish a cane at me. I wave my own needed cane back at her.

Evvie hurries to my side and we are now at the ready. She clutches her bouquet. I balance my cane with one hand and my bouquet with the other. We wait for the signal for the Cane Fus to go first and then it's our turn.

My sister and I exchange big grins.

"Pinch me," she says. "So I can believe this is really happening."

"Sorry," I say, "both hands are taken."

"This is the happiest day of my life, second only to the birth of my Martha."

I think of my happiest day, when I married my first Jack. I begin to tear up.

Evvie looks at me knowing exactly what I'm thinking. She hugs me as best she can with our bouquets and cane in the way. "He would be so happy for you."

As I wait for our signal, I relive my first wedding day, every beautiful moment of it.

The Snake waits until the Frenchwomen's baggage is stowed in the trunk of their taxi. The two redheads say good-bye to their police guards. The guards leave and the cab takes off.

The Snake feels content from where he sits up front next to the dark, curly-headed driver whose name on the dashboard reads José. At first the man refused, because the front seat was his place to put all his crap—greasy lunch bags, cell phone, sweater, notebooks, credit card machine. The Snake

*was very convincing when he told the hesitant
driver that in his country it was an insult to sit in
the back, like some filthy rich landowner.*

The Cuban driver could relate to that. He
cleared the seat quickly.

"Now!" The Snake says to his cabbie as the
women take off.

The cabbie jerks the car into motion. He's
amused and excited. "Just like in the cinema. I always wanted to have a customer say 'Follow that
cab!' "

"Today's your lucky day." If you only knew how
this day will end for you, The Snake muses. He
shifts in his seat, annoyed at the discordant music
blaring out at him from the radio.

The Snake concentrates on the two women with
a small pair of binoculars. They are chatting ami-
cably. Every so often, when they face each other, he
can tell what they're saying. He learned lipreading
years ago, a very useful tool. They're eager to get
home. Too bad. They won't be getting there. So
sorry.

"Stay very close," he demands of his driver.

"But maybe they will see you?"

"They won't," he insists.

The driver half turns. "This is an affair of the
heart? Your woman runs away from you?" He giggles. "Which is she? The younger? The older? Both

such beautiful redheaded ladies. I hardly ever see such women in my country."

The Snake would like to push his knife into the driver's jugular right now, but he needs the fool to keep driving. Patience. *"José, my friend, I will pay you double if you keep quiet. I need to think of how happy I will be when I am reunited with my wife and daughter. It will be such a surprise to them."*

José grins. Seems like the fool listens to all those romantic songs.

"And do turn your lovely salsa music down."

"Si, señor. Of course, señor," and he switches the music to earphones. It takes all The Snake's control not to snatch the earphones off his head and smack him. Instead he taps the man on the shoulder and indicates the earphones. José nods and reluctantly takes them off and shuts off his radio.

The Snake watches the women as they lean back in their seats relaxing. He is rightfully pleased with himself. They all fell for it. The flics. The woman. The former lover.

Finding some moth-eaten homeless man was easy. There were so many of them. And this one was very eager. A meal in his hotel room. A shower, what a luxury. And the look of gratitude when The Snake helped the formerly disgusting, smelly man into one of his suits. The pathetic vagrant would have done anything he wanted of him. A squirt or two of his *cologne helped mask years of street smell. It also helped with the disguise.*

And so easy to walk him back outside and into a nearby alley with the promise of much money. The indigent loser half drooled in happiness. The Snake, of course, made sure his victim faced him when he showed his knife. The thrill for him was always the terrifying look of realization on their faces before they died. And voilà!

All he had left to do was check out of that fleabag hotel, and get the computer and his other passport and other set of airline tickets out of the hotel safe downstairs. He laughed. He wondered how many guests ever had need of the safe—he doubted there were many—but he was glad it had been there.

The garage band continues to play what they call music as the two brides wait. Seating the huge number of guests is taking longer than they expected, reports Hy as he enters the grove to reassure us. "Shouldn't be much longer." He grins in his usual mischievous way. "Not to worry, the band is entertaining us. They just played an original song they wrote, 'Kill All the Cops.' "

Evvie groans. "Sorry, my mistake. I should have checked Linda's suggestion in advance."

Hy shrugs. "Ya gets what ya pay for."

With that, he trots back to the great lawn, and his place at the chuppah, laughing rudely.

What's happening? The two taxis are waiting for the light to change. The Snake sits forward, peering anxiously into the redheads' cab directly in front of him. Something's wrong. The two women are turned, staring out the back window. The young one is gesturing excitedly. He reads her lips. "It's him! It's the man in the book room!"

The older one says, "It can't be! Are you sure? You never got a good look at him!"

Now the two women are leaning over to the front seat excitedly talking to their driver and pointing back at him.

As soon as the light turns green, the cab swerves and makes a sharp right turn.

The Snake punches his driver in the shoulder. "Follow them—they're heading in a different direction—fast!"

The startled man does as he is told. "But that is not the way to the airport!"

"Shut up and don't lose them."

He senses the driver's trepidation. He'd better reassure him. "Triple the money if you stay with them!"

The cabbie calms down and concentrates on his driving.

"Merde." *The Snake thinks that this disgusting city will be the death of him. Where the hell are they going?*

Merrill Grant readies his Cane Fu team into action. The rat-a-tat-tat of the drums calls them forward. Our daughters and the girls blow us air kisses as they proudly step out of the grove and into the lawn area, their canes on high.

We listen to the amused laughter and applause, knowing they must be setting up their crossed canes for our grand entrance.

Our turn next. I straighten up and primp my hair for our march down the aisle. I have to admit I'm excited.

Evvie pokes me, indicating that I should turn around. "Look at that!"

"Now's not the time to be sightseeing. Get ready. We're heading out in a minute."

Evvie pinches my arm. "Turn, dammit!"

"Ouch. Stop that. At what?" And then I see what she sees. To my astonishment, a taxi careens into our parking area with screeching tires. It zigzags until it gets as close to us as possible. For a horrible moment, I fear it will hit us. The cab door opens. The driver rushes to the trunk and grabs two large suitcases and dumps them on the ground.

At the same time, two women jump out of the backseat.

The taxi driver takes off as if the devil himself is after him.

I stare at the women running toward us. Two redheaded women. What? "Oh, my God! It's Michelle and her niece!"

They are screaming. "Help!"

"What the hell..." Evvie says, equally amazed. She squints to get a better look. "So, that's Jack's Michelle!"

"Never mind the commentary! What are they doing here?"

Michelle is half dragging Colette, who holds onto her injured side painfully. And I recall she has just come out of the hospital.

As Michelle reaches me I'm aware that, behind them, another cab is screeching to a stop in the parking area as well.

Michelle is panting. Colette, in agony, sinks to her knees.

"*Gladeeze,* The Snake is not dead!"

As she says this, I see a small, thin elderly man jump out of the second cab. He, too, drops his luggage and sprints toward us at a startling speed.

"He will kill us." Michelle clutches at Colette in terror.

I have to think fast. "Michelle," I say, pointing.

"Run through the shrubs and get Jack and Morrie. Run!"

To Evvie I say, "Hide Colette! Fast!" There's no running for me with my bad ankle.

Evvie practically drags the young woman, who is gasping for air.

The Snake gets closer. I hobble away from him. Evvie is back in seconds. Who knows where she dumped Colette.

"Glad, what are we going to do?"

"Stall him somehow until Jack and Morrie get here."

Evvie and I hear the Wedding March being played. Badly. Our cue.

"Are you kidding? How? With what?" asks my practical sister.

"Anything. Think of something!"

Jack waits eagerly under the chuppah for his bride. Joe, standing next to him wearing his matching tuxedo, smiles shyly at him. The rabbi is patient. The men holding the poles stand proudly in place, though Hy wobbles a bit. Merrill and the Cane Fus hold their canes crossed on high. Jack looks behind him to his best man, Morrie.

Morrie shakes his head. "I'm not going to tell you again. I've got your ring!"

The awful band mutilates the Wedding March.

Jack groans. The guests stand as they all turn toward the tree grove, respectfully awaiting the two brides. Some of them have their fingers in their ears.

Suddenly there is a wave of reverberation from the audience. Building to a crescendo of chatter. Jack assumes it's the response to the band. But that's not it.

He turns around. The wedding guests are pointing and staring.

No, he thinks. *It isn't possible. Michelle?* Michelle is marching—no, running—down the aisle toward him? Through the archway of canes? Morrie is equally incredulous. Jack shakes his head as if to get rid of this bizarre specter. Michelle throws her arms around his neck. "Jack, save us!"

Everyone's jaws drop—to say they're in shock is putting it mildly.

He hears Hy at his pole say, "Gotta hand it to you, Jack. You sure got a touch with women!"

Jack pushes Michelle away from him. "What have you done with my wife-to-be?"

"Never mind that—"

Jack interrupts her. "How did you find this place?"

Michelle points toward the grove. "A cab driver with his GPS. Thank God you told me where the wedding would be. Listen to me. The Snake is here. He is *not* dead!"

Morrie asks anxiously, "Where is he?"

"By now with *Gladeeze*!"

The Cane Fus, with Merrill in the lead, race back down the aisle toward the brush, closely followed by Morrie, Jack, and Joe as the rabbi gets out of their way.

The members of the audience are also on the move.

The chuppah, left behind, collapses.

I watch Evvie smash her bouquet of flowers into The Snake's face. Over and over she hits him. He sneezes. A triple sneeze. Oh, what can I lose? I shove my bouquet at him as well. He can't stop sneezing, but it doesn't hinder him from getting his knife out.

What else can I do but use my cane? I wish I had taken Merrill's course. I hit the assassin haphazardly on the head as he swings his knife at us. We manage to back away.

At the same time I hear Merrill calling out: "Hit hard! Hard as you can! Sound off. One two, jab into his neck." His group chants in cadence along with him as they surround The Snake. Sophie, Bella, and Ida do their stuff. Our daughters jump in as well, following Merrill's instruction as he gets into the fray with them.

The Snake struggles to get away from the swinging canes while Morrie grabs him and twists his arm and forces the knife from his hand.

The Snake is wrestled to the ground as now wedding guests who really need their canes join in.

Jack calls out to his son, "Where's your gun?"

By now, Morrie has the killer's arms twisted behind him. The Snake struggles and has fit after fit of sneezes as more flowers are thrown by yelling female guests. Even Linda gets her licks in, tossing her bouquet from her wheelchair.

Morrie shouts, "You think I'd bring a gun to your wedding?"

Jacks asks, almost poignantly, "Handcuffs?"

"No!"

With that, Jack pulls his cummerbund off and pushes it at his son. Joe does the same. Morrie, with their help, ties the struggling killer up with the bright peach fabric.

Michelle and Colette clutch each other.

Jack embraces me.

Our family is dumbfounded. Our friends and neighbors applaud even though they have no idea what's going on.

Hy can't stop gazing at Michelle. Lola puts her hands over his eyes.

The rabbi appears through the trees. He glances around, stymied by this strange panorama. "Is there going to be a wedding today?"

Toothpaste, still at their little bandstand, attempt another feeble try at the Wedding March.

Jack, out of breath, takes my hand in his. "Shall we?"

The entire congregation head back to their seats, chatting merrily in relief. I smile. This will certainly be a wedding to remember. How many weddings include a gorgeous redhead running down the aisle instead of the bride, and grabbing on to the groom? And the best man holding on to a killer while he passes the grooms their rings? And everyone participating in capturing a famous killer? There'll be dozens of free dinners to dine on with this story.

Michelle and Colette stand to the side, not quite knowing what to do. I call out to them, "Catch a later plane. You're both invited to our wedding."

Evvie and I no longer have bouquets. I don't have my cane, either. My hair is a disaster.

Frankly, we look a mess. But I have my darling's arm to hold on to.

As the ceremony finally begins, something makes me look back. The sounds of the wedding guests fade away and there is only the soft rustle of the trees. The now empty grove seems to shimmer in the shade. I sense movement and I squint to see who's standing in the mist. My new husband is un-aware.

It's my Jack Gold. My beloved first husband, long deceased. He wears his old plaid jacket with the patches on the sleeves. His eyes gleam at me through his black horn-rimmed glasses. He raises his hand and waves.

I can barely hear his whisper. "Good-bye, my dearest. You don't need me anymore. Have a good life."

I blink and he's gone.

No, don't go. I won't forget you. But I probably will. A little.

I turn back to greet my new life with tears in my eyes.

Acknowledgments

Thanks to Shirley Ragsdale of Diogenes Ridge Vineyard for connecting me to Randy Dunn of Dunn Vineyards, in Napa Valley, for his wine expertise.

Thanks to Betty and Roger Eggleston, my Florida spies, for Cane Fu (and especially thanks for Deb).

Thanks to the wonderful Toby and Bill Gottfried, just because...

And rounding up the usual suspects, Caitlin, Nancy Y., Peggy, Jonnie, and Camille.

And my boys, Howard and Gavin, every single time.

Farewell to my beloved aunt Annie—my "Evvie"—never to be forgotten.

Dear Reader,

So there you have it. Seventy-five percent of you loyal readers thought it was right and proper for Gladdy and Jack to marry. Nervous seniors have often faced these questions pertaining to leaping into so precarious an institution as marriage. Should we? Why not? If not now, when?

Gladdy and Jack answered with a resounding yes!

However, the twenty-five percent of you (mostly men, cynics all) who voted con to the prevailing pro insisted the marriage was literary suicide—that boredom and snores would follow.

The pros fought back. What about Nick and Nora Charles? What about Tommy and Tuppence? Lord Peter and Harriet Vane? On and on, the famous married character names poured in. Well, we shall see.

Reality has set in for the girls. Jack is no longer a maybe. Jack is a fait accompli. He and Gladdy are in honeymoon heaven at Niagara Falls. The girls' concern: How much is Jack going to interfere with the Gladdy Gold Detective Agency? But their greater worry: Will their friendship suffer? Will they no longer have the fun they used to have when they were "just us girls"?

Meanwhile something strange is happening in Lanai Gardens. A new resident has moved in, and within a month she is brutally murdered. Everything points to longtime resident Arlene Simon as the killer. "Save me," she begs Gladdy. "I'm innocent." But is she? Another adventure begins.

So watch your local bookstore for the arrival of the new and exciting GETTING OLD CAN KILL YOU, coming soon. Or visit my website, www.ritalakin.com, to get updates. And keep those wonderful e-mails coming to me at ritalakin@aol.com. I love hearing from you.

Rita Lakin